Kristy

JUSTICE DENIED

Thanks for making
my Christmas. I hope
you enjoy my efforts

G.M. Glanville

Author: Geoff Glanville

ABN: 49 351 254 617
Email: justicedeniedgmg@gmail.com
Facebook: Justice Denied the Novel

Produced by: Bermingham Books
First Published: January 2022

ISBN: 978-0-6487812-7-1

In memory of
St. Bloody Veronica and Porky.

Prologue

Feb 1980

Lennie Krause rolled himself off the low trolley, dragged himself off the floor, and limped into the small, lined cubicle at the end of the workshop that served as his office and lunchroom. He downed the remnants of the rum and coke that was sitting on the bench, picked up the badly chewed stub of pencil, opened his diary, composed a short simple message, and tore off the bottom half of the page. He then placed the torn page along with the contents of his wallet into an old Vegemite jar.

He made himself another drink, then eased himself back onto the trolley, carefully negotiated the timber chocks under the axles, and slid back under the old Jaguar he had been working on. "Don't know why old Joe wants the brakes replaced on this piece of shit, the parts are worth more than the car," he thought. He had not paid attention to the radio, it was just background noise with news and weather, but then the DJ came back on, full of overt enthusiasm.

"It's just gone ten past five so welcome back, folks, to our walk down memory lane. Well, it's not that long a walk really. Let's hark back now to 1964, not quite sixteen sweet years ago, when the fabulous Beatles released this classic. Sit back, lay back, stop what you are doing and enjoy the Fab Four and 'I'm a Loser.'"

Drifting through the workshop, from the tinny sounds of the cheap transistor radio came the lyrics:

I'm a loser
And I'm not what I appear to be
Of all the love I have won, and have lost
There is one love I should never have crossed
She was a girl in a million, my friend
I should have known she would win in the end....

Like a dentist's drill hitting the rawest of nerves, the words bounced off the galvanized iron walls of the industrial shed which had become less of a workplace and more of a prison over the last eight weeks.

I'm a loser
And I lost someone who's near to me
I'm a loser
And I'm not what I appear to be.

His health, his business, his finances, his love life, and his future had all been spiraling downward over the last year. But it was probably the words of that song that, strangely, were the last straw for Lennie after all the setbacks and turmoil he had suffered.

"I'm a loser, too fucking true, Lennie," he said softly to himself, as he suddenly burst into tears. "Too fucking true, you useless piece of shit. The old man had you pegged years back." The tears came as a complete surprise. They first mortified him because of the weakness he believed they signified, and then they consoled him. The release of tension they afforded after the pressures of the last few months was almost euphoric.

He let the tears flow for a good five minutes. First sobbing, then as the relief became more evident, letting go completely, heaving with huge intakes of breath, until finally he was curled up in a tight ball and sobbing again amongst the grease covered rags and metal filings of the workshop floor. The release was short-lived.

"You weak prick," he sobbed as he wiped the tears from his face. "How am I going to handle this now?" he thought, as he looked closely, through tear-stained eyes, at the naked wheel hub above his head. "I've got a baby on the way, yet I am on the bones of my arse. Is this brilliant news or one more kick in the guts?"

His head was spinning from so many options, but the analysis stopped when a greasy hand brushed the shortened handle on the trolley jack he had recently modified. This was followed by an unfamiliar noise, then one and a half ton of ageing British motoring excess quickly came to rest on his troubled skull.

Chapter 1

Len Krause might have thought that his problems began five months previously, but Alan Fitzgerald's assessment was that Lennie's whole world had taken a dramatic turn in the wrong direction around a year earlier. Alan "Fitzy" Fitzgerald considered himself Lennie Krause's best friend. He was in his early thirties and worked with his father, running a substantial grain and cattle property, "Kilmarnock," 100km west of Dalby, off the Moonie Highway past Tara.

Fitzy was a big man, well over six foot tall, thick through the chest, but lean. He seemed to taper down from his wide shoulders to finish in his elastic side boots, like an overly large exclamation mark. He had black tight curly hair with just the beginnings of grey at the temple, greyer still on the sideburns, and a few days stubble on his strong chin.

Fitzy was the third generation of Fitzgerald's to work the property. His grandfather, Nevin Fitzgerald, was a gentleman farmer from outside Kilmarnock, a town on the west coast of Scotland below Glasgow. At the outbreak of the Great War, Nevin enlisted with the Gordon Highlanders obtaining the rank of lieutenant. He served for nearly three years before he was wounded in the battle of Arras in 1917, nearly losing his right arm. He was repatriated back to Britain, and, as the family story was often told, decided during his convalescence to emigrate with his wife Mary, to anywhere that was as far away as possible from the cold, mud, and sleet that he had experienced on the Western front.

The same story, told and retold in his fading Glaswegian accent, was that his chosen destination became Australia, after he came across a fascinating article about the Jondaryan Woolshed, the largest woolshed in Australia. The numbers both astonished and fascinated him. Here was a young country with boundless possibilities and wide-open spaces. He used to recount learnedly, that the property was originally called Gundarnian, which, in the dialect of the local Jarowair aboriginal clan, translated to Fire Cloud or Place of the Fire Cloud. "*..and dinna ya agree thut Jondaryan uss easier to pronounce.*" He was astonished that the shearing shed itself was an immense three hundred feet long and that in all, it boasted fifty-two shearing stands and could hold three thousand sheep at one time. The whole thing originally had a canvas roof, until they covered it with new stuff called galvanized iron! "Canvas, a canvas roof!" he used to roar, with a huge belly laugh.

Nevin also learned that the original property, spanning 300,000 acres, was slowly being cut up into smaller properties, mainly because they had found that the land was simply too good for sheep. The rich black soil plains were now being put under the plough. That suited Nevin, because he had always been a cattle man and farmer at heart. The more he read about the region, the more he was determined to make the Darling Downs his family's new home. There was even a spectacular pristine wilderness to the east called the Bunya Mountains. It was part of the Great Dividing Range and less than hundred miles from the Pacific Ocean. As soon as Nevin was well recuperated, he sold off everything, and he and his wife, Mary, caught the next available steamer to Brisbane. It wasn't long before he had headed west and had every stock and station agent he trusted, looking for a substantial holding, suitable for the raising of beef cattle, somewhere west of Dalby.

The property he settled on was shortly christened "Kilmarnock" and the taming of his holding soon began with the extensive clearing of the brigalow scrub. Within two years of settling into his new life, Nevin and Mary were blessed with their first child, Angus, forever after to be called Jock. Two years later, Jock was followed by Donald, Uncle Don to Fitzy. Year by year their fortunes improved with "Kilmarnock" soon being regarded as one of the finest properties in the district. When young Don found out about an undeveloped holding for sale further west, in the Charleville district, Nevin was able to buy it for him. Everyone accepted it as reasonable that Don should branch out on his own, because it was the family tradition that the main family property always passed to the eldest son and Jock had not long met and married his wife Cecilia.

Unfortunately for Fitzy's grandfather, the wounds and damage of his war service, combined with his taming of a huge property took its toll early. Just six months before the start of the Second World War, Nevin died following a massive heart attack. Apart from the tragedy, this presented a major dilemma for young Jock. As a newlywed in just his early twenties, he was now the man of the family, and responsible for overseeing the family holding that was now close to 9000 acres. In addition to this huge responsibility, his mother was still in mourning and he would soon, no doubt, feel compelled to fulfill his obligations and enlist. As it transpired, army service never occurred for Jock. The list of complicating factors initially ruled it out, and then his substantial cattle business and his critical role in it was deemed by the government as a reserved occupation. Don, however, chose to enlist, leaving his Charleville property in his brother's care.

The guilt Jock felt at his inability to join his brother on active service was a matter that he never truly came to grips with. The best he could do by way of compensation was to help clear the Charleville property, so that Don would return to something resembling a viable operation. A few years after his brother returned home, Jock had a son and named him Alan Donald Fitzgerald. Jock's second son was christened Donald Nevin Fitzgerald; though from two years of age this Fitzgerald was to be universally called "Spud."

Despite the age difference, Alan and Spud were inseparable. Alan, due to the inherent responsibility of being an "eldest son," concentrated his efforts on assisting his father to run and build the property. Spud, too, was no slouch when asked, but he had no intentions of staying on the land. His abiding ambition was heading to Queensland University to study law. He was an excellent student, and it was assumed that his entry to university was as good as guaranteed. When it came to rural endeavors, he was always available, but he usually found a way to make work on the property a second priority.

Other than having to swot for exams, this usually involved sports of some sort. He was a natural at cricket and tennis, but rugby soon became his passion. Following Spud to school rugby games around the district became Alan's favourite, sometimes his only, social outing. He had played the game himself, also at Downlands College, but always in the forwards and usually at second row. Spud, however, was a speedy little winger, and you don't get two positions much further apart in the game. It became the source of constant ribbing between them, with Alan accusing his brother of touching the ball only six times in a game and

Spud casting aspersions on his big brother's mental capacity and fondness for "sticking his head up the arse of other players."

Shortly before he turned eighteen, however, Spud's sporting ability began to wane, and his school results fell away as well. Strangely, this was part of the reason that years later, Alan was to become such close friends with a young mechanic named Lennie Krause who lived and worked 100 km to the east in Dalby.

Chapter 2

A year before his death, Lennie Krause had the world at his feet. He was twenty-one, single, the owner of a thriving business, lived the bachelor's life in a rental house, and was something of a local legend when it came to cars. He was also a better than average rugby player in a better than average rugby team, where winning had become a habit. He was lucky with the ponies on those occasions he had a bet, and reasonably lucky as well with the ladies, who liked him as much for his looks as for his casual attitude to life.

Len had initially grown up in Dalby with his mother, Di, and his father, Ron Krause. However, his parents had separated when Len was only eight. His mother then raised him alone after his father left the family for the bright lights of Sydney. Despite this, Len had a pretty good life. His mother provided well, working as a barmaid in various hotels in and around Dalby. Before heading to Sydney, Ron was all but skint. As the saying of the time went, "he didn't have a brass razoo to his name", whatever a razoo was. His move to Sydney, however, had been a good decision, and the city had been kind to him financially.

Ron only had the one child, and as Di had not made his move difficult, he had stayed loosely in touch. He had helped with her general finances, put Len through school, and had later used some contacts in his old hometown to ensure that Len got the motor mechanic's apprenticeship he was so keen on. Ron was bigger than life, generous, very gregarious, and outgoing, and would bend over backward to help anyone in need. He was also a storyteller of some renown, famous for saying, "never spoil a good story for the sake of the truth."

Len, however, had always found his dad impossible to read. They could be having a great time, out camping and fishing for yellow belly, when suddenly, his mood would change without warning. The loving supportive father would become sullen and for no apparent reason the trip would be abruptly terminated, and they would head back home without a word spoken for the entire trip. Back at home the mood would continue, until Ron found some obscure reason to turn his foul mood into an argument with Di.

Ron was also a bad drunk; never violent, but loud and mean spirited. After a heavy session on the drink, he could do more to hurt his son with a few well-chosen words than some local dads did with their leather belt. Lennie was conflicted. He loved the "nice" Ron, but Ron had left Lennie in no doubt that his old man thought that he could do better at pretty well everything he tried. Ron was a returned serviceman who had put up his age so he could join the war. Still just seventeen, and meadow green about the realities of life, Ron found himself in New Guinea and the surrounding islands toward the tail end of the Pacific war.

What Lennie knew of his dad's experiences, he had collated piecemeal over the years from eavesdropping on stories that Ron and his service mates from the RSL swapped at the pre-dawn breakfast before the Anzac Day Dawn Service. Lennie never knew if his dad had ever fired a shot in anger, but he discovered that he had been shot at. He also knew that Ron's worst experience involved a Japanese soldier who simply could not shoot back. Ron had apparently jumped off the back of a troop truck and landed on top of the rotten corpse of a Japanese soldier who had been buried in a shallow grave about a week previously. The unique stench of rotting human flesh had caused a young Ron to be violently ill. This reaction earned him his army nickname of "Bert," pronounced to sound just like he did that morning in the islands, when he spray-painted the soldier's corpse with his breakfast.

After his parents separated, Lennie only saw his dad every few years. This was usually when Ron returned to Dalby to catch up with his old RSL mates and, to a lesser extent, to catch up with his only child and ex-wife. These visits usually started with Lennie being reintroduced to "nice" Ron. The dad who brought gifts and pink lemonade at the pub, took an interest in how he was travelling generally, and asked genuinely about his progress at school. Unfortunately, the visits inevitably ended with Ron spending way too long with these mates at the local RSL. As he grew older, Lennie knew that each visit would finish with Ron trying to force his way back into the family home with lecherous intent. Len's most vivid memory of his father was Ron's ruddy face and beery breath inches from his own at the rear fly screen door, and with Ron's less than favourable assessment of what a weak prick his son really was.

Despite these spasmodic confrontations, Lennie still broke down and cried with his mother when she came to tell him that his father had died in a work accident. Lennie was just nineteen and nearly finished with his apprenticeship, yet he was old enough to seriously ponder his failed relationship with his dad. He now realized that Ron's problem was not so much the drink as the war. Lennie laid the blame for Ron's problems squarely at the feet of the grandfather he never knew. He could never comprehend how Ron's own father could ever have agreed to tweak the paperwork that would allow his seventeen year old child to go off to war.

Ron had never really recovered from the experience and Lennie still vividly remembered waking up to his father enduring a night terror. Ron's standard coping mechanism to dull the damage was to get on the drink, and the drink was the cause of all the family's issues. His conflicting memories of his father were somewhat mollified six months later when Len discovered that he had inherited a nice lump of cash in his father's will. He liked to think that beery confrontations apart, his father was thinking of him right to the end.

Len promptly used some of the funds to buy himself a secondhand Holden Ute and also a particular pale green Mark 1 Ford Zephyr which his mother had once admired so much. The Zephyr was incredibly cheap, as the prior owner, a local schoolteacher, had recently wrapped it around a big gum tree on the outskirts of town. In his spare time, Lennie did the required mechanical work in secret at the workshop of a good mate who was a panel beater. He paid the same mate to straighten it out and give it a fresh coat of paint before ultimately presenting it to Di as a fiftieth birthday present.

His mum had been over the moon with her new toy. It was the same pale green colour she had always admired, but the paint work and the chrome were now much shinier. The tires looked new as well and were painted a glossy black while the upholstery was covered in clear plastic. Impressed as she was with the car, Di was more impressed with the sentiment and with his skill and work ethic involved in restoring it. She now knew for certain that her son had chosen the right career and with the help of a local solicitor, ensured that Len set aside the remaining money. She wanted to be sure that when he had some experience under his belt, he would be in a financial position to set up his own mechanical workshop.

Despite his father's assessment when drunk, Lennie had a natural flair for anything mechanical. Di had used her share of Ron's estate to buy a small acreage property with a two-bedroom house on the Oakey side of town. She and her son lived there happily together until Lennie turned 21 and began making noises about being more independent and moving into his own place. A family friend of Di's had an old three-bedroom weatherboard farmhand's house on the outskirts of town. It hadn't been lived in since the owner scaled back his operation and had no need of hired help. She came to an arrangement with him to rent it out to Lennie at a fair price, on the understanding that Lennie would give the place a good clean and arrange to have the electricity reconnected. Lennie cobbled together a pile of furniture, some from family friends and some from the second-hand shop and soon set up house.

After settling in, he used the bulk of his remaining inheritance to set up his own workshop in the unused good sized shed out the back of his mother's house. The chosen location was perfect on a cost basis, as well as for the host of ancillary benefits it offered. Though Lennie's and Di's work hours often clashed, they still got to see a lot of each other and there were now no more awkward meetings in the hallway if he "got lucky" after a night out. Like any good mother, Di also let him retain his washing and ironing privileges. His usual work hours were about seven am to four pm mid-week and depending on the workload, half day Saturday; but as a one-man band he really set his own hours. He loved the work; the customers knew he did too, and in no time, business was thriving.

Chapter 3

On Wednesdays during footie season, Lennie always closed the workshop early so he could get to the oval on time for rugby practice. It was only early pre-season around late February, and so it was still hot, even in the late afternoon. After a long day in the workshop and a 90-minute training session in near thirty degrees heat, Lennie hit the showers, changed, then decided to chance his luck getting a late meal at The Imperial Hotel in town where his mother, Di, was putting in the late shift.

Di was an amiable woman in her early fifties and around five and a half foot tall. She had been very likely an attractive woman in her earlier years, but these days could best be described as "tidy". Di wore her greying blond hair in practical tight curls and her makeup comprised no more than a little smear of lipstick. She carried no extra weight, was wiry, and the sort of person who you knew had worked hard all her life.

"Hi honey," his mum said with a genuinely happy lilt to her voice when she saw him. "You look nice and clean for a change. To what do I owe the honour of a visit from you midweek? Are you out of clean undies?"

"No, Mother, mine, I've managed to do my own laundry this week," he responded cheekily as he flashed his toothy white grin, knowing that half the bar was listening as his mother discussed his underwear status. "I've just finished training and I know I've got bugger all in the fridge at home. As my dear departed dad used to say, 'I'm so hungry I could eat a Chinaman's ass through a wicker chair.'" His mother shot him a look of disapproval, she remembered that phrase well, hadn't liked it then, and still didn't.

Lennie either ignored the look or missed it, so went on. "I know it's a bit on the late side, but if the kitchen is still open, I'm hoping the cook could rustle me up a rump steak and veggies with some extra chips while you pour me a cold one, with a dash of Sars."

"I'll get that beer, Di", said a voice from the far end of the bar. "Dash of sarsaparilla eh, I thought only old boys and women liked dashes in their beers."

Len looked around to see who was making the smart-arse comment at his expense. "Len, this is the new girl, Marion. Marion this is my son, Lennie." His mother offered the quick introduction as she headed off to the kitchen to arrange his steak.

"Pleased to meet you, Marion," said Lennie, firing off his signature toothy grin, then he quickly downed over half the beer in one thirsty gulp. "I only have Sars in the first beer, it's a little more refreshing and it goes down easier."

"Well, I'm certainly in favour of anything that helps going down easier," Marion countered brazenly, as she looked him directly in the eye. Lennie almost choked on his beer. She had timed her suggestive comment just as he took his second swig, and he had managed to breathe some of the foam up his nostrils. He had to let some of the beer fall back into his glass and quickly swallow the rest or he would have spray painted her and half the bar. His eyes watered as he broke out into uproarious laughter. Good sense of humour as well, he thought, as he took the opportunity to get a better impression of Marion.

She was shortish, about 5'4," and had red brown shoulder length hair. She was curiously attractive too, with, he guessed, a good figure underneath the smock dress she was wearing. The most noticeable thing about her was that she was wearing too much makeup for a girl her age. Len estimated she was perhaps a little older than he was but was trying to look older still. The extra make up was mostly around the eyes and it gave her a trashy, sexy sort of look, a look he decided he didn't half mind.

"Sorry about that," he finally said as he wiped a little of the wayward beer from his chin. "I didn't see that one coming. I'll have another beer now thanks." As Marion turned toward the tap he added, "And, Marion, given your comment, maybe you better put some Sars in the second one too."

Marion smiled to herself at the comment. He was cute, a little big for her liking perhaps, but good looking, sandy haired, tanned, and obviously pretty fit. If the rest of town promised as much as she had discovered in her first week in Dalby, then the move up from Brisbane would prove to be worthwhile.

Marion Kent had left Brisbane after another blazing row with her mother a fortnight or so earlier. Not that she hated her mum, quite the opposite, in fact. It was the company her mother kept that invariably caused the problems between them.

Over the years her mum had added one deadbeat after another to a long list of failed relationships. This list started, of course, with her own father, who used to take his belt to his wife after most every drinking session. Marion had discovered early on that if she ever tried to intervene, her father wasn't averse to giving her a good belting around the back of the legs as well. Her fear of that belt didn't dissuade her if her father's abuse toward her mother was particularly viscious and she was even known to climb on his back if things got particularly grim, to allow her mother time to escape.

If he was on the drink and had also had a bad day at the track, then the beatings usually escalated to the point the neighbours called the police. Of course, on the rare occasion that the ponies were kind to him, Marion and her mum could count on a long absence; one just long enough to ensure that he was broke again by the time he walked back into the most recent of their rented houses.

She didn't even refer to him as dad or Bill. In her mother's own words, he was referred to as, "Bill Kent, that's Kent spelled with a C." She had very good reason to use that epithet. Bill Kent was a low-grade clerk in the Queensland public service. He always looked on his employment position as something of a two-edged sword; the pay was poor, but it was near impossible to get fired. He used his job security to turn his lack of ambition into an art form. Not only was it his mantra to do the least possible while actually at his desk, he also was famous for stretching out morning tea and lunch breaks and for managing to always hit the street at least ten minutes before five. On many a Friday, he even managed to stretch his lunch break right through to ten minutes before knock off time. He then swanned up to his desk, said a beery goodbye to his colleagues, grabbed his crumpled briefcase that only ever contained a green form guide and his lunch, signed out in the time book, and headed back to the pub.

While his job could not be terminated, he could certainly be transferred and passed over for promotion, both of which happened on a regular basis. Sometimes this meant a change of address, which mattered little to him but greatly impacted his wife and daughter. Marion lost count of the number of schools she attended before she finally called it quits in year ten. She wondered as well, if her father ever really believed the half-baked excuses he proffered when the time came to move. It was always the fault of someone else at work. His workmates had "white anted him" or his boss "had it in for him." He certainly never took responsibility for his own failure at work, at home or as a parent and father.

Marion had no memory of him ever supporting her, of attending one of her school academic or school sports functions. She still remembered being picked in the school athletic team and her father promising to come along and watch her. When the day arrived, her father told her he couldn't make it because something important had come up. When she got home after the sports carnival, she was proudly wearing her first prize winning ribbon pinned to her tunic and after her father finally arrived home late that afternoon, she raced up to him proudly showing it off. His response said everything about Bill Kent as a father, "Well at least someone had a win today, I couldn't pick a winner all day."

While she had no memories of love or support, Marion did have vivid memories of the fights, the physical abuse and the drunkenness. When he finally disappeared, both she and her mother considered it a blessing. It even helped her mother secure a Housing Commission property as a more permanent residence. When that paperwork came through you would have thought they had won the Golden Casket.

When she finished school, Marion began working in a series of menial jobs, the first and shortest of which was in a fruit canning factory. This was followed by numerous casual positions working as a shop assistant in various suburban businesses. The income from these barely covered the rent and board that her mother insisted she pay, so when she turned eighteen she began looking for a job that came with a more substantial pay packet. Her good looks and tidy figure helped in this task, when the publican at the local hotel took a shine to her and offered to teach her bar work. Working in pubs was rewarding financially, certainly widened her horizon and gave her the confidence to develop opinions of her own.

Amongst those opinions was that Marion remained amazed that her mother had not learned anything from her married experience and that her choice in men had not improved one iota over the ensuing years since Bill Kent had departed. If she and her mother argued, it was inevitably about the latest man her mother had hooked up with. The final argument Marion had with her mother before she moved out, involved the latest in a line of very poor choices, another grub who had never contributed anything either legal or useful to the relationship or household. When he decided that their relationship had matured to the point that it was okay to give her mother a clip around the ear, her mother had mercifully finally stood up for herself and ordered him out of the house. Unfortunately, Marion discovered that the pride she felt about her mother's decision was misplaced.

Not two weeks later, she had come home to find them curled up on the couch together, and halfway through a bottle of gin. Marion firstly took aim at her mother apparent love of serial abuse and deadbeat boyfriends. He sat there with a stupid half-drunk grin on his face until Marion turned her anger toward him. She told the prodigal boyfriend he was a weak piece of shit who didn't deserve her mum and that he should grow a pair and do something with his life. When he endeavored to get up from the lounge to defend his indefensible honour, she picked up the half bottle of gin and warned him to stay exactly where he was. She finished her rant by pleading with her mother to stop throwing her life away on garbage like him and that she had decided to move out and go and live her own life.

For a short while Marion felt as though she was orphaned. She hadn't seen her father in fifteen years or more. She didn't know and didn't care if he was dead or alive and now she had given up on her mother too. After a few boozy pleas from her mother to please reconsider, Marion hastily packed what little she called her own into her tatty suitcase and hitched her way into the centre of town. After wandering aimlessly for an hour or so she eventually found herself in front of Roma Street Railway Station. She sidled up to the ticketing window and asked when the next train was leaving and where it was heading. She frankly didn't much care.

Her plan wasn't destination specific, she just wanted to get away, but unfortunately no trains were leaving for hours. Those hours were spent attempting sleep on a platform bench, until she found herself hopping on the next train that was bound for Toowoomba. Two more hours of interrupted sleep on a hard wooden seat followed, before she arrived there in the middle of the night with absolutely no idea of where to go, or what to do. Courtesy of a lift from a young air force guy and then another from an overnight truckie, she had ended up at a roadhouse on the outskirts of Dalby in the early hours of the following morning.

Dalby's main claim to fame was as a major regional agricultural centre on Queensland's Darling Downs. Though Dalby didn't reek of money, there was a lot of it around, with huge grain properties to the north, east and south, and sheep and cattle properties further to the West. The town itself serviced these industries and was vibrant in its own way as a result. If Marion had the inclination to have an in-depth look, she would have taken note of the neatly laid out streets, particularly Cunningham Street which was extraordinarily wide. She would have noticed outstanding features of the town such as the art deco Council Chambers, the Romanesque Catholic Church, manicured lawns, parks and beautiful picnic area along Myall Creek. If she had stopped for even a moment to consider where she was, she would have been astounded by the clear skies and the enveloping stillness and quiet of an early Dalby morning. None of this registered with her, though she did note that the series of huge grain silos adjacent to the rail line meant money and that there were an impressive number of pubs along the main street.

Though only a day since the big blow up with her mum, Marion was certain she had made the right decision. She had been wasting her life living with her mum in Brisbane. The hard part was making the decision to leave, and that part was now over. What was important now was to make the most of her new circumstances. After an extra strong cup of instant coffee and watery scrambled eggs on toast, courtesy of the Shell roadhouse, Marion did a little remedial work on her makeup in the ladies' restroom. She scrounged through her small suitcase to find a clean top that best displayed her charms. She then gave herself what might be termed a sponge bath, courtesy of paper hand towels and cold water from the basin in the toilet. She finished off the whole renovation with a liberal application of underarm deodorant and a couple of squirts of her favourite perfume.

Marion had done quite a lot of bar work in Brisbane and although her last position had been problematic, she figured she should play to her strengths. If pubs in Dalby were anything like suburban Brisbane, the publican would be either helping out with pre-opening clean up or setting up the tills by at least 8.00 or doing both simultaneously. So, at 8.30, Marion began methodically working her way up the main street going from pub to pub to find bar work.

As luck would have it, it was the last pub— The Imperial, where she had success of sorts with a publican by the name of Bob, who was in the process of spearing a new keg in the cold room. Bob was typical of a lot of publicans, a big broad-shouldered man with a bigger belly, a big head, and a ruddy face dominated by a bulbous veiny nose. He seemed an easy-going type when Marion first struck up a conversation, but when the conversation got around to possible employment, he was all business. He said that yes, he was a little short staffed, particularly when things got busier over the weekend. Bob engaged her in conversation for the next five minutes to get a better read on the sort of person she was. After he had finished setting up the new bank of kegs, and satisfied with his initial assessment, he took Marion into the public bar and asked her to show him her stuff by pouring him three pots.

She grabbed a large bucket and drew the beer through the lines. Once the beer was flowing, she removed three pot glasses from the fridge, arranged them in the one hand and promptly began filling them, topping up one after the other and placing them in front of him having not spilled a drop. He was impressed that she knew enough to first pull the beer through the lines. If she had tried to pull a beer straight up, all that would have landed in the glass would have been gas and froth. The three pots in the one hand was skillful too, but when she finished the test with, "There you go boss, breakfast of champions," he knew he had a winner. Knowledge, skill, and personality was the trifecta for a good barmaid. Her good looks were a bonus, but at the end of the day in a country pub, they were well down the list of must have traits. Bob told her the pay rate and agreed to try her out as a casual straight away if she wanted, provided she took the hours and times offered. He indicated they would likely be a minimum of twenty hours a week to start.

Marion's only reservation was what she was going to do for accommodation close by, as there was no public transport, and she had no car. That hurdle was soon overcome as well when Bob said, "We have ten old rooms upstairs, but we rarely rent them out except during special events like when the stock sales are on. If you need a bed, I can also throw in a room on the understanding you do your own laundry and that it's only short term until you find something permanent."

Marion quickly agreed to the terms. The decision had proved a good move for them both, with Marion soon becoming not only efficient but popular, particularly with his older regular customers, those who historically were hard to impress.

"There you go me boy, no waiting no delay." It was his mother back, not with a steak but some healthy slices of roast beef swimming in thin gravy and surrounded by an assortment of vegetables that were so well boiled they were verging on soup.

"What happened to the steak?"

"The kitchen just closed, Sunshine," his mother replied. "I managed to salvage this from the bain-marie before Cissy threw it out. Boss says it's on the house providing you and your mates beat Warwick this Saturday in the pre-season trial game."

"Tell Bob that shouldn't be a problem, Warwick couldn't beat us with a stick," Lennie shot back as he quickly got to work on the meal in front of him.

"Have you fixed Marion up for the beer yet?" his mother asked. "Or do you expect Bob to carry your bar bill as well?"

"No, mum, I haven't fixed up Marion yet, but I'm sure if she asked me nicely, I could oblige."

Marion overheard the family exchange but pretended she was busy restacking the cigarette dispenser. Lennie's mother had worked in bars too long not to have her ear attuned to sexual innuendo; she knew Len was interested in Marion. At the rate he was sowing his wild oats, she wondered if he shouldn't have studied at an agricultural college rather than a technical college. She wasn't complaining though, Len was well liked in town and considered something of a catch. He would be okay, she thought, just as long as he didn't end up prematurely starting a family in the process.

By the time Marion arrived with his second beer, once again containing a goodly dash of sarsaparilla, Lennie was almost finishing his meal. He dropped a $20 note on the bar for the beers, then quickly washed down the last of the meal with a heathy swig that emptied half the glass. When Marion returned with his change most of the rest of the pot was gone too.

Throwing the last of the beer down his throat, he leaned over the bar, gave his mum a peck on the cheek and said, "Thank Bob for the meal, I've got to rush. I've got a meeting about last year's tax with the accountant tomorrow and to put it kindly, my bookwork needs a little attention... or at least a bigger shoebox." This was their running joke.

Knowing how hopeless he was at bookkeeping, his mother had devised for him what she referred to as her "Lenniekazoo" accounting system. It comprised three elements: a shoebox for receipts, another shoebox for payments, and a day diary where he registered his jobs, wrote notes, and recorded things to do.

Passing the far end of the bar on his way toward the door, Len approached Marion as she loaded up the last of the cigarettes.

"You working Saturday?"

"Yes," she replied matter-of-fact. "On at ten off at three. Why, were you considering coming in for a little sarsaparilla?"

"Just wondering if you followed rugby? We play Warwick at the oval this Saturday at three."

"Well, I don't know a lot about it, but a paddock full of fit blokes in tight shorts all trying to kill each other does have some appeal. Providing I can arrange a lift down, I'll see you there, but I'll likely miss the first twenty minutes," she said with a smile.

"See you there, Marion. I'll catch you at the bar after full time." Lennie was beaming as he walked out the door.

Chapter 4

By half time, the Dalby boys were well in front. The two teams had retired to respective ends of the field for the half time break, a break which constituted a short lie down, an orange cut into quarters, but definitely no water. The standard orders were to wash your mouth out if you absolutely had to, but to never swallow the water as you would cramp up. As the team rested in the shade of the small grandstand, the coach felt obligated to begin his half time rev up.

"Why is he bothering?" Lennie thought; but as usual, the coach was going on with the usual hackneyed phrases that Lennie figured they handed out in booklet form at coach's school. "Keep up the fucking pressure, the game plan we practiced is working fine." "Don't let them back into the game." "It's not over until the final fucking whistle."

While Len had a lot of respect for Coach Cowley, this speech was totally unnecessary today of all days, because Warwick were no competition at all really. Last year they finished nearly at the bottom of the ladder, and they were on average about ten years older than the Dalby boys. It was patently obvious the heat was killing them, and that they were already totally exhausted. Lennie knew that as they got toward the end of the second half, Warwick would run out of puff completely and the score would blow right out.

He wasn't listening that attentively to the coach anyway. He was too busy keeping an eye out for Marion, who, he hoped, would soon be visible on the other side of the white picket fence that separated the field from the small timber grandstand. He figured that she should have been able to make it down by half time if she had finished her shift on time. Lennie half nodded in agreement with the coach as he scoured the small crowd to no avail. He had all but given up, so reached for another piece of orange and began sucking out the juice, when he heard her call out his name from close quarters.

He spun around and flashed his smile which this time was framed by the triangle of orange peel. She had obviously changed clothes after work. She was wearing a light cotton dress that accentuated her figure, had applied fresh make up, and her auburn hair was fashioned into a sort of pony tail.

"Having a win so far I see," she said motioning to the score board.

"You're looking good. Yeah these Warwick boys are seasoned players and as tough as teak. We are having a real job staying in touch with them so it's great to actually have a half time lead," he lied.

He was about to give her a slightly embellished history of the first half when the referee blew his whistle and the coach yelled, "Len, mind on the game, out you go, move up to side of the scrum, pull Johno back to No 8."

Lennie yelled over his shoulder, "See you at the bar after full time. We'll have a few, and then I'll show you the sights of Dalby."

In the ensuing months Marion was pleased to be shown more than just the sights of Dalby. The pair had quickly become inseparable. With Marion working shifts, it wasn't unusual to see her down at the workshop during the day, while Len had suddenly decided that he liked pub food and was having most of his evening meals at the bar of The Imperial.

On the odd occasion that Marion was given a weekend off, Lennie would duck the preseason game with some lame excuse, and they would head off to Toowoomba and stay the night at a motel. Lennie didn't much care what they did, or that Marion always took control and obviously had an agenda. The reason he was so accommodating was that part of Marion's agenda was always a heavy early morning session of some pretty steamy sex. He remembered vividly their first weekend away when Marion assessed his capabilities in bed. "Lennie," she said, "I quite enjoy your body, but your repertoire in bed is somewhat 'meat and potatoes'. There is more to this than missionary."

Lennie had tried to joke about the term; making some lame reference to sausages but Marion was seriously keen to introduce some more exotic manoeuvres to their sex life and educate him on the finer points of the female body. He soon discovered that he loved oral sex, not only the receiving, but the giving. He was so keen on some of Marion's favoured positions that after the preliminaries, he would sometimes say, 'Time for the trick shots!" then proceed to work his way through the new inventory.

The rest of the day usually involved some form of shopping in the afternoon, going to a disco that night, then a long sensual sleep in on Sunday morning followed by some less athletic sex than what they had enjoyed the day before. Shopping was the thing Marion missed the most since moving west. Toowoomba might only be a regional centre, but its shopping facilities left Dalby for dead, and it even had a Myer Department store.

What mystified Lennie was how Marion could manage to try on ten dresses and as many pairs of shoes in as many shops, buy none, and not upset the shop assistant at all. She was then as likely to head back to the first shop and buy the first thing she had tried on. When Lennie quizzed her on this, she said that she was "shopping not buying". That confused him all the more, because in his mind, surely shopping and buying were one and the same thing. Lennie was happy to make her happy, but said to her, "There is no way you will change my mind that shopping should be conducted as a speed event and not as an endurance event."

Their relationship grew stronger by the day and Lennie wondered what it was about her that so appealed to him. She was quite attractive and had a good figure, which used to be his only requirements in female companionship, but Marion offered so much more than the other girls he had dated. She had a wicked sense of humour to begin with, and he loved the way they matched wits, fired off each other in conversation and laughed a lot. She was also quite intelligent and well-travelled; certainly, compared to Lennie who hadn't even been out of the state. She knew people and knew about people too, which no doubt came from her time as a barmaid in Brisbane as well as in Dalby.

Lennie was mesmerized when she told him how Dennis Lillie had come into a hotel where she was working a few years earlier in Brisbane. She not only served him a beer, but they had a long conversation as well. For Marion's part, she just found Lennie easy company. He was a fit attractive young guy who had a bit of ambition. He was good for a laugh and he respected women, unlike a lot of the men she knew in Brisbane. Certainly, no one who had ever been associated with her mother was in his class. This said a lot, because while Lennie was a nice young fella, no one would have described him as "classy." On reflection, Marion decided that Lennie had a lot to offer, plus his business was doing well and he had nothing to spend the proceeds on now but herself.

After living in each other's pocket for nearly four months, it still came as a surprise to Di when Lennie had first raised the prospect of having Marion move in with him. She had no major reservations, other than that Lennie didn't know this girl all that well. She had to admit that they did seem to get along like a house on fire and she reasoned that if Lennie didn't start getting serious soon, she would never become a grandmother. The only advice she could give him was not to rush into anything, as going out together and living together were two vastly different propositions.

"Remember when you live together you see everything up close; the good is better and the bad is worse."

When Lennie broached the idea with Marion a week or so later, it took her no time at all to pack what few belongings she had brought from Brisbane into the same tatty suitcase and tell the publican that she would be moving out of the small room above the hotel where she had lived since arriving in town.

She couldn't wait to move into what had previously only been referred to, as Lennie Krause's bachelor pad. Her previous visits to the house had always been late at night and usually she headed straight to his bedroom. The lights were always down low, and she had a vague recollection that it was spartan but clean.

Truth be told she didn't much care, it wasn't her house, and as long as she had an exciting and satisfying time followed by a comfortable night and a good breakfast in the morning, she was happy enough. Once she became a new occupant, however, she had the time and self-interest to have a good look around, and quickly realised that this was indeed bachelor pad central.

The room at the pub was certainly no palace, but this place, well as they said about small towns, "It was okay to visit but you wouldn't want to live there". The furnishings were rudimentary at best, and largely consisted of hand-me-downs from his friends or his mother or stuff that had previously occupied a dusty corner of the local op shop or second-hand shop. There was not one new item she could see anywhere. The flooring throughout the place was just old linoleum, and in numerous high traffic spots, it was so well-worn that the floorboards under it were clearly visible. She even noticed now that the kitchen table was covered with the same linoleum as had been used on the floor. There were just a few cups, saucers, plates and cutlery, none of which matched, and every pot and pan looked like it was regularly used as part of a drum kit. Marion wasn't a housekeeper by nature, but she quickly realised that the place needed a lot of attention and a good clean in all the places that a bachelor was sure to miss. She soon set about that task with undisguised relish.

In a matter of a few weeks, she had totally transformed Len's bachelor pad into a half ways acceptable home, right down to lace curtains on the kitchen windows. Of course, the transformation was largely due to a complete overhaul of the furnishings, accomplished in stages. During the week or a weekend trip to Toowoomba, she scoured the stores and made the selections. Lennie contributed as well, by signing all the hire purchase agreements.

A new bedroom suite with double bed was quickly followed by a new lounge, new T.V. and stereo unit and a couple of big floor rugs. The kitchen now sported a matching crockery set, new cutlery, and a couple of new pots and pans. There was even a new kitchen setting where the tabletop wasn't the same as the floor coverings. Marion was surprised at how much she enjoyed the task, but she also knew part of the fun was because she wasn't using her own money. For his part, Lennie appreciated the order and the much-improved cleanliness of the place but wondered if, over the last couple of months, he wasn't responsible for half the new hire purchase agreements signed up in the district.

Lennie had no complaints about all the changes because everything Marion did just made life more comfortable, and he knew he could afford it. He owned his car outright, his business was trading well, his footie team was on a roll, and he had no other financial commitments. Marion was happy and she was certainly keeping him happy in more ways than one.

While he was popular around town prior to her arrival, he was "lucky if he got lucky" once a month and that was potentially risky. Sex for Lennie always involved the use of a rubber device he wasn't fond of, but that he believed was essential for his own protection rather than his partners. In his experience, a lot of the unattached girls around Dalby and district had an agenda when it came to sex.

The bride of, at least, two of his school mates had been accompanied down the aisle by their beaming father with the proverbial shotgun at the ready. Lennie thought life was too short and too interesting to settle down just yet. He had not long turned twenty-two after all, and he had big plans for his business and his football career. This new relationship with Marion was ideal, she ticked every box. She was a "looker" with a good figure, a great company, feisty, had an insatiable sex drive, and knew what she wanted. She was too smart not to be on some form of contraception, and best of all, she wasn't in the least clingy and worked in a pub too! It was absolutely everything a young bachelor could ask for.

Chapter 5

One person who wasn't happy with the new living arrangement was Coach Cowley, who had noted a distinct lack of commitment over the last month or so from his star loose forward. After Wednesday night training, he bemoaned Len's lack of form to the team captain, Kev Johnson.

"That boy has a mile of potential, Kev, but the way he's going lately, it's not going to be realised. I have had a few calls from some of the local selectors and they tell me they have been watching his form for a while as well. From these discussions, he was looking a near certainty to make the team for the next Country versus City game. But I can tell you, Kev, if the selectors are watching what I have been seeing of late, he can kiss off any chance of playing representative football. He needs to get his finger out of his arse, knuckle down at training, and start putting together a few good games on the pitch."

Kev chuckled and told the coach to have a heart because after all, Len was in love. The coach failed to see the funny side and bellowed, "LOVE, FUCKEN' LOVE!!! The kids just cunt struck, is all. That blousy pourer of piss that he has hooked up with, that barmaid… what's her name, 'Marion The Maid', she is just leading him around the shops by his prick and he's too stupid to realise it."

Kev loved the coach's clever turn of phrase, but he knew the coach was in the minority as far as his opinion of Marion was concerned. She had settled into life in a country town quickly. As a barmaid in one of the larger watering holes, she probably met more people in a day than most locals would in a week. She was good at her job, her good looks were an obvious asset, however, it was her feisty nature and cheeky sense of humour that was the constant source of amusement to The Imperial's patrons. It wasn't long before only the very game or very drunk took her on in even a mild disagreement.

She had also earned the silent admiration of a lot of the locals shortly after she had moved in with Lennie. No one was sure of all the facts, but she was credited with meting out a little long overdue justice of her own to Darcy Finnamore, the husband of one of the kitchen staff at The Imperial. Cissy Finnamore worked part time as a kitchen hand, helping the cook with meal prep during the peak times of lunch and, sometimes, dinner. She generally was also left to do the after service cleaning, washing, and drying. She was a mousy little woman of indeterminate age, who was rarely seen without a bruise on some parts of her face, or the dapple of green-black finger marks on her scrawny arms.

Darcy Finnamore was something of a roustabout, taking jobs on properties where he could, or shooting roos when it was worth his while. Whoever came up with the expression "Absence makes the heart grow fonder" wasn't thinking of Darcy and Cissy. He was a mean son of a bitch who seemed to spend just enough time out of town to allow Cissy's bruises heal, so that when he got to work on her again, she presented him with a brand-new canvas.

Marion had first encountered some of Darcy's handywork shortly after she started at The Imperial. It was just before closing, and she had gone out to the kitchen on Bob's orders to ensure it was all locked up. Cissy should have been long finished cleaning up by that stage, but a light was on inside the pantry and when she looked down, Cissy was on the floor with a wet rag in her hand. Her bottom lip was split, she had a vacant look in her eyes, and she was sort of humming as she cleaned up a mess of oil and flour that was spread all over the floor and all over her head. This time Darcy had decided to not only hurt her but degrade her as well. Marion raced in and got Bob, and between them they closed up the pub, helped Cissy get cleaned up and settled, and then he drove her home.

On getting back to the pub and while cleaning up the remaining mess, Marion asked Bob for the history and what they could do to help. "Unfortunately," he said, "I am at a complete loss." He conceded that the whole town considered Darcy Finnamore to be a first-rate prick. He confirmed that the police had been called, that he was banned from The Imperial, and that, on a few occasions, the locals here and elsewhere had tried beating some civility into him. The general conclusion was that unless Darcy fell out of love with the bottle, or unless Cissy was prepared to leave him and leave town, that nothing would ever change. Marion decided then and there that there must be a better way to sort the matter out. Cissy was the victim here, why should she be the one to sacrifice her life just to be safe from Darcy?

Meanwhile life for Lennie and Marion as a couple continued to develop, he even had his mother over for dinner one night. The conversation between his mother and girlfriend was comfortable and animated as they bustled around preparing dinner. And when the topic got around to Cissy's predicament, they were united in their contempt for Darcy Finnamore.

It was to be a month or so later, however, before Marion's next encounter with Darcy. He had come to The Imperial via about five hotels and had consumed the better part of a bottle of rum by the time he got to the kitchen at the back of the hotel.

Bob could ban him if he liked, but Bob didn't have eyes in the back of his head, so Darcy let himself into the kitchen through the fly screened rear door and began helping himself to some of the food that Cissy was preparing for the evening meals. He first scarfed down half a piece of sliced beef she was cutting up to put into the bain-marie, and then he dipped the rest into the pot of gravy before suspending it over his mouth and finishing it off.

Cissy knew she was going to have to ask him to stop, and she also knew from bitter experience, that he was patiently waiting for her to do just that. When she issued the inevitable request, he sprang with a speed that still surprised her. By the time Bob and a couple of regulars from the public bar had responded to the commotion, Cissy was on the floor of the kitchen nursing sore ribs and a swollen eye while Darcy was already on his way to the next hotel with the contents of his wife's purse pushed roughly into the fob pocket of his well-worn jeans.

Every time Marion saw Cissy in the kitchen, she was reminded of what Darcy had done and would no doubt do again. It was a replay of what she had seen her mother go through. Sure, some of the men here had tried force on Darcy, and the police had provided him on occasion with a night's accommodation in a less than comfy cell, but all this had achieved nothing.

Over the next few weeks Marion felt she had devised a solution of her own, all she needed was the opportunity to put her plan in place. With the rear kitchen door now securely locked, there had been no further sightings of Darcy at The Imperial, but it was a small town and a number of regulars had mentioned seeing him around over the last week or so. Marion had been keeping an eye out for him and sighted what she had been looking for on her way back from the bank one day.

Parked out the back of the local Foodland grocery store was Darcy's tan Land Cruiser Ute with its distinctive one blue driver's side door. As she walked up the street past the bar of The Railway Hotel, Marion noticed him drinking alone in the corner. He had just put down the remnants of a five-ounce beer beside a shot glass that most likely contained his favoured OP rum. He looked typically disheveled and unshaven and given the problem he was having with rolling himself a cigarette, he had obviously already had a few drinks. Was this the opportunity she had been waiting for?

Marion had noticed that Darcy's Land Cruiser was laden with provisions and had additional jerry cans of fuel strapped on the side, so despite his early morning drinking session, it was obvious that he was all packed to head off to the bush. She decided that fate had given her the ideal opportunity to give this prick a bit of grief of his own. She turned quickly on her heel, and walked briskly into the

Foodland store and purchased just two items—a two-kilo packet of salt and a large bag of sugar.

She lingered outside the hotel, watching from a distance until she saw the barmaid place a fresh beer in front of Darcy. She quickly calculated that she had a safe three or four minutes to act. With her heart racing she walked hurriedly back to the Foodland car park and added a couple of kilos of extra provisions to his loaded vehicle.

When the search party caught up with Darcy nearly six days later, they could not understand how a bushman of his experience had come so close to death. His Land Cruiser had evidently developed fuel problems a few days out of Dalby and to compound the problem, his drinking water was fouled with salt. He had initially followed the standard rule of staying with the broken-down vehicle, however, when things became grim, he had decided to set out on foot for the nearest homestead. Unfortunately for Darcy, by the time he decided to leave the vehicle, the lack of water had impacted both his common sense and his sense of direction.

He was staggering in large circles when by sheer chance he was spotted by a grazier looking for breaks in a remote fence line. The grazier got him back to the station; his wife rehydrated him as best she could while they waited for the RFDS to land on their remote strip. From all reports the RFDS estimated he was no more than a day or so away from meeting his maker.

Chapter 6

Like all small towns, Dalby thrived on rumour. While she was clever enough not to openly take the credit, Marion seemed to know way too much of what had happened to Darcy and why he had ended up in the state he was in. She seemed to know before the police did that his jerry cans of fuel were laced with sugar and that his water was full of salt. It wasn't long before Lennie heard that it was common knowledge that Marion was the architect of Darcy's near demise.

Lennie's initial reaction was one of pride, but he was also concerned for her safety. If he had heard the rumor, there was a good chance that Darcy had too, and while he was still weak from the experience, he wasn't too weak to plot his revenge, particularly if he knew where to direct it.

That night as Lennie was cleaning up after dinner, he raised the matter with Marion. "I heard a rumour that a barmaid from Brisbane was the one who spiked Finnimore's truck. That wouldn't be that new barmaid at The Imperial, would it?" he

53

smirked. As he returned the last of the dinner plates into the kitchen cupboard, he continued without waiting for Marion's response. "Because if it was, I would suggest she keep a very low profile for quite a while."

He had expected a bit of light-hearted banter or maybe a logical discussion and so was shocked by the tone of the response. Marion slammed the frying pan she was drying down onto the kitchen table and fixed Len with a steely stare. "To begin with, Lennie, I thought he might have been stuck for a day at best, but I wouldn't have cared if the prick had died of thirst. Maybe that would have been an even better result. Second, I'm not scared of him. Men who beat women are the lowest form of scum and in my experience, they are without exception the world's greatest cowards."

Marion waited for Lennie to engage in the argument, but he was too shocked at her reaction to say anything. "Probably the only people who come close to this low life are weak pricks like you lot at the pub. You know what he does to Cissy, but you do absolutely nothing about it. It shouldn't have been up to me to sort him out."

Lennie decided he was going to have to come to the defense of the pub's patrons and inform her of the time Bob caught up with Darcy and almost put him through the wall of the kitchen. Marion was deaf to reason, however, and the more they talked, the angrier and louder she became. He decided to back off a while and let her lose some steam, but she continued her rant.

"Look at yourself, Lennie. You are young and fit and very much the big man on the footy field, but what did you yourself ever do to sort him out? Nothing, that's what. You are as weak as piss when it comes to doing what a real man should do. Get it, Lennie, you are weak as piss; fucken weak as piss!"

Len was totally taken aback by the venom and was at a loss as to how to approach the situation. She seemed to be wanting him to apologize but for what? He walked into the bedroom and as he changed into his pajamas, decided to try and inject a bit of sweet reason and a lot less emotion to the discussion.

"Mate, I am a lover not a fighter, and I am sort of proud of you for sticking it to that prick. Thing is you are only new in town remember, and you don't know the whole history behind a lot of these domestics." Marion changed into her nightie as well, threw the sheets back and climbed into bed, but said nothing so Lennie continued. "We both know what he is like, but you don't know everything that has happened in the past. You especially don't know what has happened to Cissy in the past when various people have tried to teach Darcy a lesson."

Lennie went on to calmly explain that Bob had also had at least two major run-ins with Finnamore after catching him loitering out the back of the pub or in the kitchen itself. Both times, there had been major brawls where Darcy had come out well and truly on the losing side. The trouble was that after Darcy got a flogging and then sobered up, he just waited until Cissy got home and took his revenge out on her. In the end everyone felt that giving Darcy a toweling was counterproductive to Cissy's health.

"Cissy knows the solution is to leave him and get out of town, but she just won't take it. My advice is play dumb and whatever you do, don't take any credit for it, he shoots roos for a living, remember." Marion was staring at him now, her eyes wide and her breath rapid, but she still said nothing. Thinking he was finally making headway Lennie continued in a lower voice. "You say he is a coward; well he can still be pretty cowardly while he's looking at you through the scope of his .223. So follow the golden rule with this prick, honey, and don't tempt fate!"

Marion was beginning to see his point of view, but right or wrong, Lennie wasn't getting the last word, so she wound up for her final salvo. "Lennie, when it comes to pricks like him there are no rules, golden or otherwise, and don't you dare call me dumb. Now turn out the fucken light, I'm going to sleep."

Lennie got up and flicked off the light switch, then got back into bed and snuggled up behind her with no intention other than to offer a bit of comfort and a warm body on a cold night. Marion responded by elbowing him in the ribs, grabbing more than her share of the blankets and hissing, "Len, I said I'm going to sleep."

"What the fuck brought that on?" Lennie wondered, as he rolled away from her and crushed the pillow to his chest. He stared at the ceiling for a while contemplating how a well-intentioned jibe had quickly developed into a full-on row. He was beginning to realize that she was a lot more complex person than he had thought. In this household, in her mind at least, he might pay the bills, but she wore the pants. "Mum is on the money again," he thought, remembering her advice about the risks associated with them living together.

He and Marion had some fantastic times since the move, and the good Mum referred to had indeed been even better. If this, their first argument, was a rare example of the bad being worse, then he was prepared to live with it.

Len woke up next morning to find Marion was already up and rattling around in the kitchen. In their discussions before Marion had moved in, his mum had counselled him that couples should never go to sleep angry with each other. He had no option but to ignore that advice last night, but he knew that he had to rectify the situation this morning. Unfortunately, Marion had her own interpretation of what you do, if at the end of the day, you are involved in a blazing row. Her version was "never go to sleep angry, stay awake, and plot your revenge." This meant of course that when they caught up with each other in the kitchen that morning, they had totally different agendas.

Len walked up behind Marion, wrapped his arms around her and pecked her on the cheek. Before he could utter a word, she spat out, "For fuck sake, Lennie, brush your teeth, your breath is rank."

"..And a very good morning to you too," said Lennie, not without an edge of sarcasm and hurt in his voice.

"Don't think for a moment that I have forgotten about last night," Marion shot back. "I thought I could expect you to support me. Instead, you tell me I am in the wrong, tell me I'm dumb, then lecture me like I was a school kid. That weak Finnamore prick deserved everything he got and was lucky things didn't turn out worse for him. His poor suffering wife is less than half his size and he delights in knocking her around and not one of you weak arseholes does anything much about it."

Lennie tried again to put her straight on a few points, like the reason there was still a big section of broken wall in the pub kitchen about the size of

Darcy Finnamore's head. Like the fact that Darcy was barred from drinking at The Imperial and about five other pubs in town. Marion was still steaming though, and in no mood to listen to anything he said. She grabbed her half-eaten piece of toast and stormed out the back door leaving her unwashed plates on the kitchen bench.

Len was learning that there was no reasoning with her while her temper was up. If he knew Marion, and he wasn't all that sure now how well he did, she would be in the backyard, dragging on a cigarette roughly in time with her pacing. He decided the safest place for him at present was to leave her alone with her cigarette and her temper.

After a quick shower Len pulled on his greasy overalls, then checked the fridge to assess the options for breakfast. He soon realised that Marion had eaten the last of the eggs, there was no milk left, and even the kettle was empty. He needed to get an early start anyway as he had promised a new customer that he would definitely have the transmission job on his Fairlaine sedan finished by late afternoon. The new customer was Alan Fitzgerald, apparently better known to all and sundry as "Fitzy". Lennie knew that if he was happy with the job on the Fairlaine, there would be a lot more work to be had from him, from his family, and his contacts in that district.

Lennie was aware he still had some bridge mending to do with Marion but knew he would be wasting his time trying to achieve anything right now. He had this important job ahead at the garage and then footy practice after work, so conciliation, explanation, even an apology, was going to have to wait until later that night. Hopefully Marion's mood would have improved some by then too. He decided to give her a quick kiss goodbye and promise that they would have a long talk about last night when he got back from training.

Len grabbed his car keys and walked around the back of the weatherboard house to where he had parked his Ute last night, expecting to find both car and a sullen girlfriend. Neither were to be seen. Marion had obviously used the spare key he left in the ashtray and driven off while he was in the shower, leaving him stranded.

Lennie's day now started with an unexpected two kilometres walk to the workshop. As he trudged up the street, he worked out that his mum could rustle him up some breakfast while he opened the workshop and started working on the Fairlaine. He smiled as he saw her small weatherboard house with the fading paint job come into view, realizing as well that having his mum as the breakfast cook would actually see him in front time wise. As he walked down his mother's gravel drive, Len quickly noticed there was no green Zephyr in the car port and no lights on in the kitchen. His stomach rumbling, he reached into his pocket to retrieve his keys only to realise that the spare one to his mum's house was on the spare set that Marion had taken. He wasn't prepared to break in just to make himself some breakfast, and so resolved that he would have to survive on a mug of sweet black tea he could make in the workshop.

He pulled back the heavy sliding door to his shed and there was the copper-coloured Ford that Fitzgerald had delivered the day before. It was only about four years old but looked to have had a hard life so far. It was covered in red dust inside and out; the radio aerial had been bent at some stage and roughly re-straightened and a number of the panels were either dented or scratched. Len boiled up the kettle, and as he drank his meagre breakfast, began to work out how to best attack the job at hand. Whatever Marion was up to, he figured, wouldn't take long, and she would soon drop the Ute back. The parts he had ordered for the transmission rebuild job were due on the morning bus from Toowoomba, but he didn't need them immediately. He had a fair bit of prep work to do first, draining the transmission and then pulling it all down. Provided she was back within the next couple of hours, he would be no worse off.

Half a dozen times Lennie had gotten out from under the Fairlaine, certain he had heard the familiar note of his old Ute, but all were false alarms. At the pub, Bob had a standing rule that his "girls" couldn't take phone calls during a shift, so once the transmission was out, he decided he had no option but to walk all the way into town to The Imperial. He hoped to find both Marion and his car there waiting for him. The first person he saw when he walked into the public bar was his mother and Lennie soon discovered that he wasn't the only one who was pissed off with Marion.

Di greeted her son with a terse, "About time she turned up, she has really left us in the lurch! When she gets her arse in here she better go straight in and see Bob."

Lennie initially gave his mother a look of complete confusion then responded, "What, you mean to say she isn't here?"

"No, she isn't here," Di said. "Luckily, Bob called me in early to help him sort out some mix up with the invoices from last month's cigarette order. When it was obvious she was a no show, I had to abandon the paperwork, help him open up, and then start serving the early morning regulars."

Once his mother had gotten into the routine of serving the few early morning drinkers, Lennie had a quick chat with her and explained that he was in real bother with an important job. "Whatever the rules Bob has about phone calls," he said, "please ring me during any break you get, and let me know if Marion surfaces."

Lennie managed to hitch a lift most of the way back to the workshop, and once there took the next hour to finish stripping down the transmission and cleaning all the parts that were to be reused. Once that was done, he realized he had no other option open to him, but to just wait for either a call from Di or for Marion to reappear. Patience, however, wasn't one of Lennie's virtues; he was working at a tight timeframe on a very important job and the clock was ticking. He felt frustrated, furious, and impotent. He had done all he could without the parts, right down to cleaning up the workshop and setting up all the tools but there was still no sign of Marion or his Ute. He was hot, hungry, and well aware that he had to find another way of collecting the parts from the depot.

Despite the heat of the day having now arrived, his frustration made the second walk to the pub quicker than the first, but Marion still wasn't there. He went in and saw Bob and arranged to borrow the pub's Ute so he could drive out to the bus station for the parts. The trouble was they had just loaded up the Ute for a trip to the dump, so he had to offer to first drive it out to the tip and unload it. This meant his plan for a quick meal at the bar was traded in for two packets of crisps to be eaten on the run.

By the time he had cleaned the pub rubbish out of the back of their Ute, driven from the local tip to the bus depot and collected the parts, dropped off the parts at the garage, driven the Ute back to the pub and then walked back to the garage, it was past two o'clock. There was only one small consolation, at least the parts were the ones he had ordered. That would have been the bitter end.

Lennie got to work on reassembling the transmission but the faster he went the more stupid mistakes he made, and he soon realized, that despite his promises, there was no way that the job would be ready for his new customer by that afternoon.

Chapter 7

About 4.30, Alan Fitzgerald arrived in a weather-beaten old Land Rover Ute, driven by one of his workmen. Bob at The Imperial knew the family and had recommended Lennie as a cheaper option to resolve the car's transmission problems. From what Bob had told Lennie, this Fitzy was a confirmed bachelor who had a reputation as a bit of a lad and for having a heart as big as all outdoors. "On the flip side," Bob had told him, "He won't put up with shit from anybody and doesn't have to." When Lennie enquired as to what that actually meant, Bob gave a little awkward laugh. "Let's just say he is well known for the phrase, -I'll punch a hole in you! - and I think he actually could!"

Fitzy walked into the workshop, chuckling, mid-way through recounting some tall tale to his offsider, but his initial good humour quickly evaporated when he noticed the Fairlaine was still jacked up, parts were spread over the floor and the promised job was far from finished. Lennie slid out from under the car when he heard them arrive and looked up from the floor to see a huge man with hands the size of hams, reaching down to help him to his feet. Lennie, of course, was not in the best of moods either by this stage. His girlfriend had the shits with him for no good reason, she had taken off with his car to God knows where; he had probably walked six to eight kilometres today in thirty-degree heat while wearing greasy overalls and heavy boots and all he had managed to eat all day was two lousy packets of crisps.

Fitzy was soon right in his face and tapped him lightly on the chest three times with a thick calloused finger. "Just what the fuck have you been doing all day dead shit!"

Lennie's simple response came from pure exasperation. "How about you just go fuck yourself!" This was not the smartest thing to say to a tough as teak cockie, who promptly sat Len on his arse with a short sharp left. The steam quickly went out of Lennie. He knew he was in the wrong and he had a lot at stake, so he stayed on the floor, put his hands up in surrender, apologized and while still, gave a truncated version of the extenuating circumstances.

Fitzy extended him the courtesy of listening to his woman problems, but it was obvious from the expression on his face that he wasn't much in a forgiving mood. Lennie bounced up off the floor and said, "Seeing as all is now forgiven, Fitzy, how about giving me a lift to football training?"

Fitzy's response was slow in coming. He stood back from the mechanic, feigned as though he was about to land another heavy blow, then burst out laughing. "You are one cheeky little bugger, Lennie Krause. I am only 'Fitzy' to my mates, and things would have to improve substantially for you to qualify. Let's hope your timing is better as a footie player than a mechanic and that your timing as a mechanic improves too. If you want me to drop you off to training, you just make bloody sure that the job is done by lunchtime tomorrow, because I'll be fucked if I will put up with driving all the way into town for nothing, a second time."

Lenny was about to suggest that a phone call before the trip might have been good idea, then he felt the tender spot under his right eye and thought better of it. He quickly locked up, threw his footy kit into the tray of the old Land Rover and climbed in beside it. He tapped the side of the Ute with his still greasy hands, and they headed out to training.

The team had already warmed up by the time Lenny arrived. He quickly put on his kit, pulled on his boots and ran over to the coach to ask what they were up to. "Well I don't know what your plans are Lennie but the rest of the boys are fucken training. You should give it a try; it might help your game."

Now usually Lennie might respond with a smart-arse comment of his own, but the fight was well and truly out of him. Instead, he hung his head and quietly whispered, "Listen, coach, I've had one shit of a day, sorry I'm late. You just tell me what you want and I'm yours." An apologetic tone was the last thing the coach expected, but he was delighted to hear it. He could see Lenny was troubled and wondered if it had something to do with the swelling under his right eye.

"Listen Lenny," he said lowering his voice, "I think you have more potential than any other bloke on this fucken team, but you won't realise it unless you knuckle down and put in a shit load more effort than you have been doing of late. They will be picking the Queensland Country side in the next month or so, and from discussions I have had, you could very well be in the mix. But only if you get your fucken act together. Some see you as one of the breakaways but I don't think you have the height for 6 or 7, I see you as the number 8, and that spot is wide open. Now give me a couple of laps to warm up and let's see if you can prove me right."

The pep-talk lifted Len's mood no end and he sprinted off around the oval determined to do what it took to make things right with the coach. Fitzy and his offsider had decided it was too risky to head back to their property at this time of the afternoon. Driving at dusk was almost guaranteed to see them adding a few more roo carcasses to those already on the side of the road. Best if they stay here a while, watch the boys train, go into town for a few beers and a counter tea, then head back at around eight.

After the warmup and a series of back line moves, the coach had them all doing sprints, then a few more laps, then some short sprints. A couple of the bigger blokes in the squad, who had obviously eaten better than Lennie that day, eventually bought up their lunch on the sideline. This was apparently the clue the coach was after to indicate that he was getting toward the end of the fitness session.

"Okay, boys, to finish off, I want you to form up into two packs. We need to practice that set piece again close to the try line." As usual Lennie was at the number 8 position at the back of the scrum. The scrum half fed the ball, and both packs put their backs into it. Eventually Lennie's squad gave a little more effort and the ball was trapped at Lennie's feet. Out of the corner of his eye, he could see the goal posts close by. He waited for one more heave from his pack, unbound, picked up the ball and headed for the try line.

The openside breakaway saw him coming and readied himself for the tackle. Len turned, motioning as if he was going to pass to the flyhalf who had wrapped around behind him. The breakaway hesitated but instead of passing, Lennie backed up, wedging the breakaway against the goal posts. Lennie then simply spun around and planted the ball over the try line.   "That's more like it, Lennieeee!" shouted the coach. "You guys have earned an early shower, once around the oval and we will call it quits for today."

When Lennie emerged from the change room, he was surprised to see Fitzy and his offsider still there, standing in the shadow of the grandstand beside their old Land Rover. "The Fairlaine's not ready yet!" said Lenny with a big grin on his face. "Honestly why are you guys still here?"

When they explained their plans to stay in town for a counter meal and then head back, Lennie promptly recommended The Imperial as the best in town. "In fact, I was intending to somehow get there myself as I need to roll breakfast, lunch, and dinner into the one meal tonight after that session. With any sort of luck, I will also find my girlfriend and my car." With that he assumed he had scored a lift. He threw his bag, now filled with his training gear and dirty overalls and boots, into the tray of the Ute, climbed in beside them and issued directions to The Imperial.

He was surprised to find his mother still behind the bar when they walked in. "You can't have been here all day." he said.

"Well, I had a break after lunch, but the roster turned into a shamozzle after Marion failed to show up. Bob needed me to help him do a part of the afternoon shift himself, but I will be heading home in about five minutes."

Len introduced his two companions as Alan Fitzgerald and his mate Kev. "I am doing a big job for Mr. Fitzgerald and they offered me a lift from training. We are hoping to get a counter meal and a few beers." His mother then turned to Alan. "You're welcome, Mr. Fitzgerald. What would you like to—"

Alan quickly cut her off. "Fitzy, please call me Fitzy, all my friends call me Fitzy." When Lennie gave him a sideways look like a lost puppy, he laughed his big belly laugh, ruffled Lennie's hair and added, "Okay, mate, you can call me Fitzy too."

After a quick discussion Lennie asked his mum to arrange the three biggest rump steak meals the cook could lay his hands on. Di made the meal arrangements, ordered three pots of beer for them, one with a dash of Sars, and then prepared to head home. Lennie pulled out his wallet and paid for all three meals.

After telling Bob she was heading home, Di pulled Lennie aside and whispered to him that he should keep her informed with what was up with Marion. "She is a popular girl here, Len, and good at her job, but she really left us in the lurch and Bob is likely to give her marching orders tomorrow unless she has a bloody good excuse for today."

Len promised he would let her know when he knew. While he had been getting progressively angrier with her throughout the day, after the excellent run at training, and with thoughts of a representative jersey now firmly embedded in his head, he was feeling a lot more forgiving than were

Bob and his mother. That was pretty usual for Lennie, though. He was quick to anger but once he had some sort of emotional outburst, he put things behind him. He had never been one to hold grudges or stew on things.

After buying the second round of beers, Lennie begged off for a few minutes so he could track down Bob and explain what had happened with Marion. He found him in a small room beside the kitchen that served as an office of sorts. Bob was shuffling paperwork and obviously not in the best of moods.

"Bob, I am so sorry for what happened with Marion today. She hasn't been well for days and to cap things off, we had a blazing row about nothing much this morning and she left the house in tears. I will have her come in early tomorrow to explain things but be gentle with her please. I guess it's woman's stuff."

Bob's reaction was understandable anger. "Lennie, there are these wonderful things called telephones. It would have been pretty easy for her to give me some warning no matter how sick she was. I know she is your girlfriend, mate, but that doesn't give her special privileges. Get her to come in for a chat first thing tomorrow."

Lennie berated himself under his breath as he walked out of the office. "You are a weak prick. Marion was totally in the wrong and after all the things Bob has done for you, you try and get her out of trouble by playing the menstruation card."

Over their steaks, Fitzy and Lennie were beginning to really hit it off despite the age difference. Fitzy was appreciative of the gesture of a free meal, admired the fact that Len was having a go at building his own business, and liked his cheeky attitude. Even though he had only seen him during a training run, he was also impressed with his football ability. "That was a hell of a try there today, Lennie," he laughed." I don't think I have ever seen a Number 8 fend off a breakaway using his arse before."

Lennie chuckled back. "That one just came to me on the spot. I knew he would have gotten to me if it weren't for the goal posts, so I figured I would add them into the play. Might not have looked pretty but it did the job." Lennie bit into another hunk of steak and ordered another round of drinks; what had started out as a shit of a day was turning into a ripper.

Len asked the new barmaid to hand him a set of darts from under the counter, went over and opened the cover to the dart board, grabbed a wet cloth and wiped down the small adjacent blackboard. "Up for a game of 501, boys?" he asked. Fitzy's offsider agreed by slapping a $10 note down on the bar and the others did likewise. Four games and six rounds of beers later, and Bob was happy to be calling for last drinks. Not much thought had gone into how Lennie was getting home or whether the two bushies would attempt the trip back to the property that night. As the night progressed, Lennie gradually expanded on his reasons for not having finished the Fairlaine job and Marion's involvement was central to the story.

Thankfully not all common sense had been drowned that night. Fitzy and Kev decided to grab a six-pack for the road, get Lennie home and then grab a bit of floor at his place and head off at sparrow fart the next morning. When they rolled into his driveway, they saw Lennie's Ute out the back and a glimpse of a young woman slamming the back door shut. Fitzy laughed and punched Lennie lightly in the shoulder. "Well that's one problem solved, but I think another one is just around the corner."

Lennie opened up the back door but got no welcome from Marion who was now in bed doing a very good impression of being fast asleep. The boys got themselves settled on the couch, polished off the last of the six-pack and then Lennie dragged himself off to the bedroom and was soon dead to the world asleep.

Chapter 8

Lennie's drinking companions of the night before were almost back at "Kilmarnock" by the time he woke up much later than usual next morning. His mouth was as dry as the road to Moonie, he was close to throwing up, and he had a monster of a throbbing headache. While he was stumbling into the kitchen through the side door and out to the toilet in the backyard to urgently relieve himself, Fitzy and his offsider were heading up the main drive toward Kilmarnock homestead. They were initially both a little jaded as well but had stopped for fuel and a big burger on the way out and were now already recovered and ready for another day's hard work.

Lennie was not as lucky. While he enjoyed a cleansing ale as much as the next bloke, he rarely consumed as much as he had that night. It was obvious that he was suffering badly for trying to match it with the more seasoned bushie drinkers.

When Lennie returned from the toilet, Marion told him she was going to work early as she had a lot of explaining to do to Bob. Then she pointed

Lennie to a note scrawled on the back of an old calendar and held in place on the kitchen table by an empty XXXX stubbie half full of cigarette butts. The note read "The Fairlaine better be finished by this afternoon….or I'll punch a hole in ya!! Seriously call me before 3 if there is likely to be a problem, otherwise I'll see you at 4.30…thanks for the use of the couch." It was simply signed, A.F.

"Love note from one of your grubby new boyfriends, is it?" said Marion with thinly disguised disgust.

In the softest most reasonable voice he could muster, Lennie replied, "Come on, mate, it's too early for this and I am too crook. We haven't talked about the barney we had, and you have a big problem at work with Bob. To start off, I have sort of explained things to Bob for you. I told him it's that time of the month and you have big woman problems. As an old bachelor he won't be game to discuss that topic and you will be sweet. Let me grab a quick shower then I'll drive you into work and we can talk a few things through."

Marion accepted the lift but the short trip only gave her just enough time to complain about him crawling into bed last night smelling of beer and sweat and then seriously boxing his ear about discussing her "woman's business" with Bob. Lennie wanted to discuss their fight and the news he had about his rugby prospects, but when he stopped the car at the pub, Marion held up her hand. "Lennie you have a car to fix and I have a job to save. We will talk tonight. By the way if you want to get back in my good books, drop back to the house on the way to the workshop, wash the sheets, and clean the place up a bit. Your new drinking buddies left it stinking of stale piss and smoke."

She obviously still had the shits big time, and he wasn't well enough and didn't have the time anyway to broach matters and mend fences. Lennie figured the best cure for his throbbing head and dull headache was a greasy bacon burger from the local café, and multiple mugs of strong coffee. After he polished them off, he headed home to do a little house cleaning before returning to the workshop.

While Lennie worked and pondered how best to mend fences with Marion, Fitzy was mending real fences out at Kilmarnock with the station hand, Kev. Under the shade of a big eucalypt, they toiled in the dry heat, tensioning wires with the strainer, running new ones and twitching them up. As the morning wore on, they both continued to recount stories from the previous evening and raising various humorous options of how Lennie might be coping with his feisty girlfriend that morning.

In the end, Fitzy pushed his wide Akubra hat onto the back of his head, wiped his brow with the back of his forearm, and said to his workmate, "You know, I haven't laughed that much since I don't know when. That cheeky shit of a kid; and to think I sat him on his arse within five minutes of meeting him."

Kev's six-word response, "Doesn't he remind you of Spud," stopped the conversation dead in its tracks. Fitzy immediately went from upbeat and talkative to all business. He instructed Kev to head back to the homestead and bring back two extra coils of barbed wire and two of plain. When Kev took the leather cover off his watch face to check the time, Fitzy quickly added by way of explanation, "While we are out here, we might as well restring this all the way out to the Comet mill. Grab us some lunch as well, I'll carry on here."

As Kev and his Ute disappeared into the dusty distance, Fitzy redoubled his efforts which meant leaving the shade of the big eucalypt. Within twenty minutes he had worked himself into a lather and returned to the shade. He grabbed the canvas water bag they had slung over the gnarled ironbark fence post, took a long swig then dropped to his haunches, deep in thought. The memories of his young brother came flooding back.

It must be close to eight years since Spud died, and he still had not forgiven himself. It wasn't that he didn't regularly think about his younger brother, the shock was that he hadn't seen the similarity with Lennie Krause. They would be fairly close in age if his brother was still here; he estimated Lennie to be early twenties and Spud would have turned twenty-six a few months earlier. There were obvious similarities in Lennie's love of sport, but it was his drive and ambition coupled with an easy outlook on life and his cheek that was so familiar.

When Spud first became listless, it was his sporting prowess that was the first to suffer. He was boarding at Downlands College in Toowoomba, just as Fitzy had, and he had also followed his brother as a member of the school's First 15 rugby side. It was noticed that he was losing that little bit of extra speed and his natural footballer's brain wasn't as sharp. His school grades were the next to suffer and the school administrators decided that he had simply taken on too much. They decided that the rugby team would have to do without him so he could concentrate on his academic results and ensure his plans for university were not impacted. The school had a doctor attend initially, but when things quickly worsened, a call was placed to Kilmarnock suggesting that his parents come in to discuss the situation.

They met with the school doctor and on his recommendation immediately arranged for Spud to seek a specialist medical assessment and attention in Brisbane. The diagnosis was leukemia, and the prognosis was poor. He was removed from the school and came back to Kilmarnock where his mother could attend to his needs more closely. Fitzy, however, could not accept that his dynamic cheeky brother only had months to live. He did not want to discuss it with him, preferring to keep assuring Spud that all would be good in the end and that modern medicine was capable of working miracles.

The Fairlaine job had been more than half finished yesterday, and with the correct parts already having been delivered, there was no way it would not be finished on time today. Lenny wanted it more than finished though, he wanted it perfect, so he went the extra yard, and he did a full grease and oil change, tuned up the carby and gave it a good clean inside and out. When Fitzy collected it, Lennie handed him the keys with pride, offered him a ten percent discount off the quote for the original problem and then graciously begged off joining him for a beer.

When Lenny had woken earlier that morning, he not only had a massive hangover, but a new mission. It had been seriously suggested that there was a chance of him getting a rep jersey. Last night he had well and truly celebrated that prospect, but now he knew two things. He wasn't a serious drinker and he desperately wanted selection. From this point onward, early mornings before work involved getting in his Ute, and driving out to the oval where he ran until he dropped. He was giving a lot more consideration to what he ate, and not one cigarette had touched his lips.

Chapter 9

Soon it was nearly five weeks since that last heavy session with Fitzy and he had not had a beer or any other alcohol since. Fitzy still sought him out every Friday night for a big steak counter meal and still pressured him to "just have the one." Lennie firmly rejected the pressure; he was on a mission.

Despite what Lennie may have thought, Fitzy wasn't upset that Lennie was on the wagon; in fact he was pretty proud of the kid. He had stuffed up, then had gone the extra mile to make up for the error. Then when he had discovered that he had the prospect of advancing his football career, Lennie wasn't resting on his laurels, but was taking that opportunity and running with it. While he no longer had a new drinking partner, Fitzy decided he did have a new mate who was becoming an exciting player.

He hadn't missed one of Lennie's games since, and it was patently obvious that he was getting a lot stronger in both body and mind. He was becoming what the old timers used to call a thinking footballer. It wasn't just the coach and Fitzy who noticed the improvement. Lennie had scored in every game but one since the idea of a representative jersey had been raised, and he had set up at least three tries for other players. He estimated that the Country side was to be picked in a few weeks, and he was making every minute of every game and every training session count.

Unfortunately, while his game and his fitness were moving upward, his home and love life over the last two months had more of the direction of a roller coaster. Things were either brilliant or shit with Marion, and it was hard to predict when the change was coming. She loved that he was so fit and dedicated and though a light smoker herself, she loved that he had stopped. She wasn't backward in showing Lennie that she approved either. Given the opportunity, she would grab his arm in public and show him off like her own little trophy. These times were the highs, but the lows could follow quickly, particularly if they disagreed on an issue important to her. She was simply never wrong and to be honest, if he thought about it, it still rankled that they never did have the reasoned discussion about the Finnamore issue.

Lennie had spent a lot of time thinking about it and had actually sat down and mapped out the discussion in point form in two columns headed with a plus sign and a minus sign. The minus "my fault" column was all but empty. Marion thoughts on the issue, however, had not been as structured.

As more time passed, everything that had transpired was firmly embedded in her mind as his fault alone. In the end Lennie gave up trying and decided to count it as a loss and concentrate on the good, because there were heathy, if spasmodic, dose of that too.

Marion was loving the limelight of having a local footballing hero as a boyfriend. It was always a point of conversation at work and she quite enjoyed basking in Lennie's glory. This translated to the bedroom too, and Lennie had absolutely no complaints in that department. He had a rep jersey with a number 8 on the back to earn. His focus was on that, and Marion was supportive in most every way. She was not only thinking of how much she enjoyed Lennie being a local hero, but also how much more fun and how much more prestige there would be, if he became a representative footballer. He might even make the Queensland side, she thought, and she could tag along on interstate tours.

The next big game was the second Sunday in August, so the coach had scheduled an extra but short session for the Friday night prior. At training, Lennie noticed a few unfamiliar faces in deep conversation with his coach on the sidelines. Given the representative side was to be named any day, Lennie was right in assuming that these two burly, elderly gents with the cauliflower ears were on the selection panel. In Lennie's mind, today's training session was his last chance to prove his worth. He decided that if the opportunity arose, he would show them that he was the man they needed at number 8.

When the team broke into two groups to run some set moves near the try line, he saw his opportunity. He was at the back of a bigger pack and they were slowly moving toward the try line with the ball trapped between his legs. The set piece was to be a push over try and his role was basically to fall on the ball once the pack had crossed the try line. There was nothing outstanding or memorable about that sort of move, so when they were still about ten metres out, Lenny picked up the ball, broke from scrum and headed for the try line. It wasn't a planned manoeuvre, it was instinctive, changing on the fly as he anticipated his opponents moves. He had just side stepped around one player, jinked again and then again, when he was tackled side on while in mid-air diving for the try line.

The next moment was blank for a second or two, then he was on his back clutching his right knee in unbelievable pain. A couple of his teammates, and the two selectors were looking down at him when his head cleared enough to work out what happened. The coach knelt beside him trying to assess what had caused him to drop like he had been shot.

"Fuck I heard the sound, did you?" said the prop forward. "It sounded like a whip cracking. Has he broken something?"

The coach had disappointment and concern written all over his large pock marked face as he turned to the prop. "I doubt anything has broken, most likely a torn cartilage, though I saw the knee flex, I have a horrible feeling he may have fucked himself right up. Either way there won't be any ballroom dancing for Lennie in the near future."

After the initial pain had subsided, the coach had the two props do what they do best. They had Lennie wrap an arm around each shoulder and carried him like he was the hooker. Once settled, the coach asked Lennie to try and put some weight on his right leg. He took the weight off the arms around his teammates' shoulders and gingerly did as asked. The pain was incredible, and his leg collapsed like it was made of jelly.

"That is it for tonight, boys, hit the showers," the coach said as he arranged to get Lennie down to the dressing room. "Lennie, we have to get you over to emergency at the hospital so they can work out what you have done to yourself. What on God's green earth were you thinking son? The selectors had just come over to tell me the number 8 position was yours, and you go and pull a show-off stunt like that? I just hope I have it wrong, but it doesn't look good." It was the first time Lennie could remember a statement delivered by the coach that wasn't laden with expletives. If the pain wasn't bad enough, this fact alone made him fearful that things were very bad.

Under the coach's instruction, the two burly forwards again lifted Lennie, but the pain was now too intense and they slowly lowered him to the ground. A third player was recruited to take the weight of the leg itself and they tried again, carrying him as if he was sitting in a chair. It was still painful but bearable and they clumsily crab walked Lennie over to the coach's Holden sedan in the car park. This presented another problem, as there was no way they could feed Lennie into the front seat and the coach's back seat was loaded up with footballs and other kit. Fitzy appeared from around the back side of the oval and took command of the situation.

"I've got a Ute over there with nothing in the tray. Grab all those jerseys and any towels or whatever you have, and we will make him a bed of sorts in the back." They did as they were instructed; the various jerseys and towels were arranged as best possible to be under him, and Lennie was loaded aboard. A few more towels were then stuffed under his right knee to support it. One of the prop forwards got in beside him for support and the other prop hopped in the front with Fitzy.

The coach issued his instructions quietly and firmly. "Take it very fucken easy, boys, you are not doing laps on a Friday night! Drive around to emergency and wait there till you see me. I will head off now and warn them about what is coming."

The prop in the front motioned to the coach to come in closer and also whispered, "So how long could he be out for then, if it's the cartilage thing you guess it is?"

"Good!" the coach responded. The coach could see the puzzled look on the big prop's face at this unexpected answer. So he clarified further. "Good… he could be out for fucken good you nong! You can guarantee he has done a cartilage or both of them, but, Jesus Christ, I have a horrible feeling about this. He is in too much pain and that knee looked as stable as boiled spaghetti when he tried to stand on it. I'd say more has happened to that knee, and the chance is good that we will never see Lennie on the paddock again…fuck, fuck fuck!"

Every little bump they crossed in the car park shot a shaft of pain into the centre of Lennie's knee and he couldn't stifle the scream. After about ten such events the screams were accompanied with tears and a deep sense of fear and regret. As he lay on his back looking into the depths of the clear black starry Dalby night sky, Lennie knew this was bad. The pain was one thing but what was worse was that his whole knee just felt loose. Every time they changed direction, he could feel the joint move followed by that dagger of pain. "You fucken idiot, Lennie," he said out loud, "it was so close!"

Once they arrived at the hospital, the orderlies got him into a wheelchair and transferred him to Emergency. This position soon proved too painful and with the help of Fitzy and the two props, he was transferred to a gurney and left to wait in the hall. If you wanted a quick medical assessment, the emergency ward at any Australian public hospital is not the place you would go at the best of times, and eight o'clock on a Friday was about the worst time possible. Despite the relatively early hour, the line-up was already populated by drunks, a couple of broken bones, and what looked to be a domestic violence case that involved a thin forty-something woman with a split lip and the early indications of severe bruising around her left cheek and eye socket.

Nearly an hour had passed, and the line did not seem to be moving too fast. The coach asked Fitzy if he would not mind staying around with Lennie while he dropped the two props back to their cars. He promised to come back as soon as he could. He also promised Lennie that he would find a phone and ring Marion who was on roster at the pub and let her and Di know what had happened.

No sooner had the coach headed back to the training field, than a nurse called out Lennie's name and he was wheeled into a curtained cubicle. A thin, balding stressed-out doctor in his early forties soon joined them. He asked Lennie to sit up on the gurney to help with the assessment. Lennie winced as Fitzy helped him to slowly slide back along the gurney, gingerly eased him into position, and held him there while the nurse raised the back for support.

"We'll arrange some more pain relief once I have completed the examination, son," the doctor said.

"More!!" Fitzy snorted, "He hasn't been given any fucking pain relief at all yet, doc!" The accusation went right over the doctor's head, and he commenced the examination.

With Lennie's leg flat on the gurney, he braced the knee and moved the lower leg to the left then right. The pain was intense but bearable. He then had Lennie bend the knee to a ninety-degree angle, grabbed the leg just below the knee, and gently pulled it forward. Everything went black for Lennie.

Chapter 10

When Lennie regained consciousness, he was in a bed in the public ward and the coach was looking down on him. Out of the corner of his eye he could see his mum, with Fitzy comforting her as best he could. He looked around for Marion, but she wasn't there.

"Listen, Lennie, there is no easy way to say this," the coach started out, "but the doctor says you have done a first rate job of fucking up your knee. He believes you have torn at least one cartilage, likely both, and given your pain levels, you might have fractured something and done some ligament damage. This is fucken bad, son, I have been doing this a long time and I haven't seen anyone drop as fast as you did, or be in this much pain…well not since that bloke a few years back who fractured his shin and had the bone sticking out through his sock. The doctor will be in to see you in a while, and he is likely to have to refer you up the chain to a specialist. Your accommodation tonight will be right here."

"So you are saying I am fucked then, coach?" said Lennie.

"From a playing viewpoint, yes son, I am afraid to say you are likely on the money there. Certainly for the rest of the season at least from the looks of it. It's a crying fucken shame, Lennie, you have gone from the penthouse to the shit house. You were just on your way to great things," he said shaking his head in total disgust. "It's best to assume that your football will all be from the sidelines this season I reckon. For both our sakes I hope to Christ it isn't worse than that."

Di came over, grabbed his hand, and looked down at him with that beautiful supporting and loving smile only a mother could offer. Concealing her concern, she said, "You are a beautiful boy, Len, you remember there is a lot more to this world than footie. You have a lot of friends, people around town like you, you have your business, and you have me." Lennie was aware that his mum made no mention of Marion in that assessment. Where the bloody hell was she? If his mum was here, then Marion obviously got the message too.

He gave his mum a wan smile and motioned Fitzy over. "I have become a bit of a problem for you, haven't I? Thanks for helping out tonight. Can I ask another favour? Would you track down Marion and let her know what's happening and get her to come in and see me as soon as she can?"

"Marion is already up to speed, mate," said Fitzy. "Remember it's Friday night and the pub is chocka. Bob got behind the bar himself to ease the strain, but he couldn't afford to let two barmaids go. Marion volunteered to let your mum come and she stayed back. It's nearly ten o'clock so she will be off soon but visiting hours are over and I wouldn't expect to see her until tomorrow morning."

Fitzy was considering how best to broach the next subject with Lennie as the subject matter was still raw. After composing himself he said, "And Lennie, don't you worry either about being a problem. I haven't told you before that I had a young brother who would be around your age if fucken cancer hadn't come and took him away from me. He was really only a kid..."

Fitzy hesitated again to stifle the lump in his throat. "Spud was eighteen when we lost him, and like you, he loved his rugby. You remind me of him in so many ways, mate; but mostly because he was a cheeky little prick like you too," he chuckled. "So, mate, the news is, I have sort of adopted you." There was a short pause while he allowed Lennie to digest that commitment, then he said, "Listen, mate, I have to head off now, but I'll stay in touch and make sure you get on your feet one way or the other."

With that, Fitzy gave Di's hand a quick squeeze and a peck on the cheek and headed over to the coach. "I have a pile of your kit in the back of my Ute which I guess you want back. I'll meet you in the car park and we can transfer it across."

The coach went over to Len and said his goodbyes, then gave Fitzy a knowing wink and they headed off to the car park together. "That was a very diplomatic way of explaining his fucken girlfriend's absence if I do say so myself," said the coach. "You would think she would be busting a gut to get over here and support the poor bugger, but when Bob said it was okay for her to go to the hospital, she very quickly volunteered his mum instead. What's that about? She's a real piece of work that one if you ask me."

"I totally agree," said Fitzy. "The kid is bloody gutted, and I had to let him down a bit easy. Diplomacy isn't my strong suit, but it was the way to go in that situation. So, things are pretty grim I hear, coach? When I was speaking to the doctor on call, he explained things to me, but it went well over my head. Where to from here for Lennie do you think?"

"Well, I'm no doctor, but I have seen my fair share of knee bust ups in my playing and coaching days and this is a bad one. My guess is they will x-ray for fractures first. Assuming that is okay, which I think it will be, they will wait for the knee to settle down, then operate to take out the torn cartilages. Then when they have the knee open, they can assess if there is any other damage. I told Lennie that this season is over, but I'll root my boot if we ever see the boy playing again.

"Who knows, maybe they have new ways of stabilizing knees these days. He will be in plaster for a while after the op and he may need some sort of brace for support in the short term. Long term, I have known cases where they give you a stiffy, you know permanently straighten the leg; that was the old remedy if the knee was too unstable. Let's hope I am well behind the times, but oh fuck…things don't look good."

Fitzy transferred all the kit over to the coach's car and realized he had to decide on whether to head home or stay in town. He decided he would head back to The Imperial, see if Bob was still around, and if so try and score one of his rooms for the night. It might also give him the opportunity to track Marion down and give her an update on the situation. Luckily when he arrived, Bob was out the front hosing something unpleasant off the footpath. After explaining Lennie's situation, he asked Bob if he could put his swag down into one of the spare rooms for the night. Bob had no problem with that and took him inside to sort out a key to the room and the back door.

"Next issue is tracking down Marion and explaining why her man won't be home tonight. I'll need directions to their house as I was pretty pissed the last time I landed there."

Bob gave quick directions to Lennie's house but told Fitzy not to waste his time heading over there tonight. "One of the barmaids from the RSL was here tonight and she suggested that Marion go back to her place for a while and then she would drop her home. They took a cask of wine with them from the bottlo, so I doubt she will be getting home before midnight."

Fitzy knew it was too late for Marion to be visiting the hospital anyway, but couldn't understand how she felt it just was alright to get on the drink with a girlfriend instead. "Jesus, her boyfriend has just done himself some major damage and is laid up in hospital, and she decides it's a good time to go and get on the piss!" he said to Bob shaking his head in disgust.

Chapter 11

Next morning Fitzy called his dad early to see if he was needed for anything urgent at the property. It transpired that there were a few pressing issues, and he really couldn't stay around in Dalby until much after nine that morning. He decided he would drop in to see Marion first, then catch up with Di and then head home. When Marion answered the door, it was obvious that the session with the girl from the RSL had finished well after midnight. "Well, you look a sight!" was the most diplomatic conversation starter Fitzy could muster.

A serious hangover had dulled Marion's sarcastic edge and she responded with "You are the charmer, aren't you? You better come in for a coffee, I know I need one."

"Lennie's knee is pretty busted up," he explained. "I won't go into details, you would be best to get that from the hospital. He is also pretty devastated that the injury means he won't be making the rep team, so he'll be looking for a bit of comfort."

Marion's response was matter-of-fact. "Yeah, I am going to drop around to the hospital shortly, once I freshen up a bit and have a bite to eat."

It was apparent to Fitzy that she either didn't appreciate the extent of Lennie's injury, was too hung-over, or frankly didn't care as much as he would have expected.

Fitzy decided then and there that the best thing he could do for Lennie was to wean him off this girl. He would be needing someone to help him through the difficulties that lay ahead and in Fitzy's estimation, Marion wasn't that someone, she was a taker not a giver. His next stop was to Lennie's mum who was a lot more concerned. She also said that she would be heading to the hospital that morning, and Fitzy decided it was a good thing that he would be on his way home and not there when the two women in Lennie's life ended up with him in the same room. He explained that he had to sort out a few issues back at the property and promised to keep in contact and see how things progressed.

Di started to get herself organized after the update that Fitzy had provided. She needed to check in on Lennie and also ensure Bob wasn't left shorthanded at the pub. Her decision was to first ring the hospital for an update and to sort out visiting hours. When she did, she was told that the doctor's rounds didn't start until about ten and he probably wouldn't be in to see Lennie until sometime after eleven. She was told there would be no news until then, but that Lennie was on heavy pain meds last night, so had slept well.

Di had experienced enough time herself in hospital wards to know that heavy pain meds would be the only way anyone got a good night sleep in there. If a nurse wasn't taking your temperature or blood pressure, they were shining a light in your eyes to see if you were asleep. This level of activity, general hospital noise, and the five or so other patients on the ward either suffering the same indignity or snoring, did not add up to ideal sleeping conditions. On balance, Di felt it best to leave a message for Lennie that she would drop in mid-afternoon. Given Saturday was the pub's busiest time of the week, these arrangements would allow her to do the morning roster at the pub, so Bob wasn't left in the lurch.

After Fitzy headed home, Marion had other priorities. She had taken herself straight to bed for a couple of hours much needed sleep. Around nine-ish she made herself a light breakfast, had a quick shower, and dressed for her mid-morning shift. Luckily, a couple of Lennie's teammates had dropped his Ute back home last night, left the keys under the visor, and a note on the windscreen. Marion sourced the keys, tossed them up in the air and caught them. After a moment's reflection, she repeated the action but with a little more enthusiasm. A smile broke over her face. "Guess who just got their own car to drive?" she said aloud.

She then warmed up the Ute and drove herself unannounced to the hospital. She argued the hospital's visitation policy for a few minutes with the receptionist, but at around 9.30 she was directed to Ward 2, Bed 4. There she found Lennie propped up in bed, nursing a cup of tea, and in mid conversation with a scrawny old guy, with three days of stubble on his chin, who occupied the adjoining bed.

Lennie was still in the light blue hospital gown that they had to use after they removed his training gear for last night's assessment. The old gent though, was wearing a pair of stripy green flannelette pajamas about two sizes too big, with a gaping fly that was leaving nothing to the imagination.

"Put the tackle away, old fella," said Marion, pointing at the offending item with an affected look or horror on her face. She then turned to appraise a sad looking Lennie. "From all the fuss, I thought you were on death's door. So what the fuck have you actually done to yourself?"

Lennie wasn't sure whether to follow her lead and keep the conversation light, or lay out the whole grizzly tale. He decided to take the middle ground. "Well, I was sure the selectors were watching us at training, so I decided to show them something special….unfortunately it didn't pay off. It looks like I have torn my knee up pretty bad and I'll be out for the rest of the season at least."

"Where to from here then?" was her only response.

"Well, I am told the hospital registrar will be around in an hour or so and he will give me the latest update. After that I will be discharged along with a pile of painkillers."

Marion wasn't one for waiting around, so took it upon herself to seek out the young hospital registrar, who she found in the staff tearoom. "Hi there," she greeted him. "I understand that you are the registrar."

He looked up from his mug of tea and beamed at her. "Yes, that I am."

"Hi, I am Marion," she responded offering her hand to shake. "So, Registrar, what does that mean exactly? Are you the big boss?"

The young doctor went on to explain the various levels associated with that term. "Registrars are medical officers, doctors, who have enrolled in a specialty training program," he explained. "I'm looking to get into orthopedics. I've almost finished my basic training component, and will then do my advanced training at medical college." When he could see that Marion appeared unimpressed he quickly added, "But as far as this ward is concerned, yes you are right. I am the big boss."

"Okay, boss," she quickly responded. "I have a friend in Ward 2, if you wouldn't mind starting your rounds there, I will be able to offer him a lift home.

After he assessed Lennie, the registrar largely supported what had been observed last night. The only new news was that the x-rays now confirmed that there were no broken bones. There was obviously cartilage damage, though the young registrar said it could just be bruising, and the knee was now very stiff and swollen. To regulate the swelling and support the knee, the nursing staff had been advised to apply a compression bandage comprising alternate layers of cotton wool sheets and elastic bandages. The result was that his leg was almost as stiff as if it was in plaster. Lennie was prescribed pain medication and anti-inflammatory drugs. He was told to regularly remove then replace the bandages, so that a blood clot didn't develop, to rest, and to keep the leg elevated. The plan was that on Monday, he would arrange a time to see his GP and from there a plan of action could be developed.

After the registrar signed him out, the ward sister handed Lennie a pair of timber crutches. They were very well worn, and the prior user had personalized them to some extent, by attaching foam rubber to the armpit pad with insulation tape. Someone had also drawn love hearts down one side with a black marking pen. The sister pointed Marion in the direction of his training bag, adjusted the crutches, and told Lennie to take it easy as the pain meds would be wearing off soon. Lennie hobbled out to his Ute with Marion walking well ahead of him, tossing his car keys in the air and catching them with the same quick grabbing motion.

Using the crutches for support, Lennie gingerly fed himself into the front seat and asked Marion to take it easy on the way home. While she generally complied, he could still feel the looseness in his knee at every change of direction. During the short trip home, Lennie was embarrassed to broach the delicate topic of money, or the upcoming lack of it.

"Marion, honey," he started out tentatively, "I am unsure when I am going to get back to work and start bringing in some chips again." When there was no response from her, he continued. "Until things are back to normal, you might have to carry more of our living expenses."

"Don't bother your pretty little head about it, that won't be a problem at all."

Lennie was greatly relieved when he got that commitment. "You can never tell with this girl," he thought, "I can never know if she is going to blow her stack or pat me on the head."

Once home, they worked together to get him comfortable in bed with a few extra pillows around the damaged leg. Marion put his medication, some reading material, and a jug of water by his bedside, told him she would be back around dinner time and headed off to work.

"Don't forget to tell mum I'm home!" he called out as she left. "Ask her to drop around as soon as she gets off." He listened as the familiar note of his old Holden faded into the distance. Then the silence and the reality of the situation came at him in a rush.

How long before he could get back to work; how would he pay the bills in the meantime; would he lose customers; if he lost customers would he ever get them back; what was ahead of him as regards medical treatment; what was it all going to cost; how long would the treatment take; who would look after him until he was back on his feet; did he really have any prospect of playing footie again? A lot of important questions with no answers at all so far. One question that never occurred to him was: "Would Marion stick by him during all this?" He thought he had summed up the situation and he acknowledged things were going to be difficult for a while.

The truth was that Lennie had not envisaged the extent of the difficulties that awaited him. He was at the head of a long and slippery slope and was largely unaware of just how far he was about to slide.

Chapter 12

Lennie's first indication of the steepness of that incline came that very afternoon when nature called.

He struggled to get out of bed, found his crutches and made his way slowly to the outside toilet. Even getting down onto the toilet seat proved a much bigger problem than he had anticipated. Given that his leg was wrapped in that large compression bandage, it was as stiff as a board, so in the end he had to leave the toilet door open so he could complete his business. He was glad, at least, that the rental house was relatively remote and the toilet itself was pretty well hidden behind a few bushes. "Next time," he thought to himself, "I will take the bandage off first."

By the time his mother arrived mid-afternoon, the hospital pain relief had well and truly worn off and the new medication that they had issued was doing a poor imitation of the same job. Di made him a late lunch which he only nibbled at, and then offered to stay until Marion arrived home from her shift to take over nursing duties. She said she would arrange a time for them to see the family doctor next day and would take him personally to the appointment. In the end she stayed much longer than anticipated and arranged an evening meal for them both as well. Marion still hadn't returned home when Lennie decided to turn in for the night.

Next morning at breakfast, Lennie broached the subject. "I expected to see you for dinner last night. In the end, Mum cooked tea for me." If he expected contrition he was to be disappointed.

"Yeah, I knew Di was here. Just how many wet nurses do you need to look after you?"

By this time, Lennie was struggling to hide his annoyance. "I would have liked to at least know when you would be home."

But Marion was not going to be outdone, she shot right back, "Well, if you weren't such a miserable prick you would have had the phone put on at the house."

"Of course," thought Lennie, "I should have known it would be my fault, there is the other Marion I expected yesterday when I raised the issue of helping with the bills."

Monday started a procession of visits to the doctor, the hospital, and the hospital physio, with none of them being the bearers of glad tidings. The doctor was dismissive of the hospital registrar's suggestion that it might just be bruised cartilages.

"Not possible, Lennie, I am sorry, cartilages don't have a blood supply, they are just gristle." Luckily, the hospital was able to refer Lennie to an orthopedic surgeon who was up from Brisbane doing some consulting at the hospital. Someone had cancelled and Lennie was slotted in.

The specialist was a stooped, overweight man in his early sixties and his manner was abrupt and matter-of-fact. He rambled on about the various types of cartilage tears and their degree but said there would be no certainty until the knee was opened up. He told Lennie that he could perform the operation to remove them, either in Toowoomba or Brisbane and that recovery from the operation would take a couple of months. His schedule indicated that no surgery could be undertaken for at least two months, though he did give Lennie some hope that all might not be lost.

"The swelling and pain will be gone in a week or so," he said in a distinctly professorial tone. "In the unlikely event there is any ongoing instability and residual pain, it will be related to the torn cartilages. I propose totally removing and scraping out one or both damaged menisci. After they grow back, there is every chance all should be well again but don't count on playing any more football this year."

When Lennie heard the words, "this year," his mood lifted. "That sounds like I might only be delaying my representative career by a year—that's promising. " he thought.

After a few weeks, Lennie was well enough to start booking jobs again for the workshop. He soon found that he had to restrict these to simple things like oil changes; certainly nothing that involved any sort of heavy weight-bearing movements. The specialist's opinion that after a week he would be relatively okay had proved to be totally inaccurate. At the most inopportune of times, the knee would either lock up or just give way completely, especially if he changed direction quickly. Following each disturbance, the knee would swell up like a balloon and Lennie began to worry if it would ever start to improve.

His living and operational expenses were not huge, but those hire purchase payments for the new fridge, TV, stereo, lounge suite, and bedroom suite that he had racked up with Marion, continued to arrive in the mail, and the breakeven point of his small business was becoming a close-run thing. Not that Marion was using much of the new furnishings anymore.

She still considered it to be her home, she usually came home shortly after her shifts at the pub, they still shared a bed, but they hadn't been intimate since before the accident at training. Her once regular visits to the workshop between her shifts had ceased completely and the quality of the conversations at home had deteriorated to the point that he almost preferred the silence. The one saving grace for Lennie was his growing friendship with Fitzy. Even though Fitzy lived out of town, he was probably spending more quality time with Lennie, since the knee damage, than Marion.

With any prospect of making the team now extinguished, one of Lennie's earliest decisions was to abandon his commitment to go teetotal. While Fitzy didn't need another reason to visit and support his new mate, the reintroduction of alcohol into the equation certainly made the visits more enjoyable. Fitzy initially couldn't believe the change in Lennie's demeanor after he damaged his knee. When they first met, Lennie was a cheeky, outgoing kid with not a care in the world, and confident that he had a bright future ahead. In just a few weeks, that "joie de vivre" had slowly evaporated to the point that Lennie's self-pity was often palpable. Fitzy had seen depression up close before with Spud and he was determined that this time he would handle it differently.

He had not recognized the emotional chasm that his young brother had fallen into after his cancer diagnosis. Spud's decline in health was so rapid, he only ever experienced three of the five stages of grief. He skipped denial altogether, as he was so ill so quickly that the seriousness of his situation was patently obvious. He was as angry as his health would allow. He bargained with God for no time at all, as he recognized it was hopeless, and he never lived long enough to reach acceptance. Most of his time from diagnosis to death was in the stage four of grief and depression, and this from a kid who had never seen a cloud in his life that didn't have a silver lining.

Fitzy now knew that he should have ensured that his young brother's remaining time was packed with as much life and enjoyment as was feasibly possible. Instead, his approach had been to avoid his brother's diagnosis at all costs; as if failing to acknowledge it made it less real. Fitzy just immersed himself with work both on and off the property and while they spoke every day, Fitzy always directed the conversation away from the reality of Spud's medical situation. When it did arise, he brushed it away with the unrealistic fraudulent assurance that as a Fitzgerald, Spud would obviously "kick cancers arse."

When Spud died, Fitzy's grief was complex, and it took a lot of soul searching to work out why. He had come to realize that the grief was tinged with guilt, because he had been dishonest with Spud. Though his intentions had been pure, he had been unforgivably unsupportive. Fitzy was aware that Lennie's situation wasn't as dire as his brother's had been, but he was obviously hurting a lot and you could just see he was winding himself into a major bout of melancholy. Marion wasn't making it any easier, that was for sure, now that she couldn't parade around town with a potential rep footballer on her arm.

Fitzy's plan was to first promise Lennie that until he was back at hundred percent, he would get down and visit at least once mid-week and every weekend. They would have a meal and a few stiff drinks to wash his cares away. Fitzy also promised himself that he would not make the same mistake as he had with Spud. Once Lennie started to come out of his self-pitying funk, Fitzy decided he would confront him with the reality of his situation. He was going to be brutally honest with Lennie about all things medical, business, and sports related and, most particularly, about his personal life.

Chapter 13

In the meantime, Lennie was carrying on at the workshop as best he could. It was doubly quiet out there. Not only were there insufficient bookings to keep him that busy, but the only company he had for most of the day were the verbal ramblings of the various DJ's on the local radio station. He therefore was spending a good portion of every day, beating himself up for the situation he was in.

Lennie kept rehashing what had happened over the last month or so and trying to chart a path forward. As far as any work that needed to be done on the knee, he knew that he was singularly unimpressed with the specialist the hospital had arranged. The guy was aloof and condescending, which Lennie guessed came from him feeling that he was a big fish in the small Toowoomba pond. He decided that whatever the way forward was to be, it would not be with this medico.

Making things worse, the business was well and truly in the toilet. His plans for future expansion into bigger premises in town and taking on an apprentice and maybe an office girl too were now a complete impossibility. He would be relegated to doing oil changes for pensioners in the shed out the back of his mother's place ...what a loser.

Just when he was at his lowest, the thoughts of his future with Marion added to the pile on. He had expected her to have been a lot more sympathetic and caring and understanding but just the week before, she had let him down again big time. He had decided he needed to get himself out of the funk he was in and had arranged to take her to the rugby grand final on Saturday afternoon. After that, the plan was to go along to the post game celebrations or commiserations. But when the big day arrived, he found out from Bob, that she had arranged a few days off and didn't show back up at the house until the following Monday afternoon looking a lot worse for wear. "What the fuck," he thought bitterly. "Of all the events she knew I am interested in, this was it, and she goes missing in action. I am not putting up with this anymore!"

When she finally returned, Lennie was not in great shape physically or mentally. His team, even without their prized number 8, had taken out the title. Over the weekend, without Marion to oversee his intake, he and Fitzy had managed to demolish two bottles of Bundy rum and way too many stubbies to count. On top of this, despite Fitzy's decision to only bring up the issue of Marion at the right time, he had let the drink loosen his tongue. So, as they sat around Lennie's kitchen table Sunday evening, eating burgers and chips from the local "chew and spew" café, and finishing off the last of the rum, Fitzy's addled mind decided that the time was right to point out a few home truths to his hobbling companion.

His opening line was "Hey Lennie, you know I love you, mate, but you are a major fuckwit. You are young and fit and good looking, but you spend most of your time crying in your beer about how fucked up things are." Lennie tried to enter the debate but was quickly cut off when two big, calloused fingers were waved back and forth in front of his face.

"No, no, no let me finish. Sure your knee is probably fucked, but there is a lot more to life than footie. You have a good head on your shoulders, and you are good at what you do…even if you can be horribly fucken slow at it sometimes. You need to look on the bright side, mate, get your finger out of your arse and wake up to yourself."

"And just how am I to do that?" Lennie finally slurred.

"Well, mate," Fitzy slowly responded, with the earnest certainty of a well-lubricated mate, "First thing you need to do is to make a firm fucking booking for that operation, so at least you know for sure what's up. Then," he said, losing count, "the first thing you need to do is get rid of that slag of a girlfriend. She has been a waste of space since you did your knee and if you don't realise that she is off somewhere, fucking the brains out of some other bloke right now, you are off your rocker."

For the second time since they met, Lennie decided that Fitzy needed a good punch in the head. This time when he swung, however, it was so much of a slow-motion effort, that Fitzy just brushed it away, pushed his big open palm into Lennie's face which toppled him backward onto the lounge couch where he promptly fell asleep.

When Marion came in the back door a little after two that Monday afternoon, Lennie was sitting at the kitchen table nursing his fourth coffee with his still throbbing head cupped in his hands. She too was pale and washed out, and her hair was flat and oily.

"Where the fuck have you been?" Lennie shouted. "You missed the game, you missed the celebrations and you look like shit."

"You are no oil painting yourself, Lennie." She shot back. "I've been in Toowoomba sorting out a personal matter and now I am as sick as a dog, though mine isn't self-inflicted. I am going to have a shower, a rest, and then I have to be at work for the 6 o'clock shift. Make yourself dinner, I won't be back until late."

"Bullshit, you have been on the rantan fucking someone else haven't you?"

"Short answer, Lennie, is no, I haven't, though why that is I don't know, when what I have to come back to is this," she said, waving her hand backward in his direction. "I thought you had some go in you, Lennie, you were going to be a star. Instead, you have one setback and I'm stuck with a drunken cripple for company!"

With that she grabbed a fresh towel from the hallway cupboard, locked herself in the bathroom and freshened herself up for work, knowing the shift ahead was going to be difficult to get through. "So much for the big confrontation," Lennie thought, "she has managed to put me in my place again."

A few days later, Fitzy called into the workshop unannounced to see if Lennie had acted on his drunken, but none-the-less needed advice.

"Well, this is a surprise," Lennie said, "I don't see you much midweek, you got business in town?"

In his usual fashion, Fitzy got straight to the point. "I wanted to talk to you face to face to see if you have done anything about what we discussed about Marion.

Lennie was initially offended but took a breath and responded, "I have, mate. Even though I don't agree with how you see Marion, I confronted her about those suspicions all the same. She not only denied it, she was genuinely angry that I accused her of it, so frankly I believe her."

In truth, Lennie still had his reservations, because while she was convincing in her denial, he still had the sick feeling deep in his gut, that he was not privy to the full story. Somewhat chastened, Fitzy then directed the conversation to the issue of Lennie's knee. "Fair enough," he started, "of course the next issue is you getting some proper professional advise on the state of that knee of yours." He was about to try and convince Lennie to take action, when he was cut off mid-sentence.

"Mate, on that point we are agreed, the knee isn't going to fix itself." Fitzy was pleased to hear him continue. "I have taken your advice and put a plan in place with my own GP. One of the coach's old rugby mates is now a top orthopedic surgeon in Brisbane. They have talked and my GP has arranged a referral for me to see him, but the earliest appointment is still a couple of weeks away; the first week in October."

Chapter 14

As the day of the appointment approached, Lennie wasn't sure whether to be concerned or excited. He was dreading bad news but was also keen to get some certainty about what lay ahead. Soon enough he was in the specialist's rooms and being given a run down on his current status and his immediate and longer-term options. After a more extensive assessment in a small anteroom, the surgeon had Lennie come back into his office where they sat across from each other at his impressive oak desk.

"Mr. Krause…" he started, but was quickly cut off.

"Call me Lennie, please. Mr. Krause was my dad."

The specialist smiled and started again. "Lennie, the knee is not in a good way and unfortunately you don't have too many options." Lennie dropped his head and the report continued. "Every option hinges on the degree of damage, and this can only be accurately assessed during the operation itself." With that the specialist took a plastic model of a typical knee off an adjacent shelf and endeavoured to explain what the operation would entail. "The first step will be for me to open the medial or inside of the knee. I will suture up, that is stitch, any tears to the capsule and to the medial ligament."

As the specialist pointed out the sections of the knee anatomy on the model, Lennie was thinking that he should have bought Di along. "How am I going to remember all this?" he thought.

As if reading Lennie's thoughts, the doctor paused and added, "Lennie, I will be writing a full report to your GP and I will ensure that the process is explained to you in a way you would understand."

Lennie, who was already overwhelmed by what he had just heard, simply nodded his head in thanks and motioned his doctor to continue.

"Almost certainly I will be removing the medial meniscus, what your coach had called the cartilage. It's like a little shock absorber between the joints. I will then check for stability and if I still feel clunking in the knee, I will open the other side, the lateral side or outside of the knee and assess it as well. I will most probably have to remove the lateral meniscus as well."

Then came the body blow. "Lennie, I specialize in this area, I do dozens of knees a month and so I am as up-to-date with the latest techniques as anyone in Australia. I have to tell you that some of the stuff you were apparently told in Dalby and

Toowoomba is totally out of date." Lennie looked at him blankly, knowing that more bad news was to follow.

"To start with, Lennie, cartilages do not grow back, that is very much old school thinking." Lennie's head dropped again, but worse was to follow.

"Lennie, what I do with the cartilages will help with the pain, but from a stability viewpoint, the ligament damage is going to be the major problem. If it transpires that you have ruptured your anterior cruciate ligament, then we might be out of luck even with a surgery."

Lennie finally felt composed or resigned enough to ask for more explanation. "Cruciate is Latin for cross," the surgeon explained. "There are two cruciate ligaments that cross over in your knee to stop it collapsing forward and backward. If your anterior cruciate ligament is ruptured, your knee will always be unstable and likely to collapse." When the specialist finished, he sat back in his chair and asked Lennie if he had any questions.

"Do you have any good news?" was all Lennie could ask in an endeavour to lighten the mood.

"On the playing front certainly not, your rugby days are over," he responded. "Otherwise you are young and healthy, and if you continue to look after yourself you should live a long and relatively active life."

Despite the bad news, Lennie had a lot more confidence in this doctor and his opinion. He liked his no-nonsense forthright approach, and he had come very highly recommended. Lennie could also hear Fitzy's advice ringing in his ears: "Stop fucking around and do what you can do to sort it out." He weighed it all up quickly and decided to go ahead with the recommended surgery as soon as possible.

The surgeon's old association with Coach Cowley helped move the operation up the schedule and was booked for the end of November up "on The Terrace" in Brisbane. Lennie was advised to keep off the leg as much as possible in the interim. This meant that in the next six weeks or so he was going to have to take on even less work, and his finances were going to get further stretched. "Thank God I took mum's advice," he thought, "and kept paying my medical insurance."

When he returned home, he was pleasantly surprised, given her mood of recent times, to find that Marion was preparing dinner. "Just in time, Limpy Lennie" she said. "Sit down, sunshine, I have some chops and veg cooked for you heating up in the oven, I've already had mine." He did as he was told, and Marion quickly went on to tell him what had happened that day that explained her unexpected good mood.

"We had this bus load of tourists drop in at lunch out of the blue today, and we were as busy as buggery. Well the driver apparently had a whip around amongst them all and came up to me as they were leaving, told me I was a star and presented me with a $50 tip, $50 can you believe it!" she said waving the note above her head.

Lennie's first thought was that the tip was probably supposed to be for the whole staff, and that she had pocketed the lot. Nonetheless, he feigned happiness for her then explained how his day had also been eventful but somewhat less rewarding. He laid out the date that was set for the cartilages to come out and the knee assessed. He also flagged that he was going to have to drop back bookings in the garage and that money was likely to be tight for a while.

"Well can't I pick em?" she said, "Hero to zero!" There was a part humorous part mocking tone in her voice, but to be honest Lennie didn't find it too funny, so he shot back.

"Come on, Marion, I am not too happy about this either. I should have been playing in a premiership winning side and was told I had all but secured a spot in the rep side. Instead, I am sitting on the sideline for both games alone; and from what this guy says, there won't be any footie in my future. I should be looking to build my business, instead, I am still running it out of my mum's back shed and looking to taking on less work. I should be looking to coming home to a bit of support from my girlfriend and instead, I come home to smart-arsed comments like that."

To Lennie's surprise, for once, Marion didn't bite back. She got up from the table, came toward him, put an arm around his chest from behind, then kissed him on the top of the head and ruffled his hair. "Okay, Limpy Lennie, I'll try harder. I have to go into work and cover from seven until closing. Bob has to go to a Lions meeting or something. See you in the morning," she said as she walked out the back door waving the note above her head again.

When Lennie dragged himself up next morning, Marion was still fast asleep. It had been a typical bitterly cold winter night and she had managed to pile every blanket and heavy jacket they owned on top of hers. She wasn't so much sleeping as hibernating, so he didn't even try to disturb her. He walked out to the outhouse, across grass so frosty it felt as though it was snapping under his feet. After some quick ablutions, he put on his knee bandage, dressed and made himself a quick breakfast of cereal and hot tea. He grabbed yesterday's unopened mail off the table, took the half-finished mug of tea with him to the car and drove into work.

There was no need to be there so early as he didn't have a job booked until late morning. He was more interested in getting to the phone in the workshop early enough to be sure to catch Fitzy at the "Kilmarnock" homestead. He was keen to let him know the outcome of the Brisbane appointment, that he had made the decision to have the surgery and that his football days looked to be over.

Unfortunately, what Lennie considered early, wasn't early according to Fitzy. Fitzy's mum had answered the phone and after a few pleasantries said, "Sorry, Lennie, Alan is long gone. He left here after breakfast around six-ish to sort a problem with a leaking trough. I'd be happy to have him call you if that suits; when he comes back in for lunch around 12.30." Lennie decided that a return call was the best option, but he was all prepared in his mind to lay out his future plans to Fitzy and now there was no release. To get things off his chest, he wandered across the small paddock to his mother's house.

He found Di pottering around the kitchen, still wearing a terry toweling dressing gown that was obviously covering a pair of men's checked pajamas; pajamas that he hoped were left over from his father. His mother looked up with a smile spreading across her face. "I thought that sounded like your car coming up the drive. You are early and you've caught me at my glamorous best." Lennie accepted the offer of a cup of tea, sat down at the kitchen table, and put his hands on his head.

Lennie arranged himself at the kitchen table, took a deep breath, and before he knew it, all his fears and reservations about his knee, his job and most importantly, his relationship with Marion came tumbling out. He also mentioned what he could recall of the most recent drunken conversation with Fitzy about his mood, the need to commit to the operation and in particular, his suggestion that Marion was being unfaithful. He told his mum that on Fitzy's advice he had gotten off his arse and seen another surgeon in Brisbane.

"I am more comfortable with this new bloke, but unlike the first fella, he said things won't ever get back to normal. I have made a date to have the work done, but to be honest, I am more concerned about how things are going with Marion." Lennie told Di how he had confronted Marion and how she had denied sleeping around and that he believed her, sort of, but still had reservations. "Mum I really like her, I mean a lot. I sometimes wonder if I don't love her, but then I think that can't be right because I don't know her. Well, I think I do, but only sometimes. I am just bloody confused."

Di looked across her steaming mug of black tea at the bewildered look on her son's face. She had considered everything he had said but prefaced her response with a question. "Len do you want some support and a good cuddle, or do you want my honest opinion?"

Lennie took a deep breath. "I'm a big boy, Mum. I want your honest opinion."

"Okay," she said, "firstly let's address the Marion situation. That appears to be what has you so worked up. I think Alan Fitzgerald is a nice young bloke and I know he is trying to be the best friend to you that he can. He rang me a week or so back to say he was going to have a heart to heart with you and I am glad to know that he did. Lennie, what he says about Marion, you know, are his suspicions only, and you understand Marion better than he does. I doubt she is playing around, son. This is a small town; most of the rumors are run past me at the pub at some stage, and I haven't heard that one.

"Marion is a good-looking girl. She is cheeky and outgoing and well liked, but the person who likes Marion the most, is, well, it's Marion. That said, up until the footie accident, I can't recall seeing you much happier, and when she makes you happy, I am happy."

"Happiness is the biggest problems, mum. I love the happy bits, but they are so hard to predict. I don't know which Marion is going to walk in the door. One day she will bring on an argument for absolutely nothing and a couple of days later, she is all sweetness and light." Lennie said. "Last night when I got home from Brisbane, I was in a foul mood and after a comment she made, I bit her head off. I felt for sure I was in for a wing ding battle

127

and instead she sort of apologized, kissed me on the head, and went off to work, smiling and waving this $50 tip above her head that she got from a tour group yesterday. Mum, it's doing my head in."

It was Di's turn to settle herself. She took a long sip of tea and reached out for Lennie's hand, giving it a squeeze. "Len, you can bet the good days at home follow Marion's good days at work or come just before a good day she has planned. For what it is worth, word has got out about that tip, and I suspect she will find out today that it was supposed to be shared, so she might not be so chirpy tonight. As I said, all is sweet with Marion so long as things are going her way. I'll keep my ears open for any gossip, but I don't think it's an issue. Relationships are tricky things Lennie, and this is really your first long term one."

After a short hesitation she added, "But I have to say though, I hope it's not your last one." His mother continued to squeeze his hand and took a long look into his eyes before asking the most unexpected question. "Len, why do you think I never remarried after your dad left us?"

Lennie just gave her a blank look. It was honestly a question that had never entered his head. She was just his mum, she wasn't someone who had a love life or private life of her own. He was suddenly guilty that he had taken her for granted. He struggled to cobble together some sort of answer but nothing intelligible was forthcoming. In the end his mother answered her own question.

"Lennie, as I said, relationships are tricky. The reason I never remarried is that I only ever loved one man, your dad, right until the day he died." Di went on to explain how badly the war had affected her husband and how he had become terrified that he might hurt one or both of them during one of his "episodes." She even revealed that his father had confessed to her that he had considered driving himself and Lennie into a gum tree on the way back from a fishing trip one day. In the end, Ron decided that the safest thing for his family was to leave town and get as far away from them as he could.

"We never did get divorced you know Len", she confessed. "He was a good man, the love of my life. You know all those times you kept him out of the house when he visited? Well more than once, I wished you weren't so successful. The reason I am telling you this honey is that love comes in so many shapes and sizes.

"You shouldn't expect anyone else to tell you when you have found it. It's not all sweetness and light, it can be ugly, and it can be beautiful, but only you truly know when you have found something you never want to lose. There is something else, love, that I don't think you ever realized. Your dad really loved you. Part of the reason he left was because he loved you."

When she saw a tear form in the corner of her son's eye, Di stood up and ruffled his sandy hair again as she said, "Lennie, your situation with Marion will work itself out one way or another, you have more immediate problems with your knee and the workshop by the sound of it."

Lennie now understood that his relationship with his dad was more complicated than he had ever imagined. He resolved right then that, when the time came that he became a dad, his kids would never have any doubt that their father loved them.

After these somewhat confronting revelations, Len and his mother settled into a discussion about the upcoming surgery and what they could do to keep a moderate flow of cash into the business. Together they went through the mail, which was largely bills, and then worked out a bit of a budget and a strategy to ensure, as best they could, that the hire purchase agreement obligations could be met. The plan was to put up some flyers at the pub and the RSL offering discount oil and greases. It was one job Lennie knew he could handle alone, and as long as he had a fair number of bookings, he would be okay. Lennie even got a bit creative with the design of the flyer for the RSL. He would offer a 10% discount off his usual price for ex-servicemen and a 15% discount if the ex-digger had a TPI pension.

As Di wandered off to get ready for work, Lennie grabbed the keys and drove her Zephyr over to the workshop. Di had been complaining that the car was running a bit rough, so he gave it a quick once over and tuned up the carby.

Just as he finished the job, the phone rang, and it was Fitzy. Before he could get two words out, Lennie led the conversation. "I have taken your advice, mate, and the op is booked toward the end of November. The trouble is the new guy only operates in Brisbane which is going to be a pain in the arse." Fitzy tried to contribute to the conversation, but Lennie was on a roll. "I think I have made the right call, because the way the new guy was talking, the original advice I got in Toowoomba was absolute shit. I just have to take it pretty easy with no heavy lifting to make sure the knee doesn't blow up."

He was about to go into more detail about his prospects, when Fitzy finally managed to respond with a hint of disappointment in his voice. "Well that's good news and bad, Len," said Fitzy. "I have a big job lined up for you with one of the neighbours. His Ute has a blown head gasket and I guaranteed him he would get a good job at the right price from you. If you want it, the job is yours. If you feel you shouldn't take it on because of the knee, and you need a bit of muscle, I suppose I can lend a hand."

Together they worked out that if Fitzy could bring the car in on a trailer the following Saturday

131

morning and hang around to help maneuver the motor out and later help guide it back in, then the job was feasible. Lennie did some quick calculations and realized that a job this size would keep the wolves at bay a lot longer than a series of discounted oil changes. His mood began to lift. "Nice to have mates," he thought.

On the home front, things stayed much the same. That didn't mean they were the same all the time, but that Marion continued to run hot and cold, with a good proportion of the cold related to the bedroom. After the training mishap, he wasn't much interested in sex himself, and after the worst of the knee pain had settled, Marion had been under the weather a lot herself. Add in his low mood and the conditions for romance had been far from ideal. Just as the date for the operation drew near, and Lennie's general disposition deteriorated once again, Marion surprised him once more.

He was in bed one Saturday afternoon in just an old pair of footie shorts, listening to the races, when Marion came in and asked if he didn't have anything more constructive to do on a sunny Saturday afternoon. Lennie had become a little sensitive to answering questions like that, but a certain lilt in Marion's voice indicated that she had plans in mind that he might just agree with. Without waiting for a response, Marion reached over and turned the radio over to a station playing music. "So much more relaxing than listening to the droning voice of that race caller talking through his nose," she said in a voice intended to imitate his call from the last race. "Now Limpy Lennie, let's see if you are limp all over."

She ran her hand up his good leg and into the loose leg of his shorts. It didn't take her long to discover that the only damage suffered at training was to Lennie's knee. Marion stood behind the bed and slowly removed his shorts until a very healthy erection was visible above the band of his underwear. "Woo hoo, not so limpy," she squealed as she removed her own shorts and panties. She then asked him to stay on his back as she carefully straddled his groin while she slowly peeled off her top allowing her breasts to swing free. Swaying left to right, she grazed her nipples across his chest then reached behind and guided the least limpy part of Lennie inside herself.

As Marion was in the driver's seat literally, she adjusted her pace and position to make the most of the encounter. "How fucken good is this!" Lennie thought to himself. When he finally climaxed, he felt he wasn't just releasing a healthy two months of semen, it was as if all the tension of the last few months had been released as well. "Just like Mum suggested, I think I have found someone I never want to lose," he thought.

Chapter 15

A little over a week later, love was the last thing on his mind. He was in a hospital ward in Brisbane's Wickham Terrace, with his knee bandaged from hip to ankle and two drains emptying into small glass bottles. The surgeon had just been in to visit, and the news was as bad as he had been anticipating.

The term the doctor had used was pretty emphatic. He had done the "full belt and braces." This apparently meant he had torn both cartilages, ruptured the ACL ligament and had torn the medial ligament as well. The cartilages had both been removed so the pain and catching would ease as he healed. The longer-term outcome was less optimistic. With all that ligament damage, there was not a whole lot left holding his knee stable except the surrounding muscles and these had been weakened by the lack of activity since the accident. The muscles would weaken further as the knee would be heavily strapped initially for up to two weeks and then in plaster for a further eight weeks or so to permit healing. Once the surgeon decided the cast could be removed, he would have months of physiotherapy ahead of him to rebuild the muscles and stabilize the knee.

The doctor was of the view that no further proven surgical options was available and warned that as time wore on, there was every chance the knee might be permanently stiffened. His football days were over, along with any other activity that put unstable loads on the knee. He was scheduled to be in hospital for about four days.

His first visitors were a couple of his old teammates who were in Brisbane for the weekend and had decided to add in a visit to the hospital. Lennie was still groggy from the pain meds, so they spent most of their time giving a running commentary on the nursing staff and eating the chocolates they had bought for him. He was a little suspicious that the visit was as much to check out the nurses as to check in on his progress.

Fitzy and Di came to visit together the next day when he was a little more clear- headed. Di was concerned that the joint visit meant Lennie would have a day without visitors, but she confessed that she wasn't confident driving that far alone, and that she particularly could not have coped with the Brisbane traffic. The conversation comprised the typically sparse, uncomfortable exchanges, interspersed with the long pregnant pauses associated with hospital visits. How was it that people who had known each other for so long, couldn't manage to cobble together a decent conversation while huddled around a hospital bed. Di told him that he was due to be discharged after lunch on Friday and that Marion would visit him in the morning and wait around to drive him home.

Thursday was to be visitor free, and just as well, as that afternoon was chosen to remove the drains in his knee and bandage it up. The job had been assigned to two nurses, who the older gent in the adjoining bed had unkindly christened "Abbott and Costello" because one was tall and thin and the other short and dumpy. Lennie knew "Abbott's" real name to be Nurse Ryan, Patricia or Pat as she liked to be called. Pat had a reputation for never letting a pudding go to waste at dinner time. If a patient didn't want it, she did, and the habit did her waist line no favours. "Costello" was Nurse Hudson; Lennie never discovered her first name.

Pat was the senior of the two nurses and had been a great comfort to Lennie during his stay. She had particularly advised him on how to best get through the worst of the pain. "Medication isn't the only solution, you need to use your mind as well," she had told him. So he was glad to be in her hands as she explained what was about to happen. "Lennie, the plastic tubing drains that empty into these small glass bottles aren't the only method the surgeon has used to drain the site. He added lengths of gauge bandages that were folded to form a sort of wick and packed them into both sides of the knee before the wound was sutured."

Lennie nodded to indicate he understood, then asked an obvious question. "Is it fair to assume that this is going to hurt a lot?"

Pat had begun telling him that the removal of the tubes would be no problem at all when "Costello" offered her opinion. "Yes, the tube removal won't hurt at all, but removal of these wicks will be like nothing you have experienced before."

Lennie looked to the senior nurse for confirmation and unfortunately, she nodded her head in agreement. "Lennie, we have discussed ways of pain management before. The best advice I can give when these wicks come out is to compose yourself , then when we give the word, take a deep deep breath and hold it."

But in spite of this warning, Lennie was not prepared because this was a different sort of pain. It wasn't acute, it was a long stomach-churning pain, like the nurses were pulling out the insides of his knee. The first wick was bad enough, but the second one was worse, because Lennie knew what to expect.

"Well done, Lennie, that is the worst of it," said Nurse Ryan, with "Costello" nodding in agreement, "Yes, very well done. We had a patient throw up during that bit once." The nurses then checked the wounds and added an additional dressing. Despite the advice on breathing, Lennie was nauseous and sweating by the time the heavy bandaging was added over a plaster splint. "The splint will allow for swelling," Pat told him, "and it has the additional benefit of stabilizing the knee as best possible."

Other than the disturbance from routine nursing visits during the night, the pain meds ensured that he slept heavily until Friday morning. After breakfast, nurse Ryan decided that the time was right to see how he could travel on the aluminium Canadian style crutches. These, at least, were new and light, but given the design, required all the weight to be taken on the forearm. They had a totally different feel to the old ones, and it took a little time for him to adjust. After Lennie made a few trips up the hallway, his favourite nurse decided he was sufficiently confident and capable to be able to take himself off to the bathroom for a shower, freshen up, and be ready to get dressed for the trip back home.

He navigated his way unsteadily along the hallway toward the showers, past a group of younger nurses who had been entrusted with stringing the hospital's meagre collection of Christmas decorations across the reception desk. After settling in and removing his hospital issue pajamas, he made a little shower curtain for his leg out of the length of plastic they had provided. He then sat back on a chair in the shower recess and had one of the longest, hottest, and most enjoyable showers of his life.

When Marion arrived a little after lunch, he was sitting up in bed chatting to the elderly gent in the adjacent bed. She excused herself and drew the curtain between the beds and gave him a peck on the forehead. "How are you feeling" she asked, but without waiting for an answer, she added, "when can we get out of here?"

"I am just waiting for final clearance from the ward sister. Pat, my nurse, tells me it shouldn't be more than thirty minutes. In the meantime, I will put on my civvies and once we get the nod you can take me home."

Marion responded, "Your nurse, Pat, hm?, On a first name basis with the cute nurses, are we?"

The hospital's time estimate was typically inaccurate, and it was almost an hour and a half later before the sister came over to his bed with the requisite paperwork. Lennie had come to expect that medical staff of all stripes were never on time, but that didn't ease his frustration in the least. He roughly grabbed the clipboard and signed the paperwork with a flourish; keen to be out of there and on his way. An elaborate wheelchair was arranged which Lennie eased himself into. It was designed so that his stiff right leg was able to rest on an elevated shelf that was parallel to the ground. Lennie introduced Pat to Marion and between them, the two women took turns wheeling him out into the car park where Lennie started looking around the car park for his Ute. "Bob decided that you would never fit in that thing, so he offered us the use of his Fairlane." Marion answered the unspoken question.

A smile finally broke out on Lennie's face as they eased him off the wheelchair onto his crutches and then manoeuvered him into the plush back seat of the big sedan. Lennie grabbed the nurse's hand and squeezed it in appreciation. "Thanks for everything, Patricia, you are the best."

As the nurse headed back to the ward, Marion started the big V8 and gave it a few healthy revs. She looked back at Lenny and said, "A bit of a porker that Nurse Pat."

Lennie just shook his head in resignation and mumbled under his breath, "She was a great help to me."

After easing her way through the traffic in town, Marion navigated toward Ipswich Road in the direction of Toowoomba and home.

Lennie had been loaded into the car such that he was sitting sideways in the back seat. They weren't long into the trip when he realized he should have had them set him up so that his head was on the passenger's side of the car. Sitting as he was, with his head against the rear driver's side door, meant talking into the back of Marion's head. The only time he could see any expression on her face was when she turned her head left or right to look at traffic. When she did turn, he could see that she had a huge wide grin on her face.

"What are you so happy about; glad to get me home?"

"Have you ever driven this car, Lennie?" was her prompt response. "It's got a big V8 and it's a beast."

With that she planted her foot to make the point and Lennie let out a huge scream as she hit the tram tracks that ran along the middle of the road. The big Fairlaine fishtailed, and though Marion wasn't going that fast, Lennie felt like his knee was coming apart. Even after the tram tracks were well behind them and she settled down to a more sedate pace, any substantial dip or patch or pothole caused a similar stab of pain.

When they finally made it home to Dalby, the sun was just going down. Marion woke up a dozing Lennie, then moved him from the air-conditioned environment of the car's rear seat, to the still stifling heat of the main bedroom. After settling him in and making him a bit of toast and a pot of tea, she drove Bob's car back to the Imperial Hotel, where he was waiting in the car park. She thanked him and raved about the power of the thing, adding that there was no way they would have got Lennie home in the Ute.

"This bloody heat would have killed him and frankly I don't think he would have fitted anyway." She transferred over to Lennie's Ute and began to head home, then stopped and called back to Bob, "Can you give Di a call and let her know her little boy is home safe and sound?" When Marion arrived home, she found Lennie in a deep sleep, ably assisted, no doubt, by the contents of the small bottle of pills on his bedside table.

To save another trip down to the capital, Lennie had made arrangements with the Brisbane surgeon to get most of his immediate ongoing treatment in Toowoomba. He contacted Fitzy to see if he was coming into town any time soon, with the hope that Fitzy could extend the stay by driving him to the appointment in Toowoomba and back. He was also thinking they could go somewhere for a drink and a talk, as he was already getting stir crazy after only two weeks or so. Fitzy agreed he could do it this once, but unfortunately had some bad news.

His Uncle Don, who owned a cattle property at the back of Charleville, had planned a major tree clearing and refencing operation and Fitzy had been "volunteered" to help. He figured he would be out there for a few months and was leaving the upcoming weekend. Lennie had finally managed to pin Toowoomba hospital down to a date for the post-operative appointment and luckily the date coincided with Fitzy's availability.

As they sat in the out-patients' area, an hour after the designated appointment time, Fitzy wondered why he had tried so hard to be there on time. Eventually, Lennie was ushered in to see the doctor while Fitzy waited outside, thumbing through some seriously old and tatty magazines. After removing the bandages and plaster back strap supporting the knee, it was obvious that the post-operative swelling had reduced substantially. Lennie was told that the incisions were healing nicely. The doctor then removed the stitches and instructed the nurse to set up so he could put the knee into a cylindrical plaster cast. He spoke to Lennie for no more than five minutes and was gone promising to come back and view the final result.

It was almost an hour before the doctor breezed back in, noted that the cast had set nicely and that the twenty-degree angle he wanted had been achieved. "That all looks good, Len," he said. "We will liaise with your Brisbane surgeon about when we can remove the cast but count on about eight weeks. In the meantime, when the pain settles a bit, try flexing your quad muscles on and off for about five minutes, five times a day. The idea is to ensure there isn't too much muscle wastage."

When Lennie finally hobbled out on a new set of crutches, Fitzy was up and out of his chair in a flash. "For fuck sake that took some time, let's get some lunch and you can give me a run down," he said grabbing his hat and heading up the hallway toward the exit. Over a burger and coke they discussed the medical assessment.

"So let me get this straight," Fitzy said. "You have to get around in this heat with your leg plastered up to your groin for a couple months, and then they might take it off!" Lennie agreed it was going to be uncomfortable but tried to put a positive spin on it by reminding Fitzy that the doctor was happy with how it healed and that with dedication from him, combined with physiotherapy, the knee should get progressively more stable.

During the trip back home, Lennie decided to broach the subject of his current situation at home. He explained that it was difficult to get around and do the most mundane of things to fill in the days. "It doesn't help that Marion is often away for ten to twelve hour stretches at a time," he said. "And I know Mum has never had shifts at the pub that long, so I assume she isn't running straight home."

Fitzy decided to make no comment, he just nodded his head and pretended to be concentrating intently on the highway. "Lennie is finally starting to wake up to the fact that something doesn't add up," he thought. "Best I shut up and let him get this all out of his system."

145

As the trip progressed, the list of Lennie's concerns grew: he was finding it difficult to get around, to feed himself or even get to the toilet. He now realized, he said, that the way the house was built, managed to make the absolute worst of each season.

"During winter, the wind gets in through every crack and cranny, even up through the floor boards in places. But at this time of year, there is never a whisper of breeze. It's so hot I nearly cook in there during the day, and it's not much better at night." On top of this list of woes, he was concerned that he had not earned a dollar in more than three weeks and it probably wouldn't be until at least Christmas that he could hope to get back into the workshop in any sort of meaningful way.

"What I really want to do is focus on getting the business back up and running, but that will be tricky with the gear I have and my gammy leg. Even when I can work, I'll probably be back to taking on small shitty jobs."

Fitzy continued to stare straight ahead as he barreled the big Fairlane back toward Dalby. "Have you quite finished with your moaning, Lennie?" he finally said. "I want to be helpful, mate, but you are being your own worst enemy. Don't focus on the problem, focus on the fucking solution."

Lennie didn't react, so he went on in a more conciliatory tone. "Len, you are a mechanic. If the gear you have doesn't suit the work you want to do, make it suit. You have oxy, grinders, and all the paraphernalia. You have the skill to do it and more to the point, you have all the time in the world."

Once again, Lennie had to acknowledge to himself that he had to get his act together, and what better time than now to get the workshop sorted for how he might have to work permanently in future. The project would fill his days, keep his mind off his problems and set him up for how he may need to work in future. Lennie knew that after all the things they had discussed were in place, he would be back on the right track. He just needed to rejig the way he worked in the shop, do the exercises, and really get into the physio when the plaster came off.

When they pulled into the driveway of his rented house around three in the afternoon, Fitzy got out first and retrieved his crutches from the back seat, then came around to the passenger side and helped Lennie out, arranged his crutches, and steered him toward the rear door of the house. As he was about to follow down the slight incline, Lennie turned and asked him to check the mail, as he hadn't looked at it for a few days. Fitzy walked back up to the dilapidated letter box, retrieved the mail, then quickly caught up to Lennie and raced ahead to open the door into the kitchen. He had knocked the top off two beers before Lennie had even settled onto a kitchen chair.

Sitting down, Fitzy tapped the three slightly weatherworn window faced envelopes he had placed flat on the kitchen table. "You better check those out, they look to have been in there a while and don't look like good news." After just the one beer, Fitzy indicated that he had to head for home.

"Sure," said Lennie, "I know you want to be back before the roos are a problem. Marion should be home shortly anyway. Thanks for the lift, mate, and thanks for reading me the riot act. I needed that. I am going to start working out how to redesign the workshop tomorrow."

Chapter 16

Lennie waited until he could hear the distinctive burble of the big Fairlaine slowly fade into the distance, before he methodically opened each envelope in turn. All three were on AGC Finance letterhead, all three dated more than a week previously, all three had near identical wording and all three had one word printed diagonally in large red type across the page; OVERDUE. Lennie felt a horrible hollow feeling in the pit of his stomach. Marion apparently hadn't even been checking the mail. They had specifically discussed his concerns about the hire purchase repayment well before his operation, and it was his understanding that she would look after them. Afterall she was still working, while the workshop remained closed, she still sat in the lounge suite, listened to the stereo and slept in the bed and used the rest of the bedroom suite.

They would just need to sort out the misunderstanding over dinner, he thought. In the meantime, he decided to take a tablet for the pain brought on by the day's prodding and probing, and lie down until Marion returned home. It was hot and stuffy in the bedroom but before too long he began to relax as the pain killer took effect.

Lennie felt he had only just drifted off when he was awakened abruptly as the fly screen door to the kitchen banged shut. He was in a fog as usual and initially wondered where he was and whether it was already breakfast. Half asleep and confused he mumbled, "Is that you, Marion? Where am... what time is it? Is it morning?"

When Marion abruptly answered that it was just after eight, Lennie realised that he had slept for over four hours and that he was incredibly hungry. When he asked her why she was so late Marion just shrugged.

"I had a couple of drinks after work at "The Sportsman" with their new bar maid. She wanted the lay of the land, and given that she is new in town, someone suggested that she talk to me. We had a counter tea and a chat and a few beers and before I knew it, it was almost 8 o'clock."

"Well, good for you", Lennie said, "but I haven't had any dinner."

Marion looked at him sideways and said, "Don't expect me to cook a full meal, I've already eaten." With that, she grabbed a big tin of spaghetti out of the kitchen cupboard, rattled around in the kitchen drawer until she found an opener then poured the contents into a saucepan. While it heated up, she made some toast and within a few minutes, she deposited the less than appealing meal in front of Lennie, saying, "Go for your life, sunshine, eat that while I have a long cool shower."

Lennie begrudgingly began to eat the canned meal and was on the cusp of letting Marion know that he was hoping for something more substantial. Then he remembered that he had financial matters to discuss with her, and that this wasn't the time to risk getting her off-side.

Once Marion had showered and dressed for bed, Lennie motioned for her to join him in the lounge room so they could talk. Before he could update her on the doctor's report or raise the matter of the finance company's letters, Marion launched into a rant about her rate of pay at the hotel.

"That new girl from The Sportsman, Karen, you know she gets more per hour than I do and she is only just starting. I think Bob is ripping me off."

Lennie's natural inclination was to go to Bob's defense, "Before you get too hard on Bob, make sure you have your facts right and are comparing the same thing. Bob has been pretty good to you and me. Don't forget he gave you a job when you were just a blow in, he gave you free accommodation to start with, he forgave you that time you left him in the lurch and went missing. He looks after me and mum, and he lent you the use of his Fairlaine to pick me up from hospital. He is a good bloke."

"All I know, Lennie, is Karen is just a blow in too, and her hourly rate is a dollar an hour more than mine. But then I suppose I should have known you wouldn't take my side."

Lennie decided to ignore her and just change the subject. "On more important matters, have you noticed my new accessory?" he said pointing to his freshly plastered leg. "The knee is progressing well, I have to wear this for about two months and then it's just a matter of building up the muscles."

The only reply from Marion was "Two more months, you will have driven me up the wall by then."

Lennie was angry that she was so dismissive, so shot straight back with a bit of venom in his voice, "...And I will be just about skint as well, that's why I am worried about this pile of old bills I found in the letterbox." He then theatrically dropped the letters from head height onto the kitchen table in front of her.

She picked the first one up and read it and then looked quickly at the second, then third. "It's the same wording on all three of these, Lennie; it's just a bloody "try on" from the finance mob. You've got weeks before you have to worry about this shit." With that she dismissively pushed the letters back toward him with the back of her hand saying, "Well I'm off to bed, I've got an early start tomorrow."

Lennie stayed up for a while longer and reread the letters. There was nothing new in the letters, but he was playing back in his head the words Marion had used. Specifically, that HE had weeks to make a decision. When Lennie woke up late next morning, he intended to finish the conversation of last night, but Marion was already gone. He hobbled around the house for a while, then around midday, made his way carefully up the driveway to check the letterbox. Inside he found three more window faced envelopes, identical to the old ones he retrieved the day before. This time the red diagonal wording was more to the point, "Final Warning."

Lennie decided he could no longer pussy foot around. He needed to have a serious face to face conversation with Marion after she returned from her shift that night. He knew it was going to get uncomfortable, but so be it. She always seemed to manage to take control of the conversation or to delay a serious discussion. That had to stop so he steeled himself to finally bring the matter to a head.

No matter how heated the argument might get, if they were to have a life together, it was past time that they both stopped avoiding a sensible adult conversation.

Chapter 17

When Lennie heard his Ute pull up outside their house late that afternoon, he opened the fridge and pulled out a tallie of XXXX Bitter, went to the cupboard and retrieved two glasses, then poured out two foamy beers. When she reached the kitchen door, he didn't wait to find out which version of Marion had decided to come home that night. "Come in, mate, have a seat, have a beer, we need to talk," he said in the most mellow voice he could muster.

Marion complied, but Lennie could see she was already on the defensive, so he quickly added, "Listen I don't want this to turn into an argument, I just need to sort a few things out because we have been avoiding a couple of big problems." Marion said nothing, she just gave a rolling motion with her right hand to indicate that she was listening and wanted Lennie to get on with it.

"I haven't worked now for nearly a month and for the six weeks before that I was bringing in a lot less than usual. Everything was paid up to date before the accident, but things have slipped since then and I was looking to you to chip in a bit more until I got back on my feet."

Marion still said nothing but was listening and again gave a rolling motion with her right hand for Lennie to continue. "The hire purchase payments are my main worry. Before the op we discussed it, and you said you would look after them, but apparently you haven't, and now I am getting letters saying that I have to either make the catch-up payments or the stuff will be repossessed." Lennie stopped again, waiting for her to comment.

This time at least, Marion chimed in, asking him to keep going. Lennie took a deep breath, then a long swig of beer and continued. "Mate, we have been through a lot together and have a lot more ahead of us to share, but that involves keeping the promises we make to each other. You said you would look after the payments until I get back on my feet and I need to know you will go into town tomorrow and sort this out. If you don't, we will soon have no lounge suite, TV, stereo or bed to sleep in."

Lennie finished the last of his beer and noticed that Marion had not touched hers. He decided he would say no more and wait on her response no matter how long it took. He did not have to wait long.

"If you are finished with your instructions, Lennie, let me tell you for starters that I never definitely said I would pay those hire purchase bills. I indicated that if things looked really grim I would chip in, and I have been chipping in towards the rent and food. Also, things aren't that grim yet because I know you haven't even asked Di for help and I know she would be happy to help you."

Lennie was shocked. "These things aren't my mum's problems, honey, they are ours. We bought the stuff, we use the stuff, why should my mum have to pay for it? She is not rolling in dough, anyway. I might be doing it tough, but you are still making good money at the pub. If we are going to have a future together, we have to take responsibility for our own stuff. We wouldn't want our kids to come crying to us for money when they grew up, would we?"

This time it was Marion with the shocked look on her face. "You have taken one giant leap there, Lennie. In the space of thirty seconds, you have gone from an overdue payment on a lounge suite to how we would want our kids to act!" As always Marion's anger rose quickly, and she was soon on the attack. "What makes you think we have a future together anyway, Lennie, let alone one with kids? My mum got saddled with one drop kick boyfriend after another and I'll be buggered if I follow her lead. I am out of here! I'll drop your car back tomorrow when I come to pick up my stuff; tonight, I'll stay at Karen's place. How about you sort out your own financial mess shithead?!"

Marion could see that Lennie was wounded and shocked but that didn't stop her from one final lunge with her sharp tongue. "As for kids, Lennie," she continued, "I had the chance of having your kid a few months back and I got rid of that problem the first chance I got. Why do you think I missed your stupid grand final?" Marion pushed herself away from the table and was quickly heading out the door.

Lennie tried to stop her exit but got tangled up in the legs of the kitchen chair when he awkwardly rose to his feet. "What the fuck," he said out loud to himself. Everything had unraveled so quickly but all he could say was "..an abortion?" He was in shock and before he could clear his head and get his balance again, Marion was backing up the driveway leaving him in a cloud of hot afternoon dust.

Lennie was truly isolated, both physically and mentally. He was on crutches miles out of town, alone, and with no car and no home telephone. Lennie could not believe the conversation that had just taken place. Everyone had been telling him to grow up, grow a pair, get a plan underway for his future and that was just what he had tried to do. Instead of giving him some clarity, trying to talk it through with Marion had devolved into another classic argument. Lennie had been coming to believe he loved Marion and he honestly thought they had a future together. He could see where he was not offering the most to the relationship right at present, but was that not always the way with relationships? Things went better for one party than the other.

His plan was simple, to get some clear lines of communication going. He wanted to talk to her about their present problems and their future together. Instead, the girl he thought he loved had told him that she had gotten rid of a baby he did not even know existed; that she considered him a loser and that she was moving out. He turned to the only company he could find, the remnants of a large bottle of Bundaberg rum and the last of the beer in the fridge. Together they stayed around the kitchen table until he finally dragged himself off to bed around midnight.

True to her word, Marion was at the house early next morning. Karen had followed behind in her own car and was waiting in the driveway. When Lennie woke up, Marion had her head in the bedroom wardrobe and was retrieving all her clothes on hangers. She then moved to the chest of drawers, pulled out the two top drawers and emptied the contents into a large brown suitcase. Lennie got out of bed and leaving his crutches on the floor, followed her into the lounge room. He moved from one piece of furniture to another to keep his balance, imploring her as he went to settle down and talk to him about the baby she had terminated and their future together.

She turned to him and said, "Lennie, it's over. I am sorry you had to find out about the baby that way, but I did not want a family and we were a relatively new item at that stage."

Holding onto the kitchen table for support, Lennie implored Marion to think things through. "It's crazy, mate, to talk about moving, just because we had an argument about money. Moving out isn't a solution for God's sake."

"Moving out is the solution I came up with weeks ago, it has nothing to do with the payments on your TV set. Our little "Home Beautiful" session has run its race, mate. I don't want to be a wife, or a mother and I certainly don't want to be your nurse. To make things easier I am taking a job at The Sportsman with Karen from this Saturday and I am going to share a house with her in town. This way I won't have to be working with your mum, I won't need shanks pony or your car to get to work, plus I will be on better money."

Lennie tried in vain to get Marion to see reason, but she wasn't for turning. She took the clothes she had collected on hangers and the suitcase out to the car and returned with a couple of empty cardboard boxes. She filled the first box with all the LP records she had accumulated and the second with all her makeup and various lotions and potions from the bathroom. "Bye Lennie, I'll see you around the ridges. I have to drop into The Imperial to give Bob my notice. If I see Di, I will tell her to drop out to see you, and if she isn't there Bob can pass along the message." She dropped the two boxes into the back seat of Karen's old Prefect and left without a tear.

Lennie made himself a simple breakfast then began clearing up the mess caused by Marion's whirlpool departure. He felt a mixture of sadness and anger when he realized that the cardboard box of LP's she left with included a good proportion of his own meagre collection. About an hour later, as he lay in bed re-reading the AGC letters for the third time, he heard his mother's familiar voice calling out to him from the rear door.

"Well what a shit fight, love, are you all right? Bob rang me with the news and I came straight over." Lennie called out to her from the bedroom and Di rushed over to him and cuddled him like she used to do not that many years ago.

"Aw, Mum, it hurts so much, I just didn't see it coming, not like that anyway." Lennie struggled with the words, trying so hard not to cry. As a caring mum, Di's natural inclination would normally have been to suggest that her son look to see how things could be patched up, particularly as he seemed so heavily involved. In this case, the timing and method of the breakup left Di firmly of the opinion that Marion had finally shown her true colours and that Lennie was well rid of her.

"Lennie, it looks like you were right to be concerned, but just not for the reasons you thought. She might not be sleeping around but she is a selfish two-faced bitch. How could she leave you just when you need her most, and after all we have done for her too?" It took a lot to get Di's blood up, but she was on a roll now.

"She has left Bob in the lurch again. She quit, gave him no notice and is going to work at The Sportsman." Di hugged her son again and he pondered whether to tell his mother the news about the grandchild she would never see. He decided not to reveal that bit of news, as he still hadn't fully dealt with it himself.

Sorting his crutches, he shuffled over to the sink and put on the jug. "Want a cup of tea, Mum?" Di shot back the standard family response to this familiar request. "Stop asking stupid questions and make me a pot of tea!"

Once the billy had boiled and the pot had sat for the appropriate time, Len poured out two cups and added the milk and sugar to their individual tastes. Without crutches, he shuffled around the kitchen table and sat opposite his mum, clutching the set of letters with the AGC logos. "This is what bought things to a head," he said, "..though it appears things were already heading off a cliff." Len handed over the letters to Di pointing out which set had arrived first. He sat back and sipped his tea as his mum read through the correspondence.

When she had finished, she took a long sip, considered how she would approach things and then said, "Len, did you kill a Chinaman or something? How much bad luck can one young bloke have?" When she asked him how long he thought it would be before he started working again, Lennie said that he could probably get around well enough inside a week.

"Well the first thing we have to do is get you out of here. You can't look after yourself alone here anyway, so you can move back into your old room with me. That will save this rental expense," she said.

Di saw one positive with the arrears of payments. Len had three individual hire purchase agreements, so he could let them foreclose on any or all three. It was decided that as Di already had a hi-fi, TV and lounge suite, that they should let AGC take those back and that she would make a few payments on the least expensive item which was the bedroom suite. Lennie had gotten used to the large bed and did not fancy having to sleep in the same old single cot that he had had since he was a kid.

"Listen honey," Di said, "I have to head back to work. Until Bob finds a replacement barmaid, me and the other girls are going to have to cover part of Marion's old shifts."

Lennie followed his mother out to her car, then dropped one crutch and gave her a warm embrace. "I'll drop in and see Murry," she told him, "on the way into town. I'll explain the circumstance and that you are going to have to move out."

The arrangements didn't prove a problem given she had known Murry most of her life, and anyway the place had been empty for years before Lennie moved in and it was in better condition now that it was before.

The next day, Lennie rang Fitzy's mum and explained the change of circumstances to her. He asked her if she could get in touch with Fitzy out at Charleville and have him call the workshop number Friday night around five-ish. When the call came though that afternoon, Lennie was already on his second beer. He didn't need to be told that at that time of day, Fitzy was sure to have one in his hand already as well.

They shared a bit of good-natured ribbing, then he explained what had happened with Marion, his financial situation and how he had needed to move back in with his mother both for financial and practical reasons. They talked for a good thirty minutes, about the operation, how things were progressing with recovery and, more to the point, how they were not progressing so far with the business. Fitzy was acutely aware that the one subject that Lennie had avoided discussing in detail was the future after Marion.

Eventually there was a lull in the conversation, Fitzy cleared his throat and took the plunge. "Len, let me first confess that I have already had a call in to your mum to get a heads up on what's been happening. Now you know what I am going to say, but I have to say it. That girl is a serious piece of work and as much as you are hurting, you are well rid of her because...."

Lennie cut him off mid-sentence and explained that there was more still to the story. "Look I haven't even told Mum this yet, it would kill her. It's what's probably fucking up my head the most about all this. Mate, I found out why she didn't show for the grand final. You were wrong, she wasn't screwing around, she was in Toowoomba getting an abortion, mate." Lennie was choking up as he got out the next few sentences. "We were having a kid and she decided she didn't want that. She didn't talk to me, the bitch just up and got rid of my kid!"

Fitzy digested that bit of news and decided it was best that for once, he wasn't honest with Lennie. He knew that Lennie saw Marion's actions as just another bit of deception and bastardry. Fitzy, on the other hand, was thinking, "Lennie, you lucky bastard, you just dodged a bullet." Three beers later,

Fitzy said they had better soon sign off as the call would be costing his uncle a fortune.

He had explained to Lennie that the properties around Charleville had party line telephone services, which meant if any of the neighbours picked up their phone they could easily eavesdrop on the conversation, but it hadn't dissuaded Lennie from baring his soul. For some people, this eavesdropping activity was their favoured means of entertainment, and this particular conversation had already contained enough information to keep the region's gossips entertained for weeks.

Before he signed off, Fitzy made the point, in a theatrically loud voice, that he knew how delicate the information was and promised to keep it confidential. It never hurt, he figured, to let the neighbours who listened in on party line calls know that he knew they were eavesdropping. While it was a standard district pastime, that he was also guilty of, it still didn't feel right when you knew you were the victim of it. "Listen, mate, chin up. I'll be back home between Christmas and New Year so we will have a serious catch up then. The job out here is on time and I reckon I'll be back full time come mid Feb."

Before finally hanging up, Fitzy asked Lennie how things were going with reconfiguring his gear and the workshop and the conversation brightened somewhat. Lennie had obviously put a lot of thought into how he could adapt things to suit his situation and enthusiastically explained what he was going to work on in the next week or so. He had even arranged with "Sarge," one of his mates from the footie club, to lend a hand with the trickier jobs. "The coach reckons having Sarge as a helper is like having two men on sick leave," he laughed. "But any help is appreciated and, anyway, I can use the company." In short, he told Fitzy that the plan was to do everything he could to rebuild what he used to have, and put Marion behind him as a bad memory.

Lennie hung up the phone and a big beaming smile came over his face, the first one he could recall for some time. At the other end of the line, Fitzy was feeling pretty good too, as he placed the phone back in the cradle. He had been worried about Len, but the conversation had put his mind at ease. He would ring Di over the weekend and give her an update and help put her mind at ease as well.

Chapter 18

A couple of weeks before Christmas Len had moved back into his mother's house. He had paid out the loan on the bedroom suite and it had moved with him. Setting up in his old bedroom was something of a draining experience both physically and mentally. The room seemed to have shrunk for one thing, but that was likely just because he had squeezed his big double bed with headboard and cupboard and dresser into a space once occupied by little more than his original single cot and set of drawers.

He had come to an agreement for AGC to repossess the stereo, TV, lounge and other gear. After selling it for what they could get, Lennie estimated that he would have to kiss off the 40% deposit he had paid up front and would have to contribute a few hundred dollars more from his remaining meagre savings to settle the shortfall. Exactly how much that would be would have to wait until they sold the gear. He figured he wouldn't know for sure until the new year. If there was any positive news in his life, it was that he was now living right beside the workshop. He could count on his mother's reliability, and he had been able to take in a few simple mechanical jobs.

It was awkward getting around with his leg still in plaster, but he now only used the crutches to get from the workshop to the house. He also discovered that if he sat in the middle of the front seat of the Ute, steered at an angle and was happy to stay in second gear, he could use his car if necessary. Necessary use involved keeping away from town and was largely confined to driving into the local garage to collect the occasional parts. If he needed anything else, Di could deliver it on her trips to and from the hotel. He hadn't been up to visiting the pub in person since the accident. Lennie had taken stock of the equipment he would use most frequently, how it would restrict him, and how he could adjust it to better suit his situation. The time had come to put his plan into action.

The first thing he and Sarge did was to manufacture a low flat trolley with wheels. Laying on this, he could easily slide under anything he was working on. He then broke down his tool chest so that most things were accessible from the floor. It meant he wasn't getting up and down all the time which was his most difficult maneouvre at present. His next project was modifying his trolley jack. He cut the handle right down and then welded a sleeve over the remnant so he could bring it back to normal length if needed. The shorter handle meant he could lift light weights from the floor. While he was at it, he decided he would need to source some O rings for the piston, as he noticed it was leaking a bit of hydraulic fluid. Each job he completed bought him a bit more joy, as he could start to see the light at the end of the tunnel.

Lennie finally felt he was getting his life back together, and to top it off, one afternoon a few days before Christmas, he looked up from the workshop floor to see Fitzy standing there with a carton of stubbies on his shoulder and a forty-ounce bottle of Bundy with a red and green ribbon very roughly tied around the neck. The next few days consisted of catching up, sharing stories, and getting royally drunk. Fitzy spent Christmas day back at "Kilmarnock", but once he had satisfied that family obligation, he had spent the rest of the time chauffeuring Lennie around town and helping where he could. He had even managed to track down the coach, and Sarge rounded up a few more of Lennie's closer team mates as well. Together they replayed the grand final win over a BBQ and a couple of cartons around the back of the workshop.

Lennie wasn't sure if he was sad or jealous to hear that Bozo was taking up a higher paying position at the bank in Toowoomba and young Douggie, the halfback, was starting an engineering degree at Queensland University, both in the New Year. What started as an afternoon BBQ was soon extending into the night.

Lennie dragged Fitzy into the back of the workshop, opened the fridge to grab out another six-pack, then reached into the back of the freezer section and miraculously pulled out a couple of $20 notes. "There is no way we are going to run out of piss, the next few cartons are my shout, mate, courtesy of the tax man. Thanks for this, I needed it." Fitzy pocketed the cash that he guessed came from what was left of Lennie's "funny money" and drove into town to collect enough beer to ensure the night was long.

All the while Fitzy was catching up, he was also assessing how Lennie was coping and decided that he really seemed to have gotten his act together with the rebuilding of the business. He was particularly impressed with the work Lennie had done in customizing the workshop to make allowances for his new handicap. He also seemed to have accepted his fate regarding the end of his rugby days. The only outstanding matter seemed to be his broken heart. Marion had really blindsided him with the sudden move, and he still hadn't been able to raise the matter of the baby with his mum. Fitzy decided to largely leave the topic of Marion alone and the only time Lennie raised it was when he told Fitzy how Marion had finally convinced him what a first-rate bitch she was.

Apparently, she had started wearing one of his old blue and yellow Dalby football jerseys as a sort of uniform at her new job. While it was once one of her favorite casual shirts, he was surprised to hear she was still wearing it, until he heard that she had made a cruel alteration. The original jersey had sported his favored Number 8 position on the back; however, Marion had crudely changed the 8 to a 0. Others might not realize the significance of the change, but Lennie was aware that it was her sly way of conveying the message that Lennie was now a zero in her life. Fitzy's only comment was to shake his head in resignation and agreement, after which Lennie never mentioned her again all night.

In what seemed no time at all, Lennie woke up with a monumental New Year's hangover to realise that Fitzy was already on the road back to Charleville. He was soon alone in the workshop again, dealing with how to move on with his life.

Chapter 19

While Fitzy was delighted with how Lennie was progressing, he was also keen to get back out to Charleville and it wasn't because he was missing his Uncle Don. It was only a week after he first arrived out at Charleville back in November that his eye was taken by an attractive jillaroo by the name of Phoebe who was working on another property in the district. The Charleville camp draft meeting was planned for the first week in January and Fitzy had arranged to meet her there, and then take her to the dance that was to follow that night.

Phoebe was a city girl, if you classed Rockhampton as a city, but had always had a love of the land, horses, cattle, and the great outdoors. Even though her bank manager father had little to do with cattle, a number of his larger customers did have major cattle enterprises. Phoebe didn't know if it was that association, or the fact that Rockhampton billed itself as the beef cattle capital of Australia, that imbued in her a love of the industry. Either way, after leaving school, that love, and her riding skills, soon saw her first working on various properties around Emerald.

Now, at the age of twenty-five, she found herself doing general rouseabout work in the western downs. Phoebe was a petite blond with the only blemishes on her tanned skin being an arc of freckles over her perky nose and the beginnings of wrinkles at the corner of her eyes. Her good looks and small frame belied a girl who had an incredible capacity for work and who was substantially stronger than she looked.

She was by far the youngest of three girls, and was, without doubt, the apple of her father's eye, which was evidenced by the fact that he spent most weekends with her at her pony club events. Her mother had died when she was young, leaving her dad to raise his three children. Only a couple of years after her mother's death, the eldest girl, Wendy, married a young Melbourne boy and moved to Victoria. The middle girl, Gaye, more than compensated for any expected reduction in parental responsibility by constantly finding herself in trouble. When Gaye left school, she was constantly on the move. Unlike Phoebe, however, she wasn't chasing work, but trouble.

Despite their difference in age and different approaches to life the sisters stayed in contact as best they could, and from what Fitzy was able to determine, while Wendy was still in Melbourne, Gaye was now to be found around the coast of northern New South Wales. By the time Phoebe finished school she was quite the accomplished horsewoman and had decided that she could make a job out of this passion.

Due to their responsibilities and the distances between the properties, the new couple only managed to catch up on weekends, but that didn't stop romance from blossoming. Fitzy was smitten and Phoebe was just as certain that despite the ten years age difference, that Alan was the man for her. Despite now having a serious love interest in his life, Fitzy continued to stay in touch with Lennie and received regular updates as well from Di.

For his part, after that heavy Christmas/New year session, Lennie decided that the coming year was going to be his year for getting his act back together. He was more mobile by the day and was quite capable of taking on more work if only he could find it.

The week after New Year, he decided he should drive into town with Di at each opportunity and spend a little time trying to drum up business at various pubs, the RSL, and other businesses where he was well known. He even arranged to place a small ad in the local paper. "I'll just have to steer clear of The Sportsman I suppose," he said to his mum on the drive into town.

Di's response provided him with some interesting information. " You'd be unlucky to run into Marion at The Sportsman, because I'm told she isn't getting that many hours." Lennie looked across at his mother waiting for more information. "Well apparently, the publican had a different staffing structure to Bob. His idea is to have a lot more casual staff, offer them a higher than usual hourly rate, but offer each person less hours."

What Lennie found hilarious was that Marion apparently hadn't initially noticed, given they were so busy over Christmas. "Once the Christmas season was behind them," Di continued with a smirk, "she was offered reduced hours and is now making a lot less than when she worked alongside me at the 'Impy.'"

As luck would have it, Lennie did run into Marion, when he dropped into the crowded Acropolis milk bar around lunch time. She was waiting her turn at the counter with her back turned to him and again wearing that Dalby jersey with the number 0 on the back. Lennie bristled but said nothing.

When Marion turned with her lunch in hand, she saw him instantly and in her usual sarcastic tone, loud enough for all to hear, said, "Well if it isn't Limpy Lennie."

Doubly wounded, Lennie spat straight back. "Well if it isn't that partially employed barmaid from The Sportsman. Leaving Bob in the lurch for a few extra bucks isn't looking like such a smart idea now, is it?"

"Fuck you, Lennie, you fucken loser," was the only response she could muster.

"You, Marion, are a selfish bitch." He shouted after her as she grabbed her burger and stormed out fuming. Lennie felt pretty happy with himself that he had finally bested her in an argument. But he should have learned that Marion played the long game, and the final score wasn't in as yet.

Heading back to meet his mum and to cadge a lift back to the workshop, he could hardly wait to recount the story of the argument he had just "won" at the cafe. "Mum you won't believe what just happened at the café up the road." Lennie said as soon as he saw Di. "I ran into Marion and she was wearing that jersey with the-"

"Were you able to secure any more jobs?" Di immediately cut in. She was clearly not interested in hearing anything about Marion.

"No, Mum, But I got into an argument with Marion and put her in her place."

"For God's sake you didn't come into town to win an argument, and you won't win one against that girl Len, so give up trying."

It transpired that his mother's advice was a little late in coming, because within twenty minutes of Marion's next shift, she was already putting a little plan of revenge into action. The local manager of the RSL, Dez Rudd, was a forty-ish balding bachelor who had taken a shine to Marion. As he was the manager, Dez didn't think it was good form to drink at the RSL after work, so he always dropped into various other pubs downtown instead. Since Marion had moved over to The Sportsman, it had become his local. As he was responsible for the shift times at the RSL, including his own, he had roughly managed to synchronize their shifts so that she was often behind the bar when he came in after work.

Marion knew from their prior conversations that here was a man with a bigger opinion of himself than was deserved or shared by the rest of town. She also knew he was keen on her and that with the slightest of encouragement she could have him spreading a little rumor that would hurt Lennie and that could never be traced back to her. As was usual, Marion moved back and forward along the bar filling orders, but now, whenever there was a short break in activity, she parked in front of Dez. It was easy for her to lead their piecemeal conversations toward the topic of her breakup with Lennie. Dez too was keen to be discussing her new status as a good looking, single and available woman. Of course, Marion painted herself as the aggrieved party.

Over the course of a week or so, she told Dez that since Lennie's accident and operation, he had become more demanding and was treating her more as a nursemaid than a girlfriend. "Pay the rent, make my dinner, do the washing, be at my beck and call. Dez, he even wanted me to make all his hire purchase payments. He just wasn't the bloke that I started out with, he turned into a selfish and sneaky grub."

Dez was eating up the insults, figuring the more distance Marion put between herself and Len, the closer she got to him. He was a bit confused though about the description of Len as "sneaky," and asked Marion to explain.

"Bingo," thought Marion, "that is the question I have been waiting for." Marion went on to explain that due to his knee problem, Lennie was trying every which way to bring in an extra dollar and lately that involved bending the rules big time. "Let's just say if I had Lennie working on a car that I owned, I would want to see the old parts he replaced before I paid for any new ones."

Within a week, Dez had spread that little lie through half a dozen pubs and the RSL. What little work Lennie had been getting, dried up further and he was none the wiser as to why. To further compound his problems, he received more unwelcome mail from AGC late in January. They informed him that they had sold the furniture and electrical equipment that were associated with the HP agreement he had broken, and that with fees, he owed them $387.50. That was money Lennie just did not have, and his only recourse was to get a loan from Di.

Late that night Lennie sat on the lounge with Di assessing his predicament. "Here I am just shy of twenty-three, nothing in the bank, still living with my mum, working in a shed behind my mum's house, borrowing off her, business going down the toilet, no girlfriend, and a buggered knee," he chuckled almost to himself . "Don't I make you proud?" Di looked at him, disappointed he could think such a thing. To take that look off her face he added, "Ah yes, but on the plus side I own a second-hand Ute and my very own double bed."

A couple of weeks later was the scheduled date for the big knee reveal which the surgeon had decided was best done at his rooms in Brisbane. Lennie had arranged to travel down by bus on the Monday, with an appointment to see the surgeon the next day. Douggie, his ex-teammate, was now in share accommodation in an old timber house near the university and Lennie had arranged to couch surf for the day before and the day after the appointment, and head back to Dalby on Wednesday. By this stage, Lennie was quite adept on the crutches and had little difficulty with the public transport that took him pretty well to the front door of the old office building on Petrie Terrace that was occupied by a host of specialists and surgeons involved in every sphere of medical practice.

After waiting the apparent obligatory forty minutes past his appointment time, the receptionist asked Lennie to join the doctor in the surgery. "Well firstly, let's get that old plaster off and have a look shall we." A big set of odd-shaped scissors were produced, and the well crumbled plaster cast was removed, revealing an emaciated and rather smelly right leg.

"Okay, Len, well all the swelling has subsided and the incisions have healed nicely, let's see you stand up and take some weight on it. It's going to be unstable as the muscle is very weak, so keep some weight on the right crutch." Lennie did as he was told but the knee felt like jelly, there was no stability at all. He then had Lennie lay down on the elevated examination table and began to assess the degree of bend that could be achieved. Surprisingly, the doctor said the effort was good and that it was all he could expect at this stage.

Next, he asked Lennie to try a straight leg lift. That was less successful with Len managing to only raise it a foot or so off the table. Without being asked, Lennie attempted to lift the leg again, grunting with the exertion, but the doctor counseled him to stop. "You look like you are about to give yourself a hernia, Lennie," he quipped, then wrapped up the knee with a short elastic bandage and spoke at length about the need now for some extensive physiotherapy to rebuild the muscle and get more movement in the joint. He told Len that he had made some investigations and then referred him to a physiotherapist in Toowoomba. "I know that's still a good way from home for you, Len, but she can get you started on a series of exercises and stretches and the rest will be over to you to do by yourself at home."

In what seemed like no more than thirty minutes, Lennie was out the front door and back onto Petrie Terrace. "It's taken me a day to get here and it will take me a day to get home and this whole appointment took half an hour," he thought. Len walked up to the nearest public phone box trying to take more and more weight as he went. He rang his mum at home, put in a pile of coins and waited for her to pick up. When she came on the line, he was all business and gave a very clinical account of what had been, after all, a clinical visit. He told his mum he was staying over at Douggie's house that night, then catching the first bus back home in the morning which was due back in Dalby around three in the afternoon. She arranged to be at the depot to pick him up.

The conversation had not eased her fears. Like any mother, she knew her son probably better than he knew himself, and she knew he was really hurting, not just physically but mentally.

Chapter 20

Lennie spent the long bus trip home assessing how to get his life back on track. He wasn't to know that around the same time he was arriving home from Brisbane, Marion was doing her own medical evaluation back in Dalby. She hadn't had a period for some time and other tell-tale signs had given her sufficient concern to obtain one of the newly available home pregnancy tests. She waited a day, hoping that it wouldn't become necessary and then faced the inevitable and duly followed the instruction. After what seemed over two hours, the result showed that she was pregnant, again. In frustration she grabbed the packaging and re-read the fine print which revealed that the test was 97% accurate.

Marion hadn't exactly been celibate since she broke up with Lennie, but it didn't take too much in the way of calculations to determine the father. "Fucken Lennie," she thought, "he's dead to me and he's still fucking up my life. One sympathy fuck before his operation and he does this to me." Marion's response to the news was atypical. Her first thought was who to blame. Her second thought was how soon she could get out of this town and start living the life she deserved.

She picked up the phone and rang the number for the workshop. The number rang out, but she figured Lennie was up to his armpits in grease, so decided to ring it again. Sure enough, he came on the line after the fourth ring.

"Lennie Krause, guess who?" she said, but Lennie didn't have to guess and didn't even answer before she went on. "I've got some good news and some bad news for you, boyo. First up, I am leaving town, and while I don't think you are good for much, apparently your sperm is top notch. I got pregnant again and given the dates, there is no doubt who sired it." Then she twisted the knife with a lie, "Now before you get all paternal, I have already terminated this one too, so I'll leave it to you to work out which news is good and which is bad."

Lennie just managed to respond with "you are a slimy bitch, Marion, how could..." before the line went dead. He decided it was time to reveal some of his anguish to his mother.

When Di arrived home later that night, Lennie was sitting at the old Laminex kitchen table, nursing a glass of beer in one hand and pensively wiping the condensation off the bottle with the other. Di could see he was troubled, so walked straight over to him, cuddled his forehead from behind, then kissed him on the top of the head.

Without as much as a word of introduction Lennie blurted out the whole truth as he knew it to be. "I haven't been able to tell you this earlier, Mum, but without discussing it with me, Marion terminated a pregnancy back in September. She didn't tell me until the day we broke up. I am only telling you now because she rang me today with more bad news that I just can't believe."

Di gave him a second cuddle as she feared he was about to cry. "She rang me today and said she just had a second abortion and that the baby was mine too. Says she has had a gut full of this town. She has quit at the pub and she's leaving town." Lennie had been marinating in some of this news for months and some for hours, and it was a huge relief to get it off his chest.

For Di, the news came as a horrible shock and accounted for the depth of Lennie's recent poor moods. If there was any joy to be had, it was that Marion was leaving town and leaving her son's life. "Lennie, like any mum, I am as keen as mustard to have a pile of grandkids running around me. But I have to tell you, tragic as this news is, we are both better off if Marion Kent isn't the mother of those kids."

Lennie nodded his head in agreement, grudgingly admitting she was right, but Di went on. "Lennie, that girl is plain bad news. Do you know what Bob told me today? That she has been spreading rumours around town that you have been padding bills and charging for parts that haven't been replaced? That is one reason the work has been drying up. She is a cold one that girl."

Lennie just shook his head reflecting on last month's dry spell of work. He reached out for his mother's hand. "Mum, don't you worry, you will have a pile of grandkids one day. You will be a first-rate grandma, just like you have been a first rate-mum. I love ya, Mum, but I'm wrung out. I am going to make an early night of it and hit the sack."

With that they both stood, he gave Di a seriously tight cuddle and shuffled off to his bedroom. Di sat up for quite a while nursing a second cup of tea and pondered what might have been.

The next morning, Marion told her flat mate that she had given notice at The Sportsman the night before and was leaving town after she picked up her pay. "The boss man took it in his stride; 'barmaids come barmaids go,' he said, but I think that creepy manager from the RSL was heartbroken."

Karen smirked when she heard reference to Dez from the RSL, but was more interested in Marion's sudden decision to leave town. Before she could compose a question, Marion volunteered "Looks like that loser, Lennie's got me up the duff, so I am off to Brissie to put things right and make a new start. At least with me gone, you will get more hours at the pub, until the bossman cons some other poor bitch into working shitty hours, like he did to me."

Karen put her hands on Marion's shoulders and looked at her sympathetically. "Listen, I am no angel, and I know from the sounds that come out of your bedroom that you aren't either. So how do you know that Lennie is the culprit?"

Marion responded, "Well, let's say I was always good at maths and that I am 97% certain. I've seen a doctor for final confirmation, and I am awaiting the results, but either way, I am off to Brisbane; sorry if this leaves you in the lurch." With that, Marion began packing her meagre belongings and changed into some slacks and her favourite jersey top. "Can I ask a final favour?" she asked Karen. "Would you mind dropping me into The Sportsman, the bossman said my final pay should be ready by now."

When Karen parked out front of the pub, Marion dragged her bulging suitcase out of the back seat, reached through the driver's side window and touched Karen's chin with her index finger, turning her head so they were eye to eye. "A final bit of advice for you," she said seriously, "find a way to even the score with this fuckwit, you shouldn't let the tight arsed prick keep on watering down your hours." With that she wandered into the pub to collect her final pay.

At the workshop later that same afternoon, Lennie was finally working on a decent-sized job repairing an old Jaguar, when he received some news that totally staggered and unsettled him. He couldn't think straight, so just abruptly terminated the conversation. He grabbed his glass, now stained with so many greasy fingerprints they almost obscured the remaining contents, and topped up his rum and coke from the fridge. After draining it, he mixed another and took a good swig from it as well. Considering his options, he placed the drink beside the small transistor radio and checked his wallet to see what he had on him in the way of notes. Finding just a single $50 note, he made a notation into the diary that was part of the accounting system his mother had created, then rattled around in the fridge once again and began pondering what was ahead of him.

He turned up the volume of the transistor radio, maneouvered himself back onto his trolley, and slid under the Jaguar. He listened to the latest news, only half hearing what it was about. He took a little more interest in the sports news, which was followed by a weather report that focused on that day's oppressive heat. "This time of year, it's always the same," he thought, and then corrected himself. "Well the weather was always the same as this anyway." He hoped Februarys wouldn't always be the same, as it was February around a year earlier that Marion had entered his life and then turned it upside down. He knew now he had some major decisions to make with his life. With the news and weather over, the DJ came back on full of phony enthusiasm.

"Welcome back, folks, to our walk down memory lane. Well, it's not that long a walk really. Let's hark back now to 1964, folks. It's not quite sixteen sweet years ago that the fabulous Beatles released this classic. Sit back, lay back, stop what you are doing, and enjoy the Fab Four's I'm a Loser."

Then the lyrics washed over Lennie: -

"I'm a loser
And I'm not what I appear to be
Of all the love I have won, and have lost
There is one love I should never have crossed
She was a girl in a million my friend
I should have known she would win in the end...."

Di found him the next morning.

Chapter 21

August 2002

When Fitzy opened the door to the workshop that winter morning, a bitterly cold Westerly wind followed him in, and a further chill ran up his spine. It had been over twenty years since he was last in there, and he never believed he would ever return. He was now nearing sixty, a lot more weathered and carrying a bit more weight particularly around the middle, but he was still strong all the way through; the sort of strength that only a man who has worked with his hands all his life can attain. "Ah Lennie," he thought, "so sorry that I didn't see this coming… biggest fuck up of my life."

Fitzy had never forgiven himself for Lennie's death. He should have known suicide was on the cards; he had looked so closely and been so involved, but he still had not seen it coming. He should have been able to stop it. Instead, he was way the buggery out at Charleville with the girl who was to become the love of his life, when Di phoned him. Her grief was palpable, she was a gibbering mess.

He came back immediately and made himself available when the police asked for a statement, but his main task was to get Di back on her feet. She took a month off work to consider her options but realized quickly that she had only one; to just keep on going. She stayed on at The Imperial, because she could almost do the job by rote, and was still there three publicans later. The self-assured woman of old, however, was no more. She wasn't bitter, she had just lost that spark that indicated that she honestly loved life and loved doing what she was doing.

Di was never a big woman when Lennie was alive, but Fitzy thought Di positively shrank after his death. Now she was gone too, and she had decided in her wisdom, that apart from a few excluded items, her possessions, including the house property and a small bank account, would be bequeathed to the Royal Flying Doctor Service. The excluded items had been left specifically to Alan Fitzgerald of "Kilmarnock" station. The excluded items comprised the contents of Lennie's workshop and any of her son's personal belongings that Alan Fitzgerald may wish to take from the house.

Di had called him Alan from the very outset, never Fitzy. They had been in regular contact before that terrible day back in early 1980 and stayed in touch over the years since. In fact, after her son's funeral, the person Di leaned most hard on was Alan. She wondered if she would ever have survived without his support. She often thought that Alan was as devastated by Lennie's apparent suicide as she was, if that was possible. She knew he felt an extra degree of guilt because he had been actively watching for the signs but had not seen it coming.

They both knew Lennie was hurting, but he was a resilient bugger, and had always worked his way out of adversity in the past. In fact, after the New Year visit, Fitzy had called Di to specifically tell her he thought Lennie would be okay. It was one of the reasons he hadn't felt the need to come back earlier from Charleville. Di was to find out the other more compelling reason when a wedding invitation arrived early the next year.

Phoebe, the young girl Alan had met not long before Lennie's death, was now to be his wife. Di wondered if maybe Alan felt guilty on this score too. Perhaps he felt he was focused less on Lennie's problems because he had a new romantic interest. If that were the case, it wasn't warranted in her mind, because she knew that Lennie had no truer friend than Alan Fitzgerald. She also knew that Lennie would be so happy that his mate, Fitzy, had finally found someone to share his life with.

The coroner had called it an "open finding" meaning either death by misadventure or suicide. Both Di and Fitzy held on to the small hope that it had been a horrible accident, but the facts made that the less likely reason. Lennie was depressed for good reason, had major financial and health issues, and just had a breakup with his longtime girlfriend. During the ensuing investigation, Fitzy also told the police how distraught Lennie was about Marion's abortion. Di then revealed that only a day or so prior to his death, Marion had told her son that he had gotten her pregnant again and that she had recently aborted for a second time. It was this second event that had convinced most everyone, Fitzy included, that Lennie had ended it himself. Of course, against that, he was working in a risky environment while drinking, using tools he had adapted for his incapacitation and hadn't taken the usual precautions.

Fitzy wandered around the shed as the memories flooded back. It appeared that Di had locked it up twenty years ago and not been back in there since. It was something of a very dusty time capsule. The tools Lennie had been using were scattered all over the place. There was a grubby old glass with the skeletons of a few dead cockroaches and a classic old transistor radio. Fitzy smirked when he came across a couple of very well-worn copies of Australian Penthouse. He guessed some of the girls with the sultry poses were likely grandmothers now and wondered how their grandkids would react if they ever came across an old copy. He supposed that would depend on whether "Grandma" was in the least recognizable. Fitzy then looked more closely at his unexpected inheritance. Some of the hand tools he could likely use, but the oxy tank was well out of test and the grinders and other electrical bits and pieces would likely fuse out given their age and the fact that the insulation on them had perished.

As he strolled around the shed, he made a point of avoiding a large faint brown stain in the middle of the floor. There was no certainty it was Lennie's dried blood, but he wasn't going to take the chance of desecrating the scene. As he poked into the corners and inspected the various mechanical items, he came across a long fencing crowbar propped against the wall in one of the corners. It was the sort of crowbar with a hammer type head at one end and a heavy chisel at the other.

He immediately noticed that the top foot or so was coated with white enamel paint and recognized this as the system his father, ever the frugal Scotsman, had devised to ensure tools that were lent out were always returned. Fitzy was in no doubt that the crowbar belonged to his family, but it was too long ago to remember how it came to be in Lennie's workshop. Maybe he had lent it to Lennie that Christmas before he died. His vague memory was that Lennie was always doing odd jobs around his mother's property so he must have borrowed it to do a bit of work for his mum. He smirked when he realised that this wasn't so much a piece of his inheritance, more like an overdue library book. He wondered as well if Lennie had ever completed that task for his mother.

Fitzy continued to scout around the shed looking at the various tools to determine if any were of serious use to him. He quickly calculated that he would come back later with a Ute and grab the crowbar, the loose tools, and maybe the fridge and leave the rest for the RFDS to sort out. The fate of the old fridge would depend on whether he came back into town with any of the station hands, as there was no way he would get that old fridge into his Ute by himself—those old models weighed a ton. He decided that he would wait until his return to determine if there was anything in the house itself that might interest him, because nothing he had seen so far could vaguely represent something to remember his old mate by.

When he was first told of Di's bequeath to him, her solicitor had provided him with all the keys and said there was no hurry. The estate was still in probate, and he had been told that the RFDS had yet to determine what they would do with the old house even when that was resolved. The solicitor even advised him that the RFDS was happy to check that he had retrieved any item of interest, before putting the house on the market. Fitzy discovered that the one thing the dust hadn't managed to subdue in the shed, was the grease. His hands were getting seriously dirty as even the dusty items had an undercoat of old grease.

When he decided he had seen enough, he reached around in a pile of rags on the bench looking for one he could use to clean himself up. Some were so filthy there was a good chance they would put on more grease than they would take off. Eventually he found a clean one amongst the pile that looked promising. He was halfway through cleaning his calloused hands when he realized "the rag" he was using was an old Dalby Rugby Union jersey. He held it up to the light by the corner of each shoulder and then turned it around. On the back was the crudely manufactured number "0".

He immediately remembered its history from the last time he and Lennie had discussed Marion. That conversation was all about how Marion loved to wear this jersey regularly just to rub salt into Lennie's wounds. It was only a small thing he knew, but something about that old bit of football kit, tucked away with all the other greasy rags had immediately piqued his suspicions about that terrible day. He wondered aloud how it came to be in the shed. The jersey had been a thorn in Lennie's side, and Fitzy was sure he would have had a call from his mate to convey the good news, the instant he had managed to retrieve it. Traipsing around the workshop had bought back a lot of memories and refreshed his guilt.

"Maybe I owe my old mate a bit more attention to all this", he thought. Something just didn't smell right about the whole situation, and he was sure the full story of what happened that afternoon had never seen the light of day. Fitzy knew in his heart that he had let his brother Spud down all those years ago, and he had thought for twenty years that he had let Lennie down as well.

Fitzy was emotionally conflicted and confused. He was happy and relieved that there was possibly more to Lennie's death than he realized, but he was angry with himself too. He should have questioned the whole episode more closely or at least have been of more assistance to the police so that they could have explored the options more thoroughly. With the event so long ago, Fitzy felt there was no urgency to get to the truth. He would undertake his own investigations and when and if things looked seriously fishy, he would then involve the police. His only day to day obligation now was to run the property and he had good people in his employ who could handle that without him, if necessary. He decided he had the time and the money to dedicate to getting to the bottom of Lennie's death. He was just sad that his wife wouldn't be able to get involved in playing detective, she had always loved puzzles.

When he and Phoebe were first married, they had worked on "Kilmarnock" together, residing in a separate cottage about fifty metres from the main homestead. His mother was the first of his parents to pass, just one year after organizing, what was termed in the local press, "a wedding for the ages". A wedding between the district's most eligible, and supposedly most confirmed bachelor, and the pretty blonde horsewoman from up Rocky way. A photo and accompanying story of both the old and new Mr. and Mrs. Fitzgerald featured in the social pages of both *The Toowoomba Chronicle* and *The Courier Mail.*

Once his wife died, "Jock" had taken a backseat in physically running the property but was no less opinionated on how jobs should be best undertaken. Then, some two years into his son's marriage, the old Scot's heart gave out too, and Fitzy found himself the sole owner of one of the biggest mixed cattle and grain properties on the Downs. Fitzy eased easily into the new role, as it was one he had been effectively doing anyway for at least the past five years. Running "Kilmarnock" had always been a rewarding life for the Fitzgerald clan; the result of loads of hard work, the gyrations of both the seasons, and grain and cattle markets. He missed his parents, he even missed his dad's ongoing instructions, but they lived on in every crack and cranny of the place.

As he sat with his wife on the verandah of main Kilmarnock homestead that afternoon, he could not believe how blessed he was. Staring west across an expanse of swaying wheat fields toward the setting sun, with the sky lit up with a glow of pink and purple and orange, Fitzy thought it couldn't get much better than this. That was until Phoebe sidled up to him, whispered "Happy fortieth, old man," into his ear then followed up with "I have another present for you that I know you really want. But you will have to wait another six months to find out what it is."

He looked at her confused for a little while, and then it dawned on him that his dream of becoming a dad was going to be realized. As Fitzy digested the implications of the news, Phoebe sat down beside him on another squatter's chair and followed his lead of putting both legs on the extended arms. She had a glow too, that rivalled the sunset.

Fitzy finally broke the silence when he commented, "In that position, you look like you are in the gynecologist's room with your feet in the stirrups."

She leaned across and promptly and playfully clipped him across the back of the head. "Trust you to spoil the mood. Is there a romantic bone in your body, Alan Fitzgerald?!"

Two months later Phoebe went into early labour, miscarrying on the kitchen floor. Fitzy drove like a madman to Dalby hospital and from there Phoebe was transferred to Toowoomba Base Hospital by ambulance with her husband following close behind. She had lost an enormous amount of blood and the surgeon determined there was no option but to perform a partial hysterectomy. There would be no Fitzgerald heir to take over Kilmarnock. Fitzy may not have had too many romantic bones in his body, but his wife was to find that he was a carer without peer. It was a good three months before Phoebe was back on her feet and another two before she was game or even allowed to try and sit on a horse.

During her convalescence Fitzy played host to both Phoebe's sisters, though it was apparent there was friction between Wendy and the middle sister, Gaye, with Wendy needing to be assured that they wouldn't be visiting at the same time. Phoebe's natural fitness helped her quickly overcome her physical issues, however, Fitzy was glad of the assistance the sisters could render, in helping with her mental pain. Wendy had also miscarried early in her marriage, so she had some lived experience, however she had gone on to have two strapping boys. Phoebe and Alan were going to have to find a way to deal with the fact that their family plans would never come to fruition.

During the convalescence, Fitzy had a lot more interaction with Phoebe's far-flung family and gained a more detailed understanding of the family dynamic. "Well, Wendy was always the serious one in the family, eldest child, having to take on part of the mothering role too and all that," she explained. "She was always very straight-laced and serious as well. I am sure she was a virgin on her wedding night…and for possibly a few days after that too, from all accounts."

Fitzy gave his wife a surprised look then made the gesture of poking his thick middle finger into a smaller hole he made with the fingers of the other hand, followed by a cutting motion with both hands.

"You got it in one," Phoebe replied with a laugh that put a bigger smile on his face. "She was apparently terrified on the wedding night and poor hubby had to be patient. Gaye, on the other hand, is something of a lost soul. She has made some pretty poor choices in her life, but I love her to bits."

"Well, that doesn't really explain why they don't want to be in the same room together," he replied, hoping for a more detailed explanation.

"From Wendy's point of view, Gaye's day to day life choices are a big enough problem but it's her sexual orientation that Wendy really can't deal with." That bit of information didn't greatly surprise Fitzy, though he did make the point to Phoebe that Gaye had a bloke with her at their wedding.

"What can I say," she responded, "I told you she is something of a free spirt."

Fitzy pondered that for a moment and replied with a smirk, "Well that would double her chances on a Friday night."

The "Fitzes" as they became known, were always at the centre of social events in the district. Whether it was a local race meeting, gymkhana, or charity ball, they were always high on the invitation list. The most obvious reason for this was because they were the District's "golden couple", but another contributing factor was that they were well known as generous sponsors and donors to worthy causes. On the home front, Alan might have handled the "Kilmarnock" finances and made the decisions on stocking and when and what to plant, but Phoebe had taken an interest in real estate investments and they had contracted to buy a couple of investment apartments on the Sunshine Coast.

She was also always by his side at the cattle sales, loved attending the occasional horse auction, and did more than her fair share of physical work around the property. The highlights of their year were the Brisbane Exhibition, "The Ekka" or "The Show" as it was called, and The Melbourne Cup. Both events were etched in their calendar, and they hadn't missed attending either since they first became a couple. Phoebe particularly loved sleeping beside the cattle in the stalls at the exhibition grounds on those occasions when they entered a beast into the competition. She said nothing made her appreciate her country life more than this experience.

The Melbourne Cup on the other hand, could not have been further removed as a social event. While "The Ekka" was all elastic side boots, double pocket shirts, straw and shit, The Melbourne Cup Carnival was a chance to show people, that the couple from the Darling Downs were all class. It was one of the few times in the year that Phoebe managed to show off her rarely used but expensive wardrobe. Fitzy scrubbed up well too, however, he still always wore his broad brimmed Akubra at functions during the day.

It was at one of those trips to Melbourne that Phoebe first became suspicious that something was amiss with her health. She lived a healthy and active lifestyle and her weight had not changed that much over her married life. At one lunch function, she decided to wear her favourite pants suit and was surprised to find that it was a real stretch to get the top button to do up. She turned to her husband to ask, "Al, am I starting to pork up a bit?" He might have been a boy from the bush, but he was smart enough to know to answer that question in the negative. She thought no more of it, but after a few months of excess visits to the toilet, she decided that she should schedule an appointment with her gynecologist on her next shopping trip to Toowoomba.

Three weeks later, she was on her back in his rooms with her feet in a different set of stirrups than she was accustomed to on the property. A raft of tests followed, and she was advised that it would be best if her husband was with her at the next appointment. When they were both seated, the specialist opened her file but didn't read from it. Instead, he looked straight into her eyes and said, "There isn't any good news I am afraid, Mrs.

Fitzgerald. You have a form of ovarian cancer and it's aggressive." Without waiting for a response and in an endeavour to be rid of all the bad news as soon as possible, he followed up with, "It's invasive epithelial ovarian cancer and there are indications that it may have already spread to the spleen."

Phoebe had just a one-word response, "Fuck!"

Fitzy was also in shock and hugged his wife to his shoulder while he searched for words. It was almost a minute before he could ask the question he was dreading, "What is the worst-case scenario here?" He was told that Phoebe would need to go into surgery as soon as possible and that this would likely be followed by several rounds of chemotherapy.

Phoebe then asked, "And what is the likely outcome of all this?"

The specialist began showing her charts of statistical outcomes, but it was apparent that all the possible outcomes were dire and that at best, she likely had only three years to live. It transpired that the estimate was optimistic, but from that date onward, it was rare for Fitzy not to be by her side.

Her sisters came and went again in shifts to help, and he employed a nurse to live full time in the quarters that he and Phoebe had used when they were first married. It was a horrible waiting game, but just under two years after the initial diagnosis and two months before his fiftieth birthday, his wife of thirteen years took one final raspy breath. He looked down on the one woman who had genuinely stolen his heart, but he didn't see an emaciated patient with greying skin and a bandana covering her bald head. He saw a beautiful blonde with a golden tan and an arc of freckles across her nose.

It was Phoebe's wish to be cremated and for her ashes to be sprinkled over the garden of roses that her mother-in-law had established around the "Kilmarnock" homestead. Wendy and Gaye, of course, attended the funeral service and were amongst the select family and friends who came back after the service to the family property. In the intervening years, the distance between the lifestyles of the remaining sisters had widened further. Wendy and her husband, Kel, had found God in a big way and she was more straight-laced than ever before. Both at the funeral, and later at the property, both Wendy and Kel were regaling Fitzy with trite observations. "The Lord works in mysterious ways, but she is now at rest and her suffering is behind her." The comment he hated the most was "Phoebe is now in a better place at the right hand of the Lord." As far as he was concerned, there was no better place for Phoebe than to be at his right hand, right here at "Kilmarnock."

Gaye, on the other hand, had come alone, but the dainty tattoo on her right arm seemed to indicate that she may have made a decision on her preferable sexual orientation. Inside an elaborate heart, were etched three words one under the other; GAYe, L, and Les. Fitzy thought it was clever that the "e" on GAYE was in lower case, to emphasize the GAY. He was never to discover if Les was a person or a broad orientation. The girl might be a handful, but she apparently had a good sense of humour, so it made total sense to him why she had always been Phoebe's favourite. The sisters might all have been born and bred in Rockhampton, but they all lived in totally different worlds. In fact, the only thing that the sisters apparently had in common was an undying appreciation of how well Alan had looked after their little sister.

Chapter 22

If Fitzy was to get to the bottom of this twenty-year-old mystery, the best course of action was to first track down Marion. He quickly realized that he didn't have the first idea of how to find her or even who might tell him how to find her. He stood still for a short while as he came to the realization that he didn't know where to start, or how to start; he actually didn't know what he didn't know. While his initial intention was not to involve the police, he made the decision to ask for a little unofficial help from Mick Cummings, the local sergeant, who he knew socially through a few local business and charity associations.

He pulled his little Nokia out of his pocket and rang directory assistance for the local police station then dialed the number. He was still amazed at how bloody handy these things were. He had resisted buying one for years, but once they got to this size and once the coverage out his way improved, he realised he couldn't do without it.

"Dalby Police, Constable Scobie speaking."

"Hello Constable, my name is Alan Fitzgerald, I was wondering if I could have a word with Sergeant Cummings, if he is available?"

"Mr. Alan Fitzgerald, is it? Would Sergeant Cummings know what this ..." but before he could finish his sentence, the phone was obviously taken from him and a gruff voice took over the conversation. "Scobie, if that is the Mr. Alan Fitzgerald from "Kilmarnock" I most definitely want to talk to you!"

Fitzy laughed and confessed it was the very same Alan Fitzgerald who still owed the sergeant the $20 he had borrowed when they had last caught up a month or so back at the sale yards. Fitzy asked if he was available to talk unofficially on a personal matter and they agreed to meet up for a bite to eat at The Imperial.

An hour later, Mick Cummings strode into the dining room where Fitzy was already halfway through nursing a seven-ounce beer. The two big men shook hands in an almost competitive fashion, both endeavouring to apply the maximum pressure, while showing no sign of pain when pressure was reciprocated. Fitzy said he had already ordered them both a steak, chips and salad and that a beer was on the way too. He took a $20 note out of his wallet, laid it on the table and said, "Now this isn't to be taken to be a bribe, but I need a little help with something and I don't know where to start."

The policeman laughed and roughly poked the repayment into his top pocket. "I suggested we eat here because The Imperial is sort of where this thing I want to talk about all started. It was back when Bob Answerth ran the place."

"Before my time but go on."

"Mick, I believe Di Krause was still a barmaid here when you came into the district, small wiry woman, pretty well ran the place."

The policeman acknowledged that he remembered her and that she had outlasted a few publicans. "The publican before last used to joke that she was such an institution at The Imperial, that her name was entered in the inventory when he bought the place."

Fitzy grinned at the accuracy of that observation. "I was very good mates with her son, who unfortunately died around twenty years back. Di Krause died just recently, and she left me some of his stuff in her will. I am trying to track down his old girlfriend from those days and frankly I need a little help on where to start."

While Fitzy and the sergeant were well-acquainted, policemen of all stripes were inquisitive and suspicious by nature so he wanted the questions to be a simple request for the best process to follow. At this stage, he didn't want to make any reference to any suspicions he might have and get ahead of himself. He was hopeful that if he got Mick involved from the beginning, he might be able to come back to him for more help if there was any need for things to progress. Mick suggested he start with the simplest methods first, and that the telephone directory was a good first stop. Fitzy knew he was having a go at him, but he had to confess that was part of the problem; he didn't know her current name, where she was living or if she was still alive for that matter.

"Well it really depends on how important this is to you, Alan. I can help you do bits yourself, but if it's really important, then I can get a recommendation for a good private investigator for you." When Fitzy gave him the slow down signal, and said it wasn't that critical, he asked for a few tips instead. Mick suggested he try and find some of her old friends who might still be in town. Fitzy thought that was a good point so wrote it down in a notebook he had pulled from his double pocket shirt and asked for other tips.

"Well knowing her current name would be good," said Mick, "but assuming you have her old name you can do a search through the Register of Births Deaths and Marriages." Fitzy thought that was a particularly good one too and it also went into the notebook. Other suggestions Mick had, all of which went into the book, were what her likely occupation might be; where her parents lived; getting together any photos of her and seeing if she left a forwarding address at her last employer in Dalby.

"All good stuff, Mick, you have earned your $20 and free lunch." Fitzy said preparing to leave. He also asked if Mick wouldn't mind getting the name of an investigator in the event that it was ever necessary. They had the handshake competition again and Fitzy headed off back to Di's old house.

It was Fitzy's intention to search around the house for any photos of Marion. He didn't expect there would be anything in pride of place, but that maybe there might be an old photo album of Lennie with something of value in it. He couldn't track down an album, but surprisingly did find a useful photo in a frame on the sideboard. The photo was of Lennie on some old wooden crutches, so it must have been taken within of a year of him hooking up with Marion. On closer inspection Fitzy could see that the photo was obviously folded. When he retrieved the photo from the frame and opened it out, there was Marion in all her smug glory trying to look like Florence Nightingale. He popped the photo in his top pocket along with the notebook, then sat down at the kitchen table and devised a plan of attack.

First things first, her name was Marion Kent, originally from Brisbane. He knew she was a few years older than Lennie so was probably born sometime around 1954. She had mostly worked as a barmaid to the best of his knowledge. She was working at The Sportsman just before she left town and used to room with another barmaid from there, by the name of Kath or Karen from recollection. She had told Lennie that she had an abortion not long before she left, so there was a good chance that she would have gone back to her parent's place in Brisbane after she left Dalby.

By the time he finished, Fitzy was feeling quite the PI. He decided his next move was to drop into The Sportsman and see if they had old records or a forwarding address for her. He also wanted to see if her old flat mate Kath or Karen was still around or if they knew where she was these days. His initial elation soon faded when the publican at The Sportsman said he was the fourth owner since 1980 and any old staff records would be long gone. He also said that he didn't know of a barmaid called Kath or Karen either; he certainly hadn't employed one in the five years he had owned the place. That had already scratched out two of Fitzy's best leads.

He was feeling less certain of success until an unshaved drinker at the end of the bar mentioned that a Karen had worked here twenty odd years ago, and then after her flat mate left town, she had moved over to work at the RSL. Fitzy thanked the publican and turned to offer to buy a drink for his new informant.

Over a couple of beers, Fitzy discovered that the drinker's name was Dez Rudd, that he used to be a manager at the RSL and that he knew Karen quite well because he had been in a relationship with her ex-flat mate, Marion. Fitzy explained that he was only enquiring after Karen to help him find out more about a Marion Kent who may now have an interest in a deceased estate. That information seemed to perk up the drinker's interest no end. He gave Fitzy a run down on what a good sort Marion was and how good she was in bed, but that unfortunately he had no way of knowing where she was these days. "Last I heard anything about her was probably ten years ago, and she had married a guy in Brisbane and had a kid."

That was new information that might well prove fruitful, so Fitzy thanked him for the lead and motioned to the barman to refill his nearly empty glass.

Dez raised the fresh glass in appreciation, "Thanks for the beers and for bringing back the memories." Fitzy waved dismissively over his shoulder as he turned to go, guessing correctly that those much-cherished memories were all in Dez's head.

Fitzy drove over to the post office and found a Brisbane phone directory. There were a host of Kents in Brisbane and he wrote down the number of the only three with the initial M. He called the numbers, but none was a Marion Kent nor did they know of a Marion Kent. That made sense he realised; he had forgotten that she was married. Next call was to the Register of Births Deaths and Marriages in Brisbane. The public servant at the other end of the phone told him that he could make an application for any of these records at the local courthouse, or if he was in Brisbane, he could drop into their offices to do a more comprehensive search.

Fitzy decided he could do with a trip to the big smoke and that if the search down there didn't lead him in the right direction, he might just have to get an investigator involved.

Chapter 23

The following Monday, after sorting out a few issues back at "Kilmarnock", Fitzy packed a bag, told the property manager he would be in Brisbane for a week or so, and that he would call him with the hotel details once he decided where to stay. He hopped into his new Landcruiser and started his quest in earnest, arriving in Brisbane in the late afternoon, where he booked a room at the Treasury Casino. He had a great steak, lost a few hundred at roulette and was in the government office at nine am sharp the next morning. He played the part of the poor ignorant bushie who was confused by all the high-tech options and managed to have one of the search clerks guide him through the process. It was a treasure trove of information.

To his amazement, the records showed that Marion had given birth to a baby girl she named Leah in June 1980. It didn't take Fitzy long to do the quick arithmetic and realize that Lennie was a dad after all, and that Di had a granddaughter that she never knew existed. He was coming to the conclusion that his gut feeling had some real substance. He wondered why Marion would lie to

Lennie about having had a second abortion, then he remembered how much she liked to turn the knife. It was immaterial anyway, because if Lennie had indeed committed suicide, it would likely have been that lie that had tipped him over the edge.

On the birth records, Marion had given her address as care of Mrs. V. Kent in Brisbane. Further searching revealed that she married a Brian Jarrett in 1988 and they had a different address in Brisbane.

Fitzy decided to call it a day at the government offices and headed back to the hotel where he arranged to get a copy of the Brisbane white pages directory to see if there was a listing for a B and M Jarrett at that same Brisbane address. There wasn't, but there were two other listings in Brisbane, so he called the first of the numbers.

The phone almost rang out and finally a young woman with a happy but harried voice answered, "You've got the Jarrett's!" It didn't sound like Marion, he thought, too young and too upbeat. He could also hear a toddler crying in the background, but then that could be a granddaughter.

When Fitzy replied, it was with a question in his voice, "Is that you, Marion?"

The change in tone at the other end of the phone was immediate. From happy and carefree, it changed to terse and angry. "If you want that bitch, you won't find her here," she said.

Fitzy quickly pacified the young woman. "Woah up, no need to get angry," he said. "I am no friend of Marion's. I am just trying to sort out a problem relating to a property estate at Dalby where Marion used to work. I'm trying to track her down, do you know where she is?"

"I'm the new, and the final Mrs. Jarrett," the woman volunteered. "My husband divorced Marion after 'that mess' a few years back." There was a pause and then she added, "You will find her and her daughter somewhere on the Gold Coast. I have to go, my little boy needs his bottle."

Fitzy wondered what mess she had referred to, so next day, he was back at the government offices again. Unfortunately, the helpful clerk from the day before was nowhere to be found. Fitzy was told that if he wanted a series of searches from various government departments, he had best use a specialist search service. As luck would have it, a young law clerk who was standing in front of the next counter had overheard the conversation and he volunteered to help, at a fee of course. Fitzy decided it was worth passing on the aggravation to someone better qualified, and was equally sure that someone else's bill was going to be padded out by his searches.

He told the budding lawyer that he wanted to know when Marion Jarrett was divorced, the details on the Brisbane house ownership, details on any property purchase she may have made on the Gold Coast. If possible, he also wanted her current address, which was also likely to be on the Gold Coast. They agreed a flat fee, Fitzy paid him half the cash up front, and sent the youngster off on his quest, while he wandered outside for some fresh air.

In a little over an hour his unofficial search clerk had returned, and Fitzy had most of the information he needed, but also a few more unanswered questions.

The Jarrett's divorced in 1996. The house was originally in both names but was later transferred to her name only, in early 1997. The notations on the title show it was part of the divorce settlement. She initially had a mortgage on it but paid that out when she sold it a few years later. There was no way of knowing the amount of the settlement, but it must have been generous because the details for the 1998 sale revealed a price of $550,000. She then put those proceeds toward a property purchase on the Gold Coast. The records also showed that she had since sold the original Gold Coast property and bought another also on the Gold Coast, where she still lived.

The title searches showed that neither the first nor the second Gold Coast houses were mortgaged. There was no record of Marion ever remarrying and the interesting thing was that she was still using the name, Marion Jarrett. Fitzy paid out the other half of the fee, grateful that he had saved himself a lot of time, aggravation, and shoe leather. The collated information was likely more than he would have discovered if he had tried to do the searches himself. It was apparent that Marion's post Dalby life had become quite complex, and Fitzy wondered if this complexity could have any bearing on what had happened to Lennie all those years ago.

After a good night's sleep and a lot of consideration, Fitzy felt that perhaps the best way to unravel Marion's life was for him to find out a bit more about Brian Jarrett. Knowledge about Jarret would help him understand the Marion of today, and he needed that before he made direct contact with her. He decided that to gather the necessary information without raising suspicion, he might finally have to use an investigator. At least now, he thought, the investigator wasn't going to be asked to track down a ghost; he had compiled a wealth of information all by himself that would get the PI off and running. Fitzy's next call was to Sergeant Mick Cummings in Dalby. He told him he was down at Treasury having a bit of a flutter, losing on the big wheel but winning at 21, and had decided that now seemed like as good a time as any to have an investigator do some of the leg work they had discussed.

The policeman rang him back in ten minutes, with the name he had been given by a detective friend in the CIB. Cummings indicated that the investigator in question was a bit of a highflyer and that if the enquiry was a matter of peanuts, Fitzy might want to save himself some "chips" and do the job himself. Thanking the policeman, Fitzy hung up, then immediately called the number.

The initial conversation was brief and businesslike. The PI had been expecting his call, so there was not much in the way of preliminaries required. He had been told by his CIB contact that Fitzy was a respected businessman and friend of a friend and that he should be trusted and looked after accordingly. Fitzy briefed the PI on everything he had discovered about Marion's later married life and asked if he could get the additional info together in the next couple of days. It was determined that what he was after was relatively basic information and that for a $500 cash, he could probably have all he needed by the following afternoon. "Great" said Fitzy, "I hope to win at least that amount at the tables tonight."

The following afternoon they met in person, and the PI indicated that he had the information, but that some of it might come as a shock. Fitzy waited for him to start, then realized the PI expected payment up front. Fitzy pulled out his bulging tatty wallet, quickly removed the $500. After laying it in his hand, the PI's began his report.

"I don't know how long they had been together prior, but Marion and Brian Jarrett were married in late 1988. Brian Jarrett was the assistant manager of a transport business in town here. Generally, law abiding but went DD at .12 in 1991. Other than that, he had no criminal record. They separated early in 1996. Apparently, he initiated the divorce. There was a property settlement, but before the actual divorce was granted, his wife accused him of interfering with his stepdaughter, Leah, a couple of years earlier. She would have been around thirteen or fourteen at the time it happened. The police ultimately charged him, the court case was toward the middle of 97 and he was sentenced to three years for interfering with the girl.

"I couldn't find out much regarding the divorce settlement, but my contacts suggested she negotiated a bloody good deal. He was jailed and served around eighteen months. Released on bail, stayed in town, ultimately got a job back with his old firm, which is unusual, though he is not as high up the totem pole anymore. He remarried two years back, bought an expensive home in a riverside suburb and now has an 18-month-old son with his new wife. The new house isn't mortgaged, so there is something funny there. I'll need more time to find out the source of the cash and that will be an additional task."

Fitzy thanked the PI and they exchanged business cards. "You may yet have a few more jobs in front of you. Every bit of new information seems to create more questions. Your next job is to find out how Jarrett came into new money. I'd like a bit more info on the divorce settlement if you can source it and find out for me if Leah Jarrett is still living with her mother at this address on the Gold Coast," said Fitzy, handing him a scrap of paper with the address he had discovered the day prior. "I also really need to get an idea about the court case against Jarrett. How can I get a handle on that?"

The PI explained that he could possibly get a transcript of the case, but it may be sealed because it involved a minor. He advised it would be expensive anyway if available, so he would first try and track down a "hot" copy through people he knew at court. If it was available, it could take a few days, but in the meantime, he could certainly find out which law firm Jarrett used for his case.

Fitzy was happy with this approach; the information he collected didn't need to come through the right channels, he just needed it to be accurate. He thanked the PI and said he would be at The Treasury for another couple of days if he had news. "I'll be here or available on my mobile. Here is a cheque for $1000 to cover upfront expenses. Deliver any information directly to me but send the bill here," he said, pointing the PI to the address on his business card. He then engaged the PI with a look that said, "Don't fuck around with me," and continued, "I look forward to you living up to your reputation, you come highly recommended."

The job ahead of Fitzy now was to track down a 48-year-old divorcee called Marion Jarrett, living on the Gold Coast, and Lennie's 22-year-old daughter, Leah, who had been sexually abused by her stepfather. This quest started as a way of answering his questions about Lennie's death, but it now had a new dimension since learning about his daughter. Of course, once he found Marion, he had to come up with a good reason for having made contact again after all this time. If he wasn't careful with how he questioned her, it would raise her suspicions, and even then, he would have to work out what to believe of what she told him.

Fitzy was also considering if he might take the opportunity to treat Brian Jarrett to a little bit of bush justice for what he had done to Lennie's daughter. A lot of thought needed to go into his next move, but he was sure he could work that out over another steak and a good bottle of red back at "The Treasury."

Chapter 24

Sitting in his car waiting for the traffic cop to approach, Brian Jarret was reminded of the last time he had been pulled over for drink-driving. He was feeling a lot more comfortable this time though, as he had not had a single drop all day. Things had not gone quite as well that windy Friday night some ten or so years previously. He vividly remembered that bitterly cold, dry and still, mid-winter evening in 1991.

It was the first time he had managed to have a boy's night out for over six months, and they had really tied one on. Luckily, he had had a huge meal along with all those beers, or things might have been even worse for him when the blood alcohol result came back. He recalled the events leading up to the night and had memories of earlier and fonder days with his first wife.

He and Marion had clicked from the first time they met. They both lived for the moment, and both believed that life was designed to ensure that they had a good time as regularly as possible. While he knew Marion had a small child, Leah seemed to spend a substantial amount of time with her grandmother and was never an issue. Their early married life was an equally wild ride until his mother-in-law died suddenly following post-operative complications from what was supposed to be a simple hospital visit.

It was not long after the funeral that Marion had first raised the topic of the great Australian home ownership dream. She had lived in rented housing her whole life and when their current landlord told her that he wanted them to vacate because he was selling the house, she realized just how much she hated the uncertainty of being a tenant at the whim of the owner. Moving again would make it the fourth house they would have shared as a couple. Not for Marion was the security her mother had cherished in her housing commission rental. House ownership was Marion's goal but hadn't been an option after they first married, not with housing interest rates at 17%.

Anyway, the only assets Brian bought to the marriage was his car and two dirt bikes. They also had little in the way of savings between them and only Brian was bringing in a wage. They both knew the only way to build a deposit was for Brian to take whatever overtime was offered, to become a lot more frugal, and for Marion to go back and find bar work. With the economy in a mess and unemployment around 10%, unfortunately she had to take whatever work was offered, meaning her shifts started around five in the afternoon. Most days this involved Brian starting early, then arriving home just after Marion had left for work.

After Brian reheated the evening meal, he often spent most nights alone watching TV, while Leah did her own thing in her bedroom. He didn't mind Leah; she was an easy enough kid to live with, a bit sullen and lazy, but she largely kept to herself. After a minimum of time spent on her studies, Leah usually tucked herself away in her own bedroom, with her mother's old Walkman a constant companion. When Marion mentioned she wasn't working for a change that Friday, Brian had quickly taken the opportunity to invent a work retirement function that he really should attend.

In short order, he had arranged his boy's night out that continued well into the night and that had ultimately resulted in his late-night visit to the police station. He recalled he had planned it so that their last drinking hole would be The King George, a pub only two kilometres or so from his home. He also clearly remembered listening to the news as he left the pub carpark, because that was the day Paul Keating had tried unsuccessfully to topple Bob Hawke as prime minister.

Days later, Brian was still blaming Keating for his DD charge. If he hadn't gotten so pissed off listening to the news item about Keating trying to roll Hawkie, he figured he might have paid more attention to the car that followed him not long after he left the pub car park. Back then, when he had seen the flashing blue and red lights in the rear-view mirror, he knew he was a "goner".

All the good manners in the world made no difference, nor did pointing out that he was only about a kilometre or so from home. After using every bit of persuasion he could muster, the result was inevitable. "Sir I have to inform you that you have registered a blood alcohol level of .12 grams of alcohol per decilitre of blood and accordingly you are under arrest for driving under the influence."

Brian still remembered with a laugh, how the police had revealed why they had suspected him as a likely drink driver candidate. He had left the car park quietly, not broken any road or speed limit rules, and they had pulled him over well away from the pub. Apparently, in Winter, if a car is still covered in dew at night, it's a strong indicator it's been sitting out in the open for a while. With the pub just down the road they had played the odds and won… clever buggers.

He was awakened from the trip down memory lane when the cop finally got to him in the line of cars that had banked up for the RBT unit. "Good evening, sir, can I ask if you have anything to drink this evening?"

Brian proffered his license and smiled, "Not a drop, officer, clean as a whistle."

The standard procedure of blowing in the bag and waiting followed. With a "you're free to go, sir," Brian was on his way. Five minutes later, he pulled into the driveway of his impressive riverside home and waited for the automatic garage door to open. There in the car headlights stood his wife, Joy, cradling his son, Matt. She grabbed Matt's pudgy arm and waved it in his direction, cooing as she did, "Daddy's home, daddy's home."

Brian parked the car, grabbed the takeaway roast chicken from the floor well, and walked towards them with a huge smile on his face. He gave his son a loud kiss on the forehead then ruffled what hair there was on his head. He reached around them both and gave his wife a tender kiss on the nape of the neck.

Joy stood back and appraised her husband as they wandered together into the kitchen. There was nothing especially outstanding about him physically, yet he often dominated a room. He was tallish, about 5 10", thin and wiry. "You can't fatten a Jarrett," he often said after a big meal, while patting himself on a flat stomach. "Tapeworms!" He wore his straight sandy brown hair just over his collar and his face was dominated by a prominent nose. It was not even his outgoing personality that set him apart, she thought, no, it was just an inherent joy for life. A joy he still had despite all he had recently endured.

"I have a little news for you, I just got pulled over by an RBT unit and was put on the bag!" he said with exaggerated horror. Joy looked at him sideways with a blank look. She knew, without saying, that the fact that he had driven the car home, meant there had not been a problem with the reading.

"Sorry fella, not taking the bait, but I have a little news for you that you might find a lot more interesting." She told him about a phone call she had had that morning from a bloke from Dalby who was chasing a different Mrs. M Jarrett, Marion in fact.

Brian was immediately attentive. He knew that the reason for the mix up was because his wife's name was actually Margaret Joy, and while she had always been known by her second name, legal documents and phone directories always used her given name. He was experiencing a mixture of curiosity and a sinking feeling in his stomach at the sound of his ex-wife's name. "You are right, I am interested; sick in the guts but interested."

"Well, he said he was trying to track her down about some sort of mix up with a deceased estate at Dalby. He didn't sound like a cop though, or a solicitor for that matter. The way he spoke…he had a bit of a slow bushie type drawl. …and he addressed me initially as Marion, not Mrs. Jarret, which is strange, now I come to think of it. I just told him I couldn't help and that he would find them somewhere on the Gold Coast."

Brian's agitation settled a little, but Joy could easily detect the tinge of anger in his response. "That would be my luck, the bitch ruins my life and as a reward for her bastardry she will probably end up inheriting a sheep station."

Joy gave him a kiss on the cheek and quickly changed the subject to the events of her day and getting him involved in putting their son to bed. They ate a quiet meal and turned in early for the night.

There was little sleep for Brian, his mind was racing and the harder he tried to get to sleep the wider awake he became. The topic of every thought was his past life with Marion. The RBT episode that afternoon had initiated the first flashback, then he got home to find that someone from Dalby was chasing her too. It had to be a coincidence. It was impossible for the matters to be related, but it certainly had him rehashing the past. He was a different person back then and sometimes the memories seemed like he was recalling someone else's life. He began to drift back to the events following his less successful drink driving experience.

He recalled just how angry Marion was after he got home and recounted the events of that night. She was right in his face, screaming that everything she had earned at the pub that week would be going toward his fine and so nothing would be going into the home loan savings account. He remembered how guilty he was, and how the next morning, he had decided to sell his favourite dirt bike, his favoured 240 WH Husqvarna.

It was amazing how forgiving Marion was when she found out he had topped up the saving account again. The only way Marion knew how to show appreciation was with sex, and that weekend he got a lot of it. She was rostered off that weekend, but without a reliable babysitter they couldn't get away.

In truth, a big TV and a pile of batteries for her Walkman, would have sufficed as a good babysitting substitute. Most weekends Leah would walk over to a friend's house, or they would visit her. Either way her weekends involved watching TV, listening to music, and gossiping, while devouring any sort of junk food she could get her hands on. At that time in her life, her preferred diet wasn't doing her any favours because she was getting quite chunky, and the skin on her face was in a constant state of eruption. Brian was happy to supply the food she liked if she would keep to herself and allow him to catch up on some well-earned sleep. He only remembered the essence of that weekend and not the detail, because most of the time he was off his face.

Marion had cultivated a relationship with a guy at the pub where she worked and had sourced a big bag of quality weed for the upcoming dirty weekend she had planned. He recalled some of the blunts they rolled that weekend were as thick as his thumb. One of the events Marion had relayed to him involved the huge argument he had with Leah, when she discovered that he had eaten a whole big packet of her Samboy chips. He did remember that as the weekend he began a serious love affair with "the ganja." If he had no work rostered the following day, and had a spare moment to himself, the Tally-Ho papers came out and he rolled himself a sedative.

On occasion Marion's contact at the pub provided her with some hash which she kept for special occasions, usually when Leah had a sleep over. The ritual Marion had invented for "hash night," was more than a little inventive. She first emptied the tea pot and took off the lid. She then put a piece of aluminium foil over the top and held it in place with a rubber band. When it was nice and tight, she put a series of pin holes in the foil, making a perforated area about the size of a ten-cent piece. Next step was to scrape off a little hash onto the holes, light them up and draw the smoke through the spout. It was usually quite effective except for the time they decided to follow a joint with some hash and forgot to empty the tea out of the old pot.

Tossing around in bed, Brian eventually realized that it made no sense for a cop to be chasing him through the street of Brisbane and making him blow smoke into a teapot that morphed into a Samboy chip packet. He woke with a fright to realise that it was six in the morning and time to hit the shower and get ready for work. The disturbed night's sleep, going over and over the life he would prefer to forget, had left him feeling wrung out and unrested. He considered calling in sick but wouldn't allow them to be short staffed at the depot. Brian still felt an abiding loyalty to his boss at the transport yard who had ensured there was work for him when he was released from prison. He decided early after his return that the reduced responsibilities he now had would suit him ideally. He had no desire to take on the more stressful role he previously held as assistant manager.

When he got out of prison, so many of his friends had either completely abandoned him or had turned into just passing acquaintances. Those with young kids avoided him like the plague and that hurt the most. Mitch Devlin, however, had never wavered in his support and his belief in Brian as a man. He just plain didn't believe Brian capable of the charges and told his superiors down South as much. When Mitch made the offer of a job back at the depot, Brian immediately accepted the position with grace and gratitude. He repaid the gesture and sentiment with hard work and dedication.

He hated his time inside, but the time it afforded him for self-reflection had fundamentally changed him. He had always been a hard worker, but he now realized that he had allowed Marion to determine how to spend the rewards for his efforts. Their married life initially comprised a never-ending round of parties but once Marion determined she wanted a house, his life had devolved into work, overtime, babysitting and little else.

When Brian finished getting dressed, he went into the kitchen to grab a quick breakfast where he found Joy trying to spoon something mushy into his young son's mouth. She commented that her "little fella" must have slept right through the night, because she had a full night's uninterrupted sleep.

Brian had to correct her. "No, I was still awake at 1am and went and gave him his bottle. He tossed the empty bottle out of the cot as usual, and I heard it hit the floor, so I figure I didn't get to sleep until close to two. Then I had one of those stupid dream where there is all this rush and panic and a storyline that make no sense at all."

His wife gave him a sympathetic look and went back to the process of scraping up a spoonful of food off her son's face. She re-inserted it, ensuring it all ended up in Matt's mouth, scraped the spoon across his lips to clean up the overflow and started all over again.

Brian walked past and let his hand glide across her shoulder before making himself a cup of strong coffee and a couple of pieces of toast. Between sips and bites, he turned to Joy and asked about yesterday's unexpected phone conversation. "That guy who called yesterday, did he say he was going to call back? I just have a strange feeling that something is up."

"It was a pretty short conversation and I wasn't all that pleasant." Joy responded. "My guess is that we wont hear any more from him unless he hits a dead-end looking for Marion on the Gold Coast." She pondered the situation for a few seconds then added. "If he wants help from me so she gets some sort of cash windfall, the next conversation will be even shorter."

She finished feeding her son and cleaned him up so Brian could lift him out of the highchair without getting covered in the remnants of his breakfast. He gave him a big tickle on the belly, and a cuddle and a kiss and handed him back to his mother. Joy got the standard kiss on the nape of the neck, then stood back to appraise her husband before waving him off to work.

Chapter 25

It wasn't quite 7am, and as usual, Brian liked to get in at least twenty minutes before he was due to start. Joy had started at the same company in the accounts section, a year or so after Brian had been imprisoned. His situation was a common topic of conversation around morning tea. She was initially surprised that most of the employees seemed to side with Brian, but she soon realised that there were two possibilities for this. Either they had come to the independent conclusion that Brian had been badly done by, or they had incurred the wrath of Mitch Devlin if they ever expressed a contrary opinion. Joy had a simple view of the matter, and it wasn't one she shared with her boss. The police must have had enough evidence to charge him, he got a fair trial, and he was found guilty. That meant he was guilty. Mitch, however, defended him at every turn, and even corresponded with Brian in prison. He was also known to occasionally read out Brian's replies during a break for coffee.

Joy recalled that the first time she came to even consider that Brian may have been wrongly convicted, was during one such occasion. The content of the letter was describing how lonely he was, and how to some extent this was a situation of his own making. He had nothing in common with his fellow prisoners and didn't want to mingle, he just wanted to get it over and done with, get out, and get on with his life. Then he described how his hopes for early release had just been dashed.

Apparently, there was a condition of early release that he wasn't prepared to accept. He was required to enroll into a program for sexual offenders and a prime component of the program was to admit his guilt and receive counselling. If he didn't enroll, he wouldn't be eligible for early parole for at least another year. He described how much he hated it in there, but passionately explained to Mitch that he just couldn't bring himself to do it. As much as he hated his new life, he insisted he did not do it, and if not enrolling meant extra time had to be served, then he would just have to suck it up and face it.

It was at one of these morning tea updates that Mitch announced that he had arranged with head office for Brian to be offered a position with the company when he was released. "They think he will take a position down south, but Brian won't run from this, he will stay in town, and he will be back with us before you know it." It certainly gave Joy cause to have a more open mind on the subject, and she had to admit that at least Mitch had known Brian, his ex-wife, and his stepdaughter personally.

It was almost a year later before Joy and Brian met. When Brian had accepted Mitch's job offer, they agreed that he could delay the start for a couple of months. His father in South Australia wasn't well, and he wanted to go down and visit him first. When he got back from Adelaide, he said he needed to get out in the sun and get some dirt under his nails. He was going to work as a labourer on a building site for a mate from his dirt bike days. Then, once he had worked off a bit of frustration, he was keen to get back into the saddle at the depot.

Joy only occasionally saw Brian when he first started back, because he seemed to want to keep to himself. He had been described to her as a bit of a lad and extremely outgoing, but this man seemed reserved, or shy if anything. He also wasn't in management any longer but worked mainly in the yard dealing directly with the truckies. He was a willing student of this side of the business, with the drivers happy to talk to him about load distribution, and the best way to secure it. He was also privy to the odd bit of gossip about which of the drivers were likely to be taking uppers, and which one might be likely to "lighten a load" if the pickings were worth it. This information meant he could keep an eye out and adjust rosters where necessary. This activity, combined with his existing knowledge of the logistics of running a depot and local office processes, meant that he soon had the yard running more smoothly than it ever had.

Mitch was tickled pink about it and so were his superiors down south, and he was soon called into Mitch's office. Brian was introduced to "Joy from Accounts," as Brian Jarrett, better known as BJ. "BJ has been working his arse off out there, and the powers that be down south have agreed to fatten his next pay packet. When you make the arrangements," Joy was told, "back date it to his start date."

That was the first time she and Brian were officially introduced, and the first time she had a good long look at him. He wasn't a bad looker, she thought. He was very tanned from the work in the yard, and was still lean and fit from the couple of months of labouring he had done before he started back. His appearance wasn't the first thing that struck Joy though, it was his reaction to the pay rise. It was only $20 more a week, but you would have thought he had won the lotto given the size of the grin on his face.

As the weeks passed Joy seemed to run into Brian more often, as, for one reason or another, he started regularly dropping into the office to check paperwork. Their conversations started out as work related, then became more casual, then lighter and cheekier. Eventually Brian asked Joy if she was seeing anyone. When she said that her last relationship broke up months ago, he asked her out for a drink after work. These meetings were more talking sessions than drinking sessions, with Brian sitting on the one beer most of the time. Brian loved to talk and regale her with stories, but while he was becoming more the outgoing type she was initially expecting, Joy always felt he was a little guarded, a little nervous.

During one of the after work catch ups, he eventually told her that he had to confess a secret and it could possibly mean she wouldn't want to see him again. He took a deep breath and said, "Look I know that you know I have been in prison, but you don't know what it was for….I was in for a child sex crime… but Joy, I didn't do it."

He was about to explain further, tears welling up in his eyes, when she grabbed his hand. "BJ, I've heard the stories, and from what I know of you so far, you don't seem the type. If I was certain you were capable of that, I wouldn't be seen dead with you. Let's take it slow and we will see where it goes."

Slow it was too, and romance didn't so much blossom as evolve. In fact, the regular after-hours chat sessions didn't progress into a full-blown date for some months. Joy decided from the outset that she was going to make her own assessment of the man based on her own experience and observations.

Of course, when it became obvious that she had an interest, Mitch became the match-maker extraordinaire. He wanted Brian to have another go at a normal life and just had a feeling in his water, that Joy was the right girl to give it to him. So, with the best intentions in the world, Mitch began providing Joy with parts of Brian's story that she still didn't understand.

At around this time Joy received a phone call at the office from the most unlikely source; it was Marion. She said that she was calling out of concern. She had heard from someone at the office that her ex-husband was taking an interest in her, and that she should be careful because he wasn't the man he appeared to be. Joy thanked her for her concern but told her that she was aware he had been in jail and the reason he was there. Marion seemed surprised that she was aware of the circumstances, so added that Joy didn't know the full story. "He didn't just interfere with my daughter you know," she said with a degree of venom in her voice, "he had a go at his nephew as well. The police just didn't have the evidence to progress with that one." With that she abruptly hung up. Joy now had the information that Mitch had volunteered, and an unexpected intervention and fresh allegation from Marion. What she did not have was the full story from Brian's perspective.

Joy felt there was only one way forward, and that was to clear the air with Brian directly. She suggested that he come around to her flat after work that night, and be prepared to give her the whole sorry story from beginning to end. She wanted nothing omitted. If there was to be any chance for them to move forward with the relationship, she explained, she needed to hear everything, warts and all. When Brian arrived at her flat that night, he was clearly nervous.

She opened two beers and looked him in the eye and said, "Take it from the top, I have got all night. But before we get too far, I want to first know what happened with your nephew?"

Brian's nerves were immediately replaced with confusion. "I don't have a nephew!"

"Brian I fielded a call from your ex this afternoon." She began softly. "She rang me to warn me off you and tell me that there was an additional matter I didn't know about because it never went to court." Sensing Brian's confusion Joy continued. "She said there was an additional charge of interfering with your nephew that the police had to drop because of lack of evidence."

For the first time since they met, Joy saw genuine anger in Brian's face. "Joy, I am so pissed off. That evil bitch fucked up my life and now she wants to fuck up my future, our future, too. I don't even have a nephew, and she is an only child, so she has no nephews or nieces either. There was only ever one charge and that one was bullshit." As angry as Brian was with Marion, he was equally angry with an unknown work mate. "On top of her shit, I also now have to wonder who it is at work who has been talking to her about us."

Brian stormed around the room in angry frustration but eventually realized how important a time this was in the relationship, so settled himself down and restarted the conversation. He was keen to get it behind him.

"Listen all this will wait, you are right, it's past time I gave you my side of the story." He took a deep breath and said, "So as requested, here it is warts and all." Brian took a long swig of his beer and began recounting the history of his marriage to Marion and where and why he believed it went so pear shaped.

By the end of the evening Joy had no doubt who was telling the truth, particularly as some elements of the story he had volunteered hadn't cast Brian in the best of lights. To get past the warts, Joy had to apply her own assessment of Brian as a man. She decided that yes, he was the sort of man she could make a life with, and that life was going to start in her bedroom that night.

Chapter 26

It was not until late 1993 that housing loan interest rates fell far enough for Brian and Marion to believe they had saved a sufficient deposit, and had the financial capacity to buy their own home. By then, as always seems to be the case with real estate, the market had moved at a faster pace than their savings rate. This meant that the style of house and suburb that Marion fancied was no longer within their price bracket. This dilemma was pleasantly resolved by Brian's father.

Brian and his father had not been on the best of terms for some time, the elder Mr. Jarrett believing his only son had taken to the Queensland lifestyle a little too eagerly after he had moved up from Adelaide. He always felt Brian had not reached his potential, lacked ambition, and was more interested in cars, motor bikes, and having a good time than he was in building a better life for himself. His father believed that things hadn't seemed to have much changed after his son married and took on responsibility for a stepdaughter as well.

He was delighted then, when he discovered that his only son and daughter-in-law seemed to have seriously knuckled down over the last few years and cobbled together a substantial deposit for a home. To reward both his son's change of attitude and their joint diligence, he offered to contribute a more than generous sum to their house fund. The offer was eagerly accepted, and the cash injection easily bridged the gap and allowed Brian and Marion to purchase outright, a sturdy three-bedroom colonial cottage in Brisbane's inner western suburbs. They moved in just before Christmas and Brian used the holiday break to repaint internally, and do what minor repairs were required. In the three years that had passed since the idea of home ownership first surfaced, Brian had taken every hour of overtime offered and Marion's shifts always started late afternoon, and nearly always involved weekends. As a result, his social life had taken a big hit as these hours had generally involved him having to rush home to look after Leah.

Now that the house purchase was squared away, with the painting and repairs behind him, he was looking forward to a more normal home life. His weekends would soon be open again to the overnight stays or late afternoon sessions with his dirt bike mates, or parties with friends that used to be standard before he and Marion went on their "savings spree". To his surprise and annoyance, however, Marion decided she wanted to keep working these same crazy hours, meaning that nothing was going to change. It wasn't just the fact that her decision didn't suit him, what was more galling was that there was no room for negotiation. They argued about it for sure, but more and more, what Marion wanted was what happened. Brian's reaction was to either get into another argument or to take the complete opposite tack, roll a joint and just let her do what she wanted anyway.

Leah was no company at all. As she got older, she became more sullen, moody, and bone lazy. Brian remembered that Marion had told him that Leah's dad had been something of a sporting hero on The Darling Downs. He wondered if he shouldn't use some of their time together to get her to become more active and to discover if she might not have some sporting potential of her own. Even if she had not inherited any skills, getting out in the fresh air had to be better for her than listening to music and eating junk food. Her response was not in the least encouraging. She bluntly told him that she would not be following in her father's footsteps because he was a real loser who became a drunk and topped himself. Brian didn't peruse it. Instead, his usual routine after Leah had gone to sleep was to get out the Tally Ho papers, light up a smoke and watch the city lights.

Some mornings, Brian would wake up with Marion beside him and no memory of going to bed and certainly no memory of Marion even coming home. One Sunday morning, he woke to find his side of the bed undisturbed and Marion rattling around in the kitchen. When he commented that she seemed to be wearing the same clothes she had worn to work the night before, she said she had just thrown them back on and was just about to go around to the local shop and buy some bread and milk. After she grabbed the car keys and headed off, Brian walked down to the front yard to retrieve the Sunday paper. He boiled the jug to make himself a coffee and went to the fridge to see what milk, if any, might be there. What he found confirmed his growing suspicions. Right in plain view was a recently opened carton of milk and half a loaf of sliced bread.

When Marion walked back into the house thirty minutes later, he confronted her with his suspicions, but as usual she had all the answers. "Before you start accusing me of screwing around, you might want to get your facts straight. If you weren't stoned out of your mind, you would know that I came in around one am, and for the record I wanted some low-fat milk and some decent multi-grain bread, not that shit you buy."

Brian tried to calm her down, explaining that he only asked because he was concerned that they were drifting apart. This explanation had the opposite effect however. Marion began a tirade about his failings, and indicated that if she was looking elsewhere, which she was not, she would have every reason in the world to do so. From that day on, pointing out his failings seemed to become her new favorite pastime.

Brian persevered for another year with the gnawing feeling that life was passing him by, growing by the day. Their arguments became more frequent and heated and her capacity to be inconsiderate became a finely honed skill. She would wait until just before he was going out with mates to tell him that her shift had changed, or she would make a major change in her appearance without any consultation or warning. Coming home one afternoon to find a short-haired blonde Marion in the kitchen was a big shock, particularly as she knew he loved her long auburn hair. His suspicions about her infidelity also grew by the month. There were little things like her suddenly truncating phone calls when he came into the room, her recent interest in weight loss, and her general change in appearance.

But the biggest giveaway, for a wife with a huge sexual appetite, was her lack of interest in intimacy of any sort. On the rare occasion that they did have sex, it seemed different somehow, though he could never identify exactly why that was. No matter the reason for his suspicions, there was never any proof, and certainly no admission of guilt by Marion. Ultimately, he simply decided he was unhappy, unfulfilled, and unappreciated. He felt he had contributed more than his fair share to their marriage, and while he admitted to himself that he had not been the most attentive step-father, he had taken on the financial responsibility of providing for Leah. On top of that, largely with the help of his dad, he and Marion now owned a lovely house, and had no financial problems, in fact, they were slowly building up a decent saving account balance.

Just before Christmas in 1995, one final insignificant issue made up Brian's mind about the future of his marriage. As assistant manager, Brian obviously had to attend his staff Christmas function, and with his boss on sick leave, he and Marion were to stand in as hosts. At the very last-minute, Marion told him that she had been offered an extra shift and had decided to take it, so she wouldn't be going. Brian didn't even attempt to argue, he just finally decided that he had had enough. Once everyone was back at work in the New Year, he made some enquiries about the best firm to use for divorce proceedings. He needed to get some specific preliminary advice before he even broached the subject with Marion. If there was one thing he had learned, in the nearly nine years he had known her, it was that if you were going to go into battle with her, you needed to be very well prepared.

Late in January he had the first meeting with his solicitor, explained the circumstances, and answered his solicitor's standard list of questions. Yes, he was certain his wife was being unfaithful, and no, there was simply no proof. No, he had not raised the issue of divorce with her or discussed counselling for the simple reason that it would be a waste of time. Yes, from his perspective, there were irreconcilable differences. No, they had no children together, though he had a stepdaughter who would soon turn sixteen. Yes, they had a modest joint savings account and yes, he had a small superannuation fund, but he doubted there would be more than a few thousand in it. No, he didn't think his wife had a superannuation fund at all, as she had always worked as a casual. Yes, they owned a house in both names, and no, there was no mortgage on the property because his father had gifted them the balance required to buy it outright a couple of years earlier. No, he didn't have a will. These questions and answers went on for close to an hour before Brian raised one issue that was of major concern to him.

He explained that his father was a widower and that as he was the only child, was also most likely the sole or at least major beneficiary of his father's estate. "My wife knows that my dad has a fair bit of property in Adelaide. Can that come into consideration when we work through the settlement?" His solicitor explained that the Adelaide property was his father's, and that as Marion was married to him, and not his dad, his father's wealth would have no impact, provided his father didn't die and Lennie inherit the funds, before the property settlement was finalised. This prospect was an immediate cause of concern for

Brian and he asked for specific advice on how to cover that contingency.

The solicitor explained that even if his father bequeathed his estate to him before the property settlement, that he would still get to retain most, if not all of it. "The same, to a lesser extent, is true with the house," he explained. "While the money your father contributed toward the house purchase was a gift to you both, it only happened relatively recently, so your wife should not expect to get 50% of the house sale proceeds." This was pleasant news to Brian who had assumed that it would be a 50/50 split.

With the financial side addressed, the solicitor then explained that the process was for Brian to first initiate separation. After he and Marion had separated for twelve months, he could apply for a divorce. Given his concerns about the finance side, the suggestion was that the property settlement occur after separation as soon as possible; he didn't have to wait for the divorce to be granted. Brian was advised he could either move out, or, if things were amicable, he could continue to live under the same roof as his wife. He immediately knew he would soon be looking for a flat to rent.

"Brian, the only real risks at this stage are unexpected death of you or your father. We will initiate the process for a property settlement as soon as possible. I will also arrange to have one of my partners contact you, and, on your instructions, he can draw up a simple will for you. As things stand, if you were to die unexpectedly, your wife would get the house and the rest of your possessions and I gather you don't want that." He went on to recommend that the best course of action from here was to have the paperwork prepared to initiate the divorce process. This would be by registered post, acknowledging they had separated, that their differences were irreconcilable, that he wanted to immediately initiate a property settlement, and that he would file for a formal divorce once the statutory twelve months separation has passed.

His solicitor's final bit of advice was personal and not legal. "Brian, it is my experience, and remember I do this every day, that it is always best to broach the subject of divorce face to face, before the paperwork arrives. I am not a particularly religious man, but I am a great believer in the old biblical expression that you should do unto others as you would have them do unto you. What I mean is, broach this to your wife, the way you would like it to happen, if the shoe was on the other foot."

Brian's dad had an old expression of his own. "It's no good having a dog and barking yourself." Brian had sought out a divorce specialist and paid handsomely for professional advice, and so he knew his interests would be best served to follow that advice. The difference was that his solicitor didn't know Marion and didn't realise what a scary prospect it would be if he were to forewarn her about his intentions. Ultimately, Brian weakened, and decided to take the legal advice but reject the biblical and the personal advice. He had a will prepared immediately as suggested and rented a flat in town.

Then one afternoon, when he knew Leah was having a sleep over with a girlfriend, he packed up his personal belongings, borrowed a small truck from work and moved into the small unit. He arranged all the prepared paperwork to be delivered to Marion at work. Marion, of course, was furious. It wasn't because she thought the marriage was worth saving, but because Brian had initiated things, and had caught her totally unawares in the process. Her first reaction was not to call Brian and arrange to talk, but rather to make enquiries of her own as to who was the best and most aggressive law firm to use.

Within a week she was sitting down with her own family law expert, Wing Family Law, and answering a similar set of standard questions. The answers she gave though, were somewhat biased in her own best interest. No, there was no infidelity she knew of on his part. Any infidelity on her part would not be an issue because there would be no proof. No, her husband had not raised the issue of divorce with her or discussed counselling and she certainly didn't want counselling anyway. Yes, she agreed there were definitely irreconcilable differences. No, they had no children together, though she had a child for a previous partner who was now deceased, and her daughter Leah would soon turn sixteen. No, she had no superannuation though Brian did. Yes, they owned a house in both names, and no, there was no mortgage, but she had saved most of the deposit. No, she didn't have a will. Yes, he had moved out and taken all his personal belongings. When the questioning finished, Marion had a few questions of her own.

The first of these was why, in her solicitor's opinion, her husband was in such a rush, to finalize the property settlement. "The usual reason," she said, "is that your husband is concerned there could soon be some substantial additional funds that could end up in the communal pot for distribution, and that he wants matters settled before they come into consideration." Marion immediately thought of Brian's dad, and realised for the first time, that divorce would mean she would never be sharing in that future pot of gold. Further discussions with her solicitor also revealed that her understanding of her entitlement was hugely optimistic. She was unlikely to get half the value of the house given the substantial contribution made by her father-in-law, and also, she would be bearing the full cost of bringing up Leah.

"Why is the system so biased in favour of men?" she thought. "It is plain unfair." Her next thought was how she could level up that playing field.

Chapter 27

Brian, meanwhile, was reveling in his newfound freedom. The very first weekend after moving out, he arranged for three of his old dirt bike buddies to head out to the back blocks of the Brisbane Valley. They arrived early Saturday morning and rode all day before heading back to the Esk pub. After a short session in the public bar, they hit the showers and spruced up, then came back down for a counter meal. Jodie, a local country singer was performing in the lounge that night, so they enjoyed a great meal, quite a few beers, and some topflight entertainment. As the night wore on and the locals loosened up to Jodie's catalogue of country classics, the boys even had a couple of dances with the barmaids.

Next morning, they were up early so they could get in another good session in the hills, before heading back home late Sunday night. They arranged a big Chinese take away and finished it off with a few more beers on the deck of his rented, pokey, inner city unit. It had taken them until now to bring up the touchy subject of his pending divorce.

Brian gave them an outline of the advice he had received as regards the likely property settlement, and how he was still pondering the best way forward. "I can come in hard and she can have her solicitors negotiate me up, or I can go in with a fixed figure in mind and stand firm." One of his divorced mates agreed that he should start low, but not miserably low, and have her solicitors work him up. The other, who had never married, suggested that he had already closed off the most effective way to protect himself financially. "You went and got married in the first-place cockhead, that's where you went wrong." After another round of stories and beers, his mates headed off.

Laying back on the small sofa alone, Brian began to ponder on his new life and wondered why he had let things slide so far before cutting himself loose from Marion. He looked around for his pouch to roll a joint but remembered that a part of moving out of their house involved him losing his weed supplier. He had finished the last of it the night before he had moved out but decided he could do without it anyway. He hadn't felt this relaxed in what seemed an eternity.

A constant exchange of letters between the two law firms followed, before a conference was arranged to first discuss the property settlement. Brian's initial intention was to offer Marion the minimum the law would likely allow which according to his legal advice, was her car, 20-30% of the value of the house, and half the relatively meagre balance of their joint savings account. The legal advice also stated that he should be prepared to be a little pragmatic to the point of generosity. As his solicitor put it, "Brian, these settlements can be a turning point in your life. Don't try and win this battle only to lose the war."

After considering all the advice he had received from various quarters, both personal and professional, Brian told his solicitors that he was prepared to negotiate a quick resolution. He proposed that his team could start at 30% of the value of the house, all the existing household furniture, unencumbered title to her car, and the full current balance of the joint saving account. He would retain his superannuation fund which only had a $5000 balance anyway and allow her to live in the house rent free until the property was sold or for four months, whichever happened earlier. At a pinch, he told them he was prepared to increase her share of the proceeds on the sale of the house to 35%.

Brian anticipated Marion would try and make things difficult, and so it proved when her response arrived. She accepted the positive bits, of course. She would accept the unencumbered car and the full balance of the joint bank account that Brian had frozen, and Brian could keep his lousy superannuation balance. However, she wanted $10,000 a year for Leah's upkeep and contribution to her education until she turned eighteen. Brian initially felt offended by that demand; that was until the next item on her list was revealed. She believed she was entitled to 75% of the value of the house and she required the time to enter arrangements to raise the finance to buy Brian's quarter share. To achieve that aim, she was prepared, subject to raising finance, to give Brian $75,000 for his 25% interest. Brian quickly calculated that $75000 for a quarter share valued the house at $300,000 which was less than they paid for it over two years previously and made no allowance either for the work his painting and general maintenance work.

She made the point that the price was fair because the market was flat and that he would avoid having to pay agents' commission, or any promotional costs if she was the buyer. A saving on agent's fees nowhere near covered the discrepancy due to her low-price estimate and her requirement for an unrealistic percentage of the value. If these demands were not enough to make his blood boil, Marion also said that she wanted to live there rent free with all rates and insurances paid by Brian, until the property settlement was affected.

Brian, of course, was livid and sought confirmation from his legal team, that what he had proposed was more than reasonable. They agreed but stated that they rarely saw a lot of reasonableness when negotiations became toxic. Multiple proposals and counter proposals were put, but Marion remained insistent that she would not budge on her requirements relating to the house. Brian was about to take his solicitors advice and even consider seeking relief via the courts, when he had an unexpected call at work from Marion. She suggested that they meet that night for a drink to try and come to an agreement without the interference from all the legal people. Brian believed that Marion was finally coming to her senses and they could bring things to a satisfactory resolution.

When they met, Marion was civil, but all business, so Brian decided to take the initiative. "Marion this has been going on since New Year and we are no closer to an outcome. Give me your bottom line and be reasonable for a change or this is heading to court."

Her response would ring in his ears for many years. "Brian, my bottom line is, and always was, 75% of the house value to be covered by me, giving you $75000 and you giving me the full title." Brian got up, shaking his head in rejection, and ready to walk out when Marion added, "Brian, you should know by now that I get what I want, one way or the other. I would think long and hard about whether it's a good idea to fuck me around. Give me what I want, and what I am due, or I promise I will find a way to make you regret it. Remember, you were the one who wanted out of the marriage, Leah and I were quite happy before you decided to blow things up."

"I am so glad they were happy," Brian thought, "because I certainly wasn't."

First thing next morning, Brian was on the phone to his family law firm. He explained how Marion had approached him, suggesting they meet privately to come to agreement on terms, and how she had just come back to her original position instead, with a veiled threat thrown in. An appointment was arranged for later that afternoon, and they discussed the best way forward. He was reminded of the four ways that property settlement could be affected, once both sides had agreed that all their assets had been identified as forming the pool that was to be divided.

The first method was the formation of a binding financial agreement between Brian and Marion. This had to be prepared and agreed to and signed after it had been vetted and verified by solicitors for both parties. Given what had transpired the prior evening, the first method was now off the table. Option two, going up the scale of complexity, was a binding financial agreement that was prepared entirely by the solicitors for both sides, then agreed and signed. That also seemed improbable at this stage.

Next option was a consent order that had to be approved by the Family Law Court, and the last stop on this road to misery was a court-imposed settlement. Brian was warned not to go there, if possible, because his lawyers considered it "something of a raffle". "You never know what might come out of it," they said, "and at least with the other options you are a party to the negotiations."

Brian was assured that her requests were totally unreasonable and that she would be getting advice to that effect from her own lawyer. It now became solicitors at ten paces with all communication, offers, and counters submitted though the two legal firms. In the end, Brian blinked first and suggested that he would accept $150,000 for his share of the house on two conditions. Firstly, Marion needed to secure the finance to buy him out and settle within two calendar months. Secondly, he would be contributing nothing toward Leah's future upkeep and education.

Marion was all ready to reject the offer and head off to court when her solicitor called her for a meeting. Her backside had just hit the chair when her solicitor looked her directly in the eye and said, "Marion, you obviously feel aggrieved and believe you should get more out of this, but I can tell you this is a fantastic offer. In short, Marion, you have won, and I seriously recommend you accept the current proposal."

In the end, she accepted the offer, sought and obtained finance but that didn't change her view. In her mind she was still owed, and as promised, she would find a way to ensure Brian made up the difference. Brian, on the other hand, had not really given her earlier veiled threat much thought at all. In fact, he had discovered a newfound freedom and was soon endeavouring to make up for lost time, enjoying the sort of life that had eluded him over the last five or six years.

Chapter 28

September 2002

When he woke up the next morning, Fitzy had a much clearer idea of his next move. He realised that of all the players involved in this unfolding saga, the only person he really knew was Marion. He decided that he was going to delay catching up with her until he had a handle on Brian Jarrett. He would then be better placed to catch up with her and assess what she really knew about Lennie's death. That after all, was the primary reason he had embarked on this quest. While the P.I. hadn't yet come up with more information on Jarrett, he had been able to provide him with Marion's Gold Coast address. As the coast was only an hour's drive away and Fitzy wasn't pressed for time, he decided to do a little reconnaissance himself down there over the next day or so and come back to The Treasury at night.

After the monotonous drive down to the outskirts of the Gold Coast, Fitzy stopped at a service station and consulted his dog eared UBD directory to find the address he had been given.

He eventually navigated his way through Florida Gardens, on the western side of the Gold Coast Highway at Broadbeach and drove across a bridge to what he supposed would be a massive canal estate. It turned out that while some of the homes had a canal frontage, a good proportion were dry blocks. It was the sort of address that would look more impressive on paper than it was in the flesh. "That is Marion to a tee," thought Fitzy.

He drove around the estate until he came across 12 Childers Street, a still impressive large brick home with a silver BMW in the driveway. He cruised slowly past to make sure he wasn't noticed, but slow enough to note that both front door panels of the BMW were covered with what he suspected were magnetic signs displaying the words "Florida Reality". Underneath, in a cursive script, was the name, Marion Jarrett and her mobile phone number. Fitzy read the number back to himself out loud, parked around the corner and jotted it down in the small notebook he carried in his top pocket. He was starting to really enjoy playing detective; with the minimum of effort, he had discovered what Marion now did for a living, her personal mobile number, and what her house looked like.

He rang directory assistance for the agency phone number, called it and obtained the street address which was only a kilometre away on the Gold Coast Highway. Within a couple of minutes, he was standing in front of a new group of strip shops, where Florida Real Estate occupied two well-presented tenancies, sandwiched between a tax agency and a florist. He looked casually in the window display, noting that Marion's name was well represented on the window cards promoting a variety of beach front units and residential houses for sale. Not only were Marion's listings prominently displayed, but she also had an A4 photo of herself with a short bio underneath extolling her virtues as the suburbs most active and successful agent.

Fitzy had to look long and hard at the photo before the Marion of old was recognizable. Twenty years on, her hair was now bleached blonde, she was still applying too much make up, and despite the stylish clothes, she looked somewhat bloated from the extra weight she had piled on. Also displayed in front of the office was the agency's property guide, and a little cabinet with a pile of copies of the property lift out from the *Gold Coast Bulletin*. He picked up a copy of both, casually headed back to his car and drove around until he found a café where he could grab a quick snack while reading up on the local property market.

Now armed with a little local property knowledge, he headed further north back along the highway until he found a competing real estate office. He fronted up to the reception desk, and after flashing his most charming smile, asked if he could talk to a salesperson about investment property. Without a moment's hesitation, the receptionist introduced Fitzy to the salesman on duty and they sat down for a long and interesting chat about the market, the real estate industry generally, and the personalities in it. They exchanged details and Fitzy promised that he would keep in contact if he decided to progress matters.

On his way back to Brisbane, Fitzy received a call from the PI with an interesting development. He had been nosing around a few contacts trying to get his hands on a copy of the Jarrett court transcript as requested. Obviously, word had drifted around the legal circles, and he had received a call from a very irate guy, John Cameron, who implied that he was associated with the case. The guy threatened that unless he told him why he was making enquiries, he would be contacting the police or Fair Trading or whichever government department "was responsible for issuing licenses to creeps like him."

"Well I settled him down when I told him I was glad he had called because I wanted to speak to someone associated with the case, but I didn't know where to start. To ensure Cameron was legitimately involved with the matter, I had him give me his direct number to call back. Sure enough, John Cameron is a partner at Nicholas and Cameron, the firm Jarrett used for his divorce and was also the instructing solicitor on Brian Jarrett's court case."

Fitzy was keen to hear more and just said, "Go on."

"Well, I told him I had a client who had an oblique interest in the Jarrett case, but only because it looked to have a bearing on a potential criminal matter related to his client's ex-wife, Marion Jarrett." The mere mention of Marion Jarrett had apparently piqued the lawyer's interest to the extent that he suggested he would take a call directly from Fitzy. If that call went well, he said he would be prepared to meet, and if the meeting went well, he would broker a meeting with Brian Jarrett.

On the drive back to The Treasury, Fitzy was on the phone to the solicitor giving a truncated version of the circumstances that had led him down to Brisbane. Cameron was contributing very little to the conversation, until Fitzy suggested that following his friend's death in 1980, Marion Jarrett, then Lennie's ex-girlfriend, had almost certainly lied when interviewed by police and in her subsequent written statement. The solicitor bought the conversation to a halt, asking if Fitzy could meet with him that afternoon.

Within the hour, Fitzy fronted up to the solicitor's office in Toowong, an inner-city suburb in Brisbane's west. After giving his details to the receptionist, he was soon ushered into a separate office where he was met by a stocky man in his late forties who offered his hand in introduction.

Fitzy quickly found a seat, and before the solicitor could find his own, led off the conversation by saying he was not one for the niceties and would cut to the chase. He said that until a week or so back he hadn't known Brian Jarrett even existed or anything about the case. His interest had been in finding more about the death of Leah Jarret's father, and that he had stumbled on Brian's situation in the process.

"It was my original intention to make contact with Marion, but I didn't like her twenty years ago, and felt it would be best to get as much background on her later life as I could before we met again."

The solicitor abruptly interrupted Fitzy's flow, asking , "Mr. Fitzgerald I am interested in knowing your background relationship with Leah Kent's father."

Fitzy as quickly responded, "In good time, I will discuss that and a whole lot more when I know about the case that sent Jarrett to jail."

Cameron asked for a moment and held up a finger indicating he needed to make a call. After hanging up, he indicated to Fitzy that his client had agreed to have him provide a copy of the trial transcript with Leah's name redacted.

"Thanks for your time, Mr. Fitzgerald, I think you will find that your interests and the interests of my client will likely intersect." Handing him a copy of the transcript, the solicitor said, "I believe you will find this is an interesting read. Please get through this as quickly as you can and call me with any questions. I want you to be fully appraised before we all meet again Friday afternoon. Does two pm suit you?"

No sooner was Fitzy back at The Treasury, than he opened the file and began reading, taking notes as he went on the writing block the hotel had provided. The preliminaries were pretty boring but once things got down to witness statements and evidence and the cross examination it got very interesting. He ordered room service as he devoured each page, and the list of questions and notes accumulated. It was mid-afternoon the next day before he felt in a position to call John Cameron and seek his answers to a host of questions and points of clarification.

The first question was totally unrelated to the court case, and the answer had not yet been provided by his PI. "How" he asked, "had someone not long released from prison, and who had been cleaned out in a divorce, managed to buy a house for cash in a ritzy riverside suburb?"

The solicitor smiled to himself and responded, "The answer to that question probably goes to Marion's motivation to have Brian charged in the first place." Fitzy waited for clarification on what was obviously a very important answer. After a moment's consideration the solicitor went on to explain the comment.

"Brian Jarrett's father died a short time after Brian was released from prison. The father was a man of considerable means and Brian was the sole beneficiary of his estate. He inherited property and cash assets in excess of $5 million. This was money Brian's ex-wife knew he would eventually come into, and money that was excluded from the divorce property settlement. I am of the belief that this was likely the reason she was so difficult to deal with during the settlement process." This bit of information explained a lot to Fitzy and he allowed the solicitor to expand on the answer.

"My partner handled that matter, but the divorce was how the firm acquired Brian as a client in the first instance. We thought Brian was relatively generous in the negotiations, but the wife obviously disagreed, because it was after she begrudgingly agreed to the settlement and before the divorce, that she went to the police and accused him of interfering with her daughter."

"Well that was a long answer to a short question," thought Fitzy. "My next question is how Jarrett could be found guilty, if the only witness to the event was the victim."

Cameron explained that this was the situation in most sexual crimes. "While having witnesses and DNA evidence is always preferable, it often comes down to how the jury assessed the testimony of the victim or supposed victim."

Fitzy considered the response insufficient, so asked Cameron to elaborate. "It's usual legal advice for the accused not to give evidence, after all it is the Crown's job to prove guilt. Our client took our advice and didn't give evidence. Unfortunately, the jury placed a great deal of weight on Marion's police statement and the "in-camera" evidence of Leah."

"Okay," Fitzy followed up, "but the family doctor gave evidence that Leah had admitted to him her mother had put her up to it, and she just went along with what her mum wanted."

The solicitor nodded, suggesting it was a good point. "Again, unfortunately, when Leah gave her evidence in a closed session, she admitted she had indeed told the doctor this, but said it was only because he was a really scary man, and she figured he wanted her to say that."

Cameron then ventured an opinion. "Look I don't want to suggest that Brian was cocky, but some in the jury may have interpreted his demeanor that way. He never really took the issue as seriously as he should. He knew there was no truth to the accusation, and he knew there was no evidence they could rely on. He was so certain he would be cleared that he had even booked to have a weekend away dirt bike riding with his mates the weekend after the case was due to finish. When they came in with a guilty verdict he passed out in the dock and split his chin open!"

There was further pause while the solicitor considered whether to make the next statement, then he added, "… and of course there is the fact that Marion Jarrett is a consummate manipulator and very convincing liar."

The more Fitzy heard, the more interested he was in meeting Brian Jarret in the flesh. "Okay, I'm starting to get my head around this," Fitzy said. "I need to get a handle on dates and timing. When was the assault supposed to have happened and when was Marion first aware of it?"

"That is another bloody good question," replied the solicitor. "I think you have a natural flair for this because I always thought this was one of the weakest parts of Marion's case. In evidence, she said the events occurred shortly after they moved into their house which was late 1993 or early 1994, when Leah would have been thirteen going on fourteen. Yet she was apparently prepared to have Brian as a babysitter for Leah, until he decided he had had enough, and moved out about two years later." Fitzy nodded in agreement. "We thought this alone would weaken her case sufficiently, but as you know, it didn't seem to cut through to the jury."

"Okay, last question for now. How much did the case cost Brian, given that a big chunk of what he owned at the time was lost in the divorce.?"

"Well, he certainly came out of the divorce on the wrong side of the ledger," the solicitor replied.

"She got a $400,000 house for $150,000 plus the other bits and pieces including a car and a $10,000 bank account. As the case dragged on, he became short of funds. He had taken unpaid leave from work and was spending heavily. After all the legal and other costs, I doubt there was a whole lot left of the $150,000 settlement by the time he left prison.

"He refused to approach his father for help. He indicated to me that he had not long reconciled with him, and didn't want to spoil that, given his father's advancing years and poor health."

Fitzy then had Cameron explain a few finer points of law and sentencing, before admitting that he now had sufficient doubts of his own and would like to meet with Jarrett personally, if all agreed.

Chapter 29

Friday afternoon saw Fitzy again arrive at the offices of Nicholas and Cameron, and this time he was pointed toward a small conference room where a tall skinny guy sat holding the hand of an equally thin but younger woman with a cap of tight blond hair. Brian gently prized Joy's hand from his own, and stood up to meet the man from Dalby who had just reopened some barely healed wounds.

Alan Fitzgerald, this is Brian Jarrett and his wife, Joy." Fitzy was immediately surprised by the strength in Jarrett's hands. Usually, he delighted in observing the initial wince when he shook hands with someone from the city, but Brian's grip, no doubt improved by his years on a motorbike, was almost the equal of Fitzy's. He shook Joy's hand more daintily, just lightly cradling her fingers, then took a seat directly opposite Brian.

Cameron explained the unusual circumstances that led him to arrange the meeting. He suggested that while most clients who pleaded not guilty were not always being honest, he still believed Brian was being truthful and that he was the victim of a miscarriage of justice.

Once again Fitzy took the lead. "I would like you to hear me out on this. I told John here that I would only tell you why I have an interest in your story, after I got a handle on your side of it. Now thanks to John, I have just read the transcript and he has answered a pile of questions I had about it. Because of those answers and because I used to know your ex-wife well, and I know the sort of person she is, I am prepared to give you the benefit of the doubt, for now.

"You should know that Leah's dad, Lennie, was a great mate of mine. He died before Leah was born, the inquest findings were inconclusive saying it was either a work accident or he committed suicide. I now have my suspicions that both these findings were wrong, and these suspicions are what first led me down to Brisbane to try and get to the bottom of things."

"Mr. Fitzgerald.. Alan?" the solicitor asked, fishing for the best means of address.

Fitzy cut him off. "Alan will suffice."

"Sorry to interrupt, Alan; but can you please explain how there is a connection between your friend's death and Brian's conviction for interfering with a minor?"

Fitzy figured he had nothing to lose, so went into great detail to explain how Marion had come into Lennie's life. He described how what started out as a standard enough romance had slowly changed; how Marion had slowly dominated Lennie's life, then wronged him, abandoned him after he had suffered a bad sporting accident, then defamed him, and finally either persecuted him to the point of suicide or was either witness to, or involved in, his death.

Until the last few words of his story, they were all starting to think that all Alan was doing was reinforcing their existing opinion of Marion as a first-rate bitch. However, the suggestion that she might be involved in someone's death made them all sit forward a little in their seats.

Fitzy noticed the change in their level of interest and went on, "You can see I am no fan of your ex-wife, and why I might be more likely than most to believe Brian's version of events."

He then explained the basis of his suspicions; how, due to Di's will, he became reacquainted with the twenty-year-old tragedy. He also disclosed the importance of the discovery of the jersey; a bit of information that would have meant nothing to the police investigators but meant everything to someone who knew its history.

"I now have serious suspicions about what really happened that day, and I am searching for proof, that Marion was there when Lennie died." Fitzy stopped for a breath and looked around the room before adding with emphasis. "There is even the strong possibility that Marion may have been more than just an onlooker that day."

Brian, his wife, and his solicitor all sat there transfixed, until finally Joy summed up what Brian was also thinking, when she exclaimed to the surprise of everyone, "Fuck me; that bitch!" She asked John Cameron what he thought, and he confirmed, with a wry smile, that she had summed up the situation well.

Fitzy finished his explanation by acknowledging that he was just a simple man with a strong suspicion, and that he was clearly unsure on how to progress matters from here.

Privately, he had also admitted to himself that Brian was not the man he was expecting to meet. He had imagined Brian to be a weak, reserved man with "paedo" almost visibly tattooed on his forehead. Instead, he had been introduced to a man who worked in a tough industry, a man who enjoyed rough sports, yet was also a loving father and husband to a woman who appeared to know her mind. Fitzy's gut feel, supported by the weakness of the case against Jarrett and the nature of the person who had bought it on, suggested to him that Brian was a principled man who had also suffered greatly at the hands of Marion Kent. Based on his assessment over the course of the last few days, and particularly over the last hour, Fitzy acknowledged to the group that he now doubted Brian's guilt.

"But you have to understand that Brian's issue is less important to me. I have come down to Brisbane to find out if there is anything in my suspicions about how Lennie died. That was my focus from the start and remains my focus."

Brian, Joy, and John Cameron had a different agenda, of course. The suspicions that Fitzy had raised about Marion's past deeds did sound substantial, and manslaughter or murder was obviously more serious than a miscarriage of justice associated with a concocted accusation. In the latter case, however, it was Brian who had suffered, and that was the priority as far as he was concerned. They all looked toward John Cameron who was clearly thinking deeply on the way forward as well.

"Okay, chief, you are the legal expert," said Fitzy. "How do we get to the bottom of this, how do we move things along?" But the solicitor wouldn't be drawn into an immediate reply. A good five minutes passed while he pondered the situation and occasionally looked up reference books and jotted down phone numbers.

Finally, he gave his preliminary assessment, part of which was stating the bleeding obvious, that there were two agendas. "My clients want to clear Brian's name, and hold Marion to account for raising the false allegation in the first place. Alan wants to determine if foul play was involved in his friend's death or at least rule out suicide. If he can prove foul play, he obviously wants to hold Marion to account." The common denominator in both cases was Marion, plus the lack of compelling evidence. He suggested that before they take further action on either front, that he would place a call to the barrister that Brian used in the trial and seek his opinion on what would be needed as evidence in both cases and if success with one case might be used as leverage to assist with the other. John Cameron excused himself and returned to his own office.

Luckily, the barrister had just come in from court and offered to give him a few minutes. After the solicitor gave him a precis of the latest developments, the barrister quickly assessed that from Brian's perspective, there was essentially nothing new in this that would assist his old client. The cases were clearly unrelated. He did feel the police now had sufficient cause to re-examine the Dalby matter, but that was not a matter he could initiate. He went on to suggest to Cameron that there was a huge difference between reopening a case and uncovering sufficient evidence that would warrant them laying any charges.

John Cameron re-entered the conference room and gave them the outcome of the call. Fitzy face lit up at the prospect of having the matter reopened.

He volunteered that he had a good friend in the force in Dalby, who had a contact at CIB in Brisbane. Between them he was sure they could have the case reopened. As he headed off toward the car park, Fitzy promised that if there was evidence to be had to tie Marion to Lennie's death, he was determined to find it. Brian offered to be of whatever help he could be; they said their goodbyes to the big man, then Brian and Joy walked back into the solicitor's rooms to discuss the outcome of the unexpected meeting.

Brian just shook his head in disbelief. He knew his ex-wife was a handful, but he doubted that even she was capable of murder. Anyway, as the barrister had pointed out, even if she was, it would have no bearing on his situation.

John Cameron could almost read Brian's thoughts. He realized he had helped re-open a can of worms, but it had not helped Brian's cause in the least. He looked at Joy and then Brian and then asked, "Brian, can I ask if you would feel vindicated if the real Marion was revealed, and she paid for a past crime? You know that whatever the outcome with Dalby, it won't help in formally clearing your name."

Brian surprised him with the speed and clarity of his answer. "Look I am aware that whatever the outcome, nothing helps my legal status. I have been found guilty... and I can't deny that fact. But being able to rebut the doubters with the fact that Marion was charged with murder, or better still, found guilty of murder, would certainly ease the pain."

He had decided that there was nothing for him to do but to help Fitzy with the Dalby matter where he could, and hope upon hope that something would fall his way during the process. What he could do by way of assistance he did not know, but he knew this was the only chance he had been given since he ended up in prison, that could possibly make a difference.

Chapter 30

Next morning Fitzy fielded an early call from John Cameron. "Good morning, Alan, hope I didn't wake you."

"Not bloody likely," replied Alan. "I've been up since five. I got the impression I must have been the first up in Brisbane, there wasn't a soul around."

"Of course I should have realized, but eight is early for me to be at the office. Listen I have been thinking about what was discussed yesterday and I believe it would be best if you were to move things on by yourself through your police contacts in Dalby."

That suited Fitzy who had already concluded, that while Brian was keen to assist, he doubted that he could be of much help.

"But Alan," the solicitor continued, "please keep me updated on any progress that you make with the case. Maybe in the future, if things get involved, I can offer more assistance."

Fitzy agreed with the solicitor. "I now have no intention of following up Marion myself just yet. I want to be better prepared because I know she is no idiot. First up, I am going to head back to Dalby and speak to the local sergeant of police."

After finishing his call to the solicitor, he gathered his notes and thoughts and made the next call to Sergeant Mick Cummings. When the usual pleasantries were done, Fitzy began explaining how a particular old football jersey found amongst a pile of greasy rags had led him to Brisbane. He knew some might find that a thin piece of evidence, but he imposed on the sergeant to retrieve the police file on the death of Leonard Krause outside Dalby in February 1980. He asked Mick to call him once he had it so they could meet to discuss some important developments he had uncovered on his trip to Brisbane. The sergeant indicated that was possible, but the most detailed report they would need was the coroner's report and that might take a little longer to retrieve.

Early the following week, they were both sitting in his office at the Dalby station and Mick told Fitzy that he had also been able to make contact with the sergeant who was on duty back in 1980 to get a little background briefing. The retired sergeant had revealed that Lennie's death had been reported as a suicide by his mother. Because all the evidence strongly indicated suicide or an accident, the local CIB handled the investigation. To further complicate matters there had been a major traffic accident on the road to Miles that weekend with three people killed, and the station had been short-staffed.

Together the sergeant and Fitzy pored over the old files and photos of the grizzly scene and read the accompanying autopsy report, and findings of the inquest prepared by the coroner.

The inquest had determined an open finding, deeming the cause of death was either a suicide or death by misadventure. The coroner's report was more instructive than the police report, going into details of Lennie's state of mind, his recent personal, health, and financial issues. The report noted that they had searched for a suicide note and found none, even looking inside the old diary in the shed's makeshift office. As was the case with the autopsy, the report confirmed the cause of death was a fractured skull caused by the old Jaguar crushing the victim. It further speculated two possible scenarios. One, Lennie had purposely caused the jack to suddenly release, which in turn caused the weight of the car to dislodge the timber chocks under the axle. This scenario suggested suicide.

Alternatively, the jack had malfunctioned causing the chocks to give way in which case it was death by misadventure. Inspection of the jack did show it as faulty and leaking hydraulic fluid. Fitzy and the sergeant had discussed what he had uncovered to date and concluded that it certainly proved that Marion had lied to police about her whereabouts after the accident, and consequently no longer had an alibi. With the new evidence that she could well have been at the scene around the time of Lennie's death, and the discovery that Marion had not aborted the pregnancy, they possibly now had motive and opportunity. What they were missing was how she may have caused his death.

As they browsed through the files, Fitzy noted that they also contained photos taken from different angles and showing the scene before and after Lennie's body was removed, as well as general shots of the garage itself. Fitzy had a lifetime's experience of killing and butchering his own meat and had seen lambs with their eyes pecked out by crows, or beasts drowned in muddy dams on the property. Despite this, he wasn't prepared for the graphic shots of Lennie's death. He initially tried to turn away and then decided he needed it to strengthen his resolve to ensure Marion paid for her sins.

The worst of the photos were close ups of Lennie's head after the Jaguar was jacked up again. He must have turned his head as the car fell because half of his face, while distorted, was still recognizable. The other half was barely identifiable as human, let alone his old mate. One eye was protruding, and the face was covered with blood and what was obviously brain matter. As they waded through the files, they then noted the old diary, and the sergeant turned to the date of Lennie's death, 9th February.

As expected, there was no suicide note, but the bottom half of the page had been torn off. Fitzy now looked closely at the photos of the scene itself. He noted how little had changed in the shed over the last 20 years or so, other than the accumulation of dust. He concentrated on the photos that showed the overview of where all the items were located in the shed, and then close-up photos of each of those items. The close ups included photos of the hydraulic jack, photos showing the leakage of hydraulic fluid onto the concrete floor, and photos of the timber chocks.

Something about those chocks initially piqued Fitzy's interest, but he didn't know why. It was only when he looked again at one of the overview photos that matters became clearer. In that photo, Fitzy could see the long-handled crowbar with the top painted white that he had seen when he visited the shed some weeks previously. He now remembered the real reason it was there.

He had broken off part of the chisel end when he was working out at Charleville for his uncle, so had bought it back with him that Christmas for Lennie to patch weld for him. Most of that Christmas break had involved drinking and reminiscing, and that small patch job hadn't been completed. Fitzy then retrieved the close-up photos of the timber chocks, the ones that had given away to cause the old Jaguar to terminate Lennie's mechanical career. This meant something he thought, and when he explained his suspicions, the sergeant face lit up too.

He grabbed Fitzy by the shoulder and half dragged him to the adjacent offices of Dalby CIB. Once they convened around the detective's desk, Fitzy and the sergeant laid out the relevant parts of the files and photos and then Fitzy gave a potted history of the circumstances surrounding the death. The sergeant then had the bushy-cum sleuth, describe to the detective, the history of the old jersey. The detective stood erect, looked down at all the material, rubbed his chin and directed Fitzy to sit down. "I want you to give me a full written statement as to how, when, and where he came to be in possession of this new information."

Next morning, Fitzy, the sergeant, along with the assigned homicide detective, Con Peters, and a couple of local forensic officers, met at Di Krause's old home. Fitzy unlocked the large padlock on the chain that had kept the large roller door closed for all but one day over the last twenty plus years. He directed the detective over to the pile of greasy rags and pointed to the old jersey. The detective turned it over with his pen and then spread it out, back side first, on the workshop bench. Mick Cummings took over, explaining the suspicions Fitzy had about the crowbar and the timber chocks, one of which had a sharp indentation the exact shape of the chisel end of the crowbar. Acknowledging that the case was now out of his hands, the sergeant thanked the detective, said his goodbyes to Fitzy, and headed back to the station alone.

More photographs were taken including the current position of the timber chocks, the crowbar, and the jersey. Finger and palm prints were taken off the large crowbar and then the crowbar and the chocks were placed in evidence bags, secured, and sent to the Scientific Branch in Brisbane for further testing.

After both men returned to the station, Fitzy bought Con Peters up to speed about what he had discovered in Brisbane and the Gold Coast about Marion Kent, now Marion Jarrett, and offered to help with the reopened investigation. Within a week he had a call back from the detective.

"Mr. Fitzgerald, Alan, I can confirm that the forensic results both locally and from Brisbane were very instructive, this case certainly has some legs."

Fitzy couldn't help but grin at this. "That's great news Detective..Con. Is there enough to lay charges?"

"I cant say for sure, the evidence is strong but far from complete and the case is old, cold, and complex. Cold cases are notoriously difficult to solve, let alone have the charges stick in court. Without your efforts this case would never have progressed this far though." Peters then went on to explain that he believed they now had motive, opportunity, and means, but was concerned about Fitzy's discovery of the jersey. "When you discovered the bit of old football kit, it was just a memory jogger about an old friend. Now, however, it looks like you have physically handled what is likely to be crucial evidence in the reopened investigation."

"Just how good a piece of evidence is it?" Fitzy asked.

"Well it strongly indicates that Marion was at the workshop close to the date of Lennie's death. This directly contradicts her statement to the inquest. To firm things up and strengthen the case we need to find a way to confirm for certain that Marion was at the garage that night."

Feeling a little embarrassed that maybe he had watched too much American TV, Fitzy hesitantly asked if the CIB used "wires", to collect evidence in such cases. When the detective confirmed that they did, Fitzy said, "Well it looks like I am going to the Gold Coast to buy an investment unit."

Chapter 31

It's Alan Fitzgerald here, Tom," Fitzy said to the real estate agent. "I will be back on the Gold Coast next week and I am hoping to look at a few investment units while I am down there."

Tom Byrne was delighted to hear his voice as he had all but given up on Alan as a prospective buyer. At the weekly sales meetings, Tom had referred to Fitzy as an "ice cream licker." This was a less than flattering term to describe someone on holidays who looked through real estate office windows while eating an ice cream. A dreamer and time waster with no intention or capacity to buy anything. As it was to turn out, Tom's initial assessment was close to the mark, but here was this very same "ice cream licker" making an appointment to look at specific properties next week.

Fitzy revealed he had been buying the Gold Coast Bulletin weekend edition with the property section, and mentioned that he liked the look of three properties. The one that most appealed to him was being advertised by another agent, a Marion Jarrett from Florida Real Estate. The salesperson indicated that he would have to call the other agent to see if she would enter into a conjunctional arrangement, as she had an exclusive agency. When Fitzy asked if there would likely be a problem, he suggested she would only reject the arrangement if she had a sale of her own pending. He rang back an hour later to confirm he had reached an arrangement with Marion and that he should set up a suitable time to inspect the unit.

Fitzy's accommodation that weekend was paid for by the Queensland Police Service. Con Peters had overseen the positioning of the wire and reminded him the information they were trying to secure. Fitzy met up with the salesperson and inspected the first two of his own listings before meeting Marion in the lobby of the third. He was all business and gave no indication that he knew who Marion was, though he noticed several times that she was closely scrutinizing him. Halfway through the inspection she pulled Alan aside.

"You know, there is something about you that is quite familiar. I think we have done business together before, where are you from?" Marion asked, a quizzical look on her face.

"Oh, I've got a grazing and grain property out the back of Dalby." he replied.

Marion's face lit up. "Of course, Alan Fitzgerald, Fitzy, I should have made the connection."

She punched him lightly on the arm and said, "Good to see you, you are looking good." Fitzy did his best to look confused, so Marion went on. "Sorry, I'm Marion Jarrett, used to be Marion Kent. I worked at The Imperial in Dalby as a bar maid back in the late 70's."

Fitzy noted that she made no mention of Lennie, which was strange given Lennie was their connection, not the hotel. Fitzy meanwhile continued to play it cool, referring to Lennie and the old days. After the inspection was finished, he told Tom that he would have Marion drop him at the office, as they wanted to catch up on old times. The agent was crestfallen. There would be little chance now that he would retain this buyer, his best sales lead in weeks. From bitter experience, he knew that if Marion Jarrett could find a way to cut him out of any deal, she would. Fitzy and Marion arranged to meet at a local coffee shop for a quick catch up and the wire began to work its magic.

After a pleasant thirty minutes chat, Marion dropped Fitzy back to his car that was parked outside the other agency. Before getting into his Landcruiser Fitzy said, "Getting back to the business at hand, I think that unit is a possibility. Marion, but I need to be sure, so I am looking at a few more tomorrow with Tom. I'll let him know if I want you to arrange a second inspection."

Marion handed him her business card. "Don't worry about that, I have a great relationship with Tom. Just call me direct, I'll look after you and then keep Tom posted. That first unit in "Beachfront Towers" is a fantastic opportunity, but in the unlikely event it doesn't suit you, I have couple of other options I can take you to see."

Fitzy drove from there to the hotel and met up with the homicide detective. They discussed further tactics and Peters revealed that what he had seen and heard of Marion made him, believe they were on the right track. He indicated to Fitzy that whatever the outcome of the secret recording with Marion, he intended submitting a brief to the Director of Public Prosecutions. He finished their meeting by saying, "If we can just get her to confirm that she was at the garage the day he died, the prospects of any charge being successful would improve astronomically."

With those words of encouragement ringing in his ears, Fitzy rang Marion the next morning as she had suggested, and arranged to meet her outside the same apartment complex. He now believed Marion had accepted that their reacquaintance was just a coincidence, and all she was thinking about was the prospect of a nice commission cheque. He was equally certain that she had no intention of sharing anything with Tom, the poor bugger.

Marion led Fitzy out onto the balcony and positioned herself such that he was looking at the expansive view of the Pacific Ocean. She then went through the same sales spiel as the day before, with one exception. "I have to warn you though, Alan. A party I showed the unit to last week has come back to me wanting another inspection. They were keen initially and I suspect they will likely make an offer."

Fitzy did his best to look and sound genuinely concerned that he might miss the opportunity. Sensing this, Marion decided now was the time to close the deal. "Alan, I can see you have a genuine interest in the unit and it is fantastic value, but if you don't want to miss out, I suggest you have me submit an offer in writing as close as possible to the listed price. I will fax it to the owners in Sydney and with a little bit of negotiation back and forwards, we can have the deal all agreed upon and sorted out by tonight." She shot him a smile that revealed every one of her white capped teeth, then turned her head marginally to the side as if pleading with him to accept her suggestion.

Instead, Fitzy just casually asked, "So how is your daughter, Leah, doing?"

The question caught Marion completely off balance, and she stammered something about her daughter living with her latest boyfriend in Melbourne. After slightly regaining her composure,

Marion's emotions were now a mixture of irritation and suspicion. In a clipped tone, she asked Fitzy, "Are you checking up on me?"

Fitzy's response was as calm and emotionless as he could manage. "It's come to my attention that your daughter, Leah, has just turned twenty-two. Even an old bushie like me can count to nine, so it wasn't a huge leap to work out that you never proceeded with the abortion and that Leah is Lennie's daughter." After giving Marion a few moments to digest the news, he changed tack, this time asking in a deliberately aggressive and accusatory tone, "Why didn't you tell Di that she was a grandmother?"

This change of focus put Marion off balance once again, but her self-interest soon kicked in and she asked, "Are you interested in buying this unit, or are you just here to dredge up the past?"

Fitzy's response was calm and measured. "No, I don't have the slightest interest in buying this second-rate unit. I am still very interested in why you didn't console Di with the news following Lennie's death. It would have eased her pain no end if she knew she was about to become a grandmother."

Over the last half hour Marion's mood had ranged from hopeful to optimistic, then to irritated and suspicious. As Fitzy continued to press her for an answer, her mood became righteous anger. How dare he fuck her around and waste her time?

She started on a loud aggressive rant and the longer she spoke, the angrier she became, until she loudly ordered him out of the property with a few chosen and oft-used expletives. Once downstairs she hopped into her BMW, slammed the door and accelerated away in the direction of Surfers Paradise.

Fitzy was imagining he could still hear her swearing when his mobile phone rang. It was Con Peters with a simple message. "That is probably as close as we are going to get." Fitzy was advised to have no further contact with Marion, and to keep the ongoing investigation completely confidential.

Never one to take orders, Fitzy placed a call to Brian Jarrett and swore him to secrecy before giving him another status report on the investigation. He indicated that Marion would almost certainly be charged and that the only weakness in the case was firming up the proof that she was actually at the scene on the day of Lennie's death. Brian was grateful for the update and told Fitzy not to be concerned about confidentiality, as he had more to gain than most by ensuring the case didn't get screwed up.

After the call ended, Brian tried to assess how he felt about how matters were progressing. It was wonderful that Alan was unravelling a tragedy that had hung over him for so long. It was also gratifying that it now appeared that Marion might finally experience a little karma as well. Gratifying...

gratifying… that was the word and it rankled. It was a soft word for a soft feeling; Brian wanted more than a soft feeling. It was a soft feeling because even if Marion ended up in court, Brian would not have contributed to her situation, he would have been a mere spectator. He resolved to become more than that.

Alan had provided him with everything he and the police had discovered thus far. He resolved to seek advice of his own on how they could tighten up the case. In the event Marion faced court, he wanted to be sure that he was part of the reason she was convicted.

Chapter 32

While Fitzy was bringing Brian up to speed, Con Peters had headed back to the CIB offices in Surfers Paradise and arranged a cubicle where he could organise the situation and arrange for the taped meeting with Marion to be transcribed. He then contacted the DPP, and given the strength of the evidence, submitted an informal brief. As always, he focused on out-lining the evidence that had been collected and ensured that the three critical elements of opportunity, motive, and means were clearly established. These elements he believed were proved by physical and forensic evidence, corroborated by the content of the wiretap, and further supported by the statements given to the coroner during the inquest following Lennie's death. The fact that Marion had given a false statement during that proceeding was also included.

The response was slower than he expected. It was the recommendation of the DPP that Marion Jarrett, nee Kent, should be arrested for murder. However, the recommendation came with the verbal proviso that additional evidence may be needed if the Crown were to be successful in proving the case of murder. Failing additional compelling evidence, the charge may have to be downgraded. Detective Peters was therefore encouraged to continue the investigations. He then called Fitzy and told him of both the written and verbal advice.

Later that afternoon, wearing a freshly pressed grey pin stripe suit, and accompanied by two thirty-something detectives from Surfers Paradise Branch, the CIB detective from Dalby entered the premises of Florida Real Estate asking to see Marion Jarrett. The receptionist looked over to Marion who was sitting in the adjacent interview room compiling the upcoming weekend's advertisements.

As the young girl reached for the phone, Con Peters and his entourage casually walked around the reception desk and stopped in front of Marion. When she looked up, he simply asked, "Are you Marion Jarret?"

When she acknowledged that she was, he opened his police ID, showed it to her and continued, "My name is Detective Con Peters, and this is Detective Yung and Detective Greig." The other officers followed his lead and presented their credentials to her as well. With that he placed his hand lightly on her shoulder and said, "Marion Jarrett, you are under arrest, I require you to accompany us to the Surfers Paradise police station."

Marion was shocked and immediately indignant. "I'm not going anywhere until I know what this is all about," she said as she forcefully pushed the detective's arm away from her shoulder.

He quietly and calmly explained that she was indeed going to the station. "It is your decision, Mrs Jarrett. I can explain matters here in front of your colleagues, or I can explain it in more detail and in private at the station."

When Marion asked if she could speak to a solicitor, she was again offered the option of either making a call, in front of colleagues, or making a call in the privacy of a room at the station. She opted for the latter option in both cases, and was quietly ushered out of the real estate office and taken to the station in the detective's unmarked car.

As the car pulled away from the curb, she asked the reasons for her arrest. "Mrs Jarrett I can tell you that you are under arrest for the murder of Leonard Krause, at Dalby in February 1980." The rest of the trip was spent in stony silence as Marion began to assess how an event that happened so long ago could come back and haunt her now. It took her no time at all to conclude that the recent reappearance of Alan Fitzgerald had to be connected in some way. What she knew of the law was that people were not arrested on a whim, and that she would need good representation.

Once at the Watch House, she was allowed the one phone call, and she knew she needed to make it a good one. Unfortunately, the only lawyers she knew well dealt almost exclusively in the conveyancing of houses and apartments, and they likely had never seen the insides of a courthouse. She chose to call the managing partner from the biggest firm she knew and asked if he could help. His advice was simple. She was required to provide the police with her name and address and nothing else, and she was under no obligation to answer any questions. He warned her that given the seriousness of the charge, she would be spending the night at the watch house. When he suggested a good criminal law firm she agreed immediately and asked him to have them contact her as soon as possible. She then followed his advice religiously.

After it became apparent that she would not be giving a statement, Peters arranged that she be charged with murder.

The reality of Marion's situation truly began to dawn on her when her mobile phone, wallet, watch, and jewelry were removed and placed into safe custody. Her palm prints and fingerprints were then taken, as well as a sample of her DNA. She was led to her cell where she would spend a restless night, then prepare herself, as best she could, for the arrival of her new solicitor; the man who would likely control her destiny. That wait seemed the longest of her life, as she pondered just what evidence the police believed they had uncovered after all this time.

As soon as the Florida Real Estate office opened, she arranged a call to them, explaining that there had been a big mix up relating to mistaken identity. She told them that her ex-husband's new wife was also an M. Jarrett, and that the police had confused the two of them because at one time they had both been the wife of Brian Jarrett. She further mentioned that she would not be in for a few weeks while the matter was resolved. This, she mistakenly thought, would give her time to sort matters out or at least get bail, so she could continue with her life as soon as possible.

Chapter 33

About two hours after she called her office, an attractive, fit looking gentleman of Indian heritage, in his late thirties, joined her in the interview room. "Mrs. Jarrett, I am Arun Param, so sorry for keeping you waiting, particularly in the circumstances. I have a number of matters coming to a head at present that had to take priority, I hope you understand."

Marion just nodded her acceptance then asked, "Aaron, was it?"

The solicitor indicated that the name was spelled a little differently, but that "Aaron," was fine for pronunciation purposes. They broached the awkward mater of fees, and then the solicitor suggested that she give him an initial summary of what had happened the day before, after which he would give her a broad explanation of the legal process that would follow. He would then ask her to explain why she thought she had been arrested.

She immediately launched into the whole extended history of the event, her speech rapid and disjointed. He politely interrupted and suggested that she needed to calm down, as such matters were lengthy and considered processes. He offered Marion a legal pad and pen, and suggested that she keep a note of any queries she may have. He settled down opposite her, his own legal pad and pen poised, and asked her to start afresh.

Marion explained how the police had arrived unexpectedly at her place of work yesterday morning, grabbed her on the shoulder and arrested her.

"They would not tell me what it was about, they didn't give me any warnings about my rights and I was told it was best I didn't make any phone calls until they had me at the station." Marion looked up expecting "Aaron" to be shocked, but he simply responded with a forward roll of his hand, indicating he wanted her to continue.

She explained that once they had her in the car, the detective had told her that she was to be charged with the murder of her ex-boyfriend, Lennie (Leonard) Krause, in Dalby, back in 1980.

"I was pretty much in shock, but I don't think I said anything at all, though I may have said it was horseshit." She again looked toward her solicitor, but again he betrayed no emotion, suggesting only that she continue.

"Well, I am a pretty well-known agent on the Coast, and I know a pile of lawyers, but none do your sort of work. So, I rang Brendan Anthony from

Anthony Law for advice and a recommendation, and of course he recommended you. I followed his advice and didn't make a statement or agree to be interviewed. All I gave them was my name and address."

The solicitor continued to take notes then told her that he now understood the basics, which was sufficient at that stage. He suggested that he would explain the procedures that were to follow, which should clarify matters for her. Marion was advised that in the near future, she would be served with a Notice to Appear in the magistrate's court, for the first mention of her case.

"Given that I am now in the system as your solicitor of record, there is every likelihood that the notice will go directly to our office." He then explained that the arrest process she had experienced had been fairly procedural. "You may have thought that the police were heavy handed but from what you have described, it was pretty standard; that's the way it's done in Queensland," he said in an offhand fashion.

He went on to outline the other processes that would occur from here forward, starting with the "First Mention" of her case at the magistrate's court. The "First Mention" was described as more of an administrative process that required little in the way of preparation. "No witnesses will be called," he said. "The magistrate will read out the charges, and from what you have told me thus far, I gather we will enter a plea of not guilty."

After a moment of silence, Marion realised he was looking blankly at her for confirmation about the plea, then she nodded her head rapidly.

When he felt that his new client had digested this step, he went on to explain that the magistrate would then set a date for a committal hearing. "The Committal Hearing", he further explained, "is to determine if there is enough evidence to send you, the defendant, to trial. Such a trial would almost certainly be held in the Supreme Court in Brisbane."

When he mentioned that the committal would likely be two to three weeks away, and that Marion should expect to be transferred to the remand centre in the meantime, Marion stood up in shock saying, "Surely you can get me out of here before all that process starts. I am fairly well off and can easily afford bail. I don't want to be locked up for two or three week for God's sake."

"Mrs Jarrett unfortunately that won't be possible."Arun advised. "Bail is usually withheld in murder cases due to the prospect of flight risk, and in any case, bail applications have to be processed through the Supreme Court, all of which takes time."

"Well, that is why I will be paying you the big bucks," Marion growled in a low deep voice. "Get me the fuck out of here. I got fuck all sleep in here last night. It's bad enough they put me in here, but everyone else is either high as a kite, pissed, or both."

The solicitor was well used to a client's agitation at this stage of proceedings, and in as calm a voice as he could muster, said, "Look Ms. Jarrett, I can see you are understandably upset, nervous, and still somewhat confused, but you need to compose yourself and accept that you will be in the system for a short time. You should also be aware that if the police case is weak, the whole process may stop after the committal, and you will be released and free to carry on with your life."

"And if not?" Marion asked.

"Well then the matter proceeds to a jury trial, and we would need to brief counsel... that is employ a barrister. But let's not get ahead of ourselves. Now give me your explanation of why you believe the police have charged you."

Marion cast her mind back to 1979 and began to recount her version of what had happened all those years ago in western Queensland.

As her solicitor had explained, the First Hearing was a simple affair. Despite this, Marion arranged for one of Arun's female staff to visit her home and pick out an outfit that identified her as a successful businesswoman. She arrived in court wearing killer heels and dressed in her most professional two-piece, jet black business suit, worn over a crisp white linen open-necked shirt. But for all the preparation, she spoke only two words, "Not Guilty" and was promptly taken back to the correctional centre.

A week or so later she heard from Arun that the date for the committal hearing was set for late spring and was to also take place at Southport on the Gold Coast. As the day drew closer, Marion and Arun met on two occasions, mainly to clarify her side of the events in Dalby over twenty years ago.

Chapter 34

When Marion arrived for her meeting with Arun just before Committal, her mood was black. She had been on remand for close to a month and had not enjoyed one minute of her time there. Her fellow inmates were a mix of first -time offenders such as herself, and some more seasoned women who were going through a process that was familiar to them. Marion found it wasn't hard to tell one group from the other, despite them all wearing the same drab prison tracksuit-based uniform.

The biggest give away, apart from their attitude, was the amount and quality of the tattoos. Tattoos from the outside were generally multi-coloured professional pieces of art. The one done at various times inside were monochromatic and amateurish. Marion also quickly learned to discern the meaning of some of these. Cobwebs on the neck and tears from the eyes seemed to reside on women who were more likely to cause her trouble, and she had enough of that already.

To begin with, her well-coiffed blonde hair was no longer blonde all the way through; a distinctive white/grey strip was now noticeable down the centre. Her weight had already ballooned as well, which she put down to the expanding waist on the track suit pants and the quality of food served at the remand centre.

Given her recent experience, her black mood darkened further when her legal team informed her that they would not be presenting any evidence at all at the hearing. Marion was incensed because this was supposed to be her best chance to secure the "Get out of Jail Free Card" that Arun had spoken about. After calming her down, they explained that it was the Crown's job to prove she had a case to answer and that the committal process was their opportunity to get the whole of the Crown's evidence revealed to them, and not give back anything in return. Marion's mood immediately improved on hearing this. She finally felt the mounting legal bills might be paying dividends. She liked this idea, as it seemed very one sided in her favour. It also meant she had a false sense of optimism.

It was only an hour or so after the Crown began to reveal their evidence that Marion's optimism began to evaporate. The Crown prosecutor was a thin statuesque woman in her mid-forties. She began the case for the Crown by outlining to the court the history of the relationship between Leonard Krause and the defendant, with the initial facts seeming to be inconsequential.

The deceased was from an established family in the Dalby district, and was self-employed in his own mechanical business, while the defendant was something of an itinerant at the time they met. She very quickly developed an intimate relationship with the deceased, and soon after they met, moved into a house he had rented and furnished. The prosecutor detailed that the available records established that Marion had contributed very little financially toward the upkeep of the household. Though no doubt was cast on Marion's fidelity in the relationship, the Court was advised that the defendant fell pregnant to the deceased in 1979, and obtained an illegal abortion of which the deceased was unaware.

The defendant was known to have a quick temper, and she and the deceased were known to argue. She was heavily suspected in the near death of a local kangaroo shooter, and while no police investigation ensued from this event, she openly bragged about her actions. This was confirmed by a written statement provided by the prior publican of The Imperial Hotel in Dalby, her ex-employer at the time.

When the deceased suffered a debilitating football injury, she terminated their relationship leaving him with substantial debts. She changed employment, and shared accommodation with another barmaid, but her income dropped and her cost of living increased. Her bank records showed that her savings had seriously dwindled just prior to her leaving Dalby. After leaving the relationship, the defendant found she was pregnant once again.

When the body of the deceased was discovered in his workshop, a police investigation ensued, followed by an autopsy and inquest. The defendant gave a statement to police at that time, in which she stated that she had not been to the deceased's workshop since before the breakup, some two months previously. She also claimed that she had told the deceased, by phone, three days prior to his death, that she had discovered she was pregnant to him again, and that she proposed terminating the second pregnancy as well.

She further mentioned that shortly after the call she hitchhiked out of town, arriving at her mother's home in Brisbane late that evening. Her statement concluded that it was her belief that the deceased was depressed due to their breakup, his football injury, and financial problems. She assumed the news of the proposed termination of her second pregnancy was the last straw, and that he took his own life. Her alibi, that she was living in Brisbane at the time of his death, was supported by her mother, who has since passed away. The inquest determined that the death was either a suicide, or death by misadventure.

She was then granted leave to call her first witness. "The Crown calls Alan Fitzgerald to the stand." Alan, dressed in a smart corduroy trousers and tweed jacket walked slowly to the witness box. Under guidance from the bailiff he placed his hand on the small bible and spoke those well-known words, "I swear to tell the truth, the whole truth and nothing but the truth, so help me God."

Fitzy's evidence also initially seemed of no consequence to Marion. Under questioning, he revealed that he considered Lennie Krause as one of his best friends. He knew Marion Jarrett, then Marion Kent, when she was in a relationship with the deceased and could also confirm the story about the kangaroo shooter and the fact that Marion and Lennie were known to argue. He revealed that he had stayed in contact with Lennie's mother, Di Krause, after Lennie's death, and had assisted her with her property when her health began to fail.

He pointed out that contrary to her police statement, Marion had not told the deceased that she proposed having an abortion, rather that she told him that she had already terminated the pregnancy. The deceased had conveyed this information to his mother, and it was part of Di Krause's statement to police at the inquest into her son's death.

On further questioning, Alan also revealed that no second abortion had happened and that, in fact, Marion had proceeded with the pregnancy and delivered a daughter, Leah, for Lennie. More revelations followed as more questions were posed to him. He revealed that the deceased's mother had padlocked the workshop after Lennie Krause's death, and it remained untouched until just after Di's own recent death. He told the Court that he had been a beneficiary in the will of Di Krause. Specifically, he had inherited the contents of the shed mostly comprising the deceased's tools, as well as any of his other personal possessions to be found in the house property. Because of the provisions of the will, he had unlocked the shed to assess Lennie's tools.

As the case progressed, Marion thought that this just sounded like the sad story of a failed relationship that she had put behind her over twenty years ago. She thought that if this was the best they had, she would be walking out of court and onto the streets that afternoon. When the prosecutor asked Fitzy if he had discovered anything other than tools in the shed, the tide then began to turn against Marion.

Fitzy gave evidence of the football jersey with the distinctive changed number that he had found amongst a pile of rags in the shed and explained the significance of finding this piece of clothing at the scene of Lennie's death. The Crown then produced Marion's statement from the inquest into Lennie's death and had it entered into evidence. It was already established that parts of her statement were untrue, and the prosecutor indicated that she would soon be showing evidence that would cast doubt on the veracity of her statement as a whole.

Fitzy was dismissed as a witness, but the Crown prosecutor indicated that he may be recalled later in the proceedings. During all this time, Arun Param had been furiously scribbling notes to himself and placing asterisks and exclamation marks where he felt appropriate.

The next evidence for the prosecution was provided by the police forensic officer. After the bailiff had sworn him in, the prosecutor asked him to tell the court about his position in the force, qualifications, and experience. He answered these as requested and during the course of questioning, observed that parts of the evidence pertaining to this case were sourced from prior enquiries going back over twenty years.

When the prosecutor asked him for clarification he said, "A great deal of the evidence in this matter has been sourced from the original investigation and subsequent coroner's inquest into the death of Leonard Krause. This evidence includes photos taken at the scene, materials collected, such as the hydraulic jack, and statements taken. All these items were collected contemporaneously in early February 1980, your honour." The judge nodded his assent.

"These items have now been supplemented by the more recent photos of the scene of Leonard Krause's death and forensic results. Amongst the photos obtained from the original investigation were ones that showed the position of the chocks relative to the old car and yet another was a wide angled shot with a long-handled crowbar circled in the background. A comparison of the old and new photographs supported the fact that the scene had been undisturbed since the original enquiry." The prosecutor thanked the witness and advised the court that their first focus would be on the crowbar, detailing the bulbous end and the chisel end in a close-up image.

A magnified photo of the chisel end of the crowbar was then projected onto the court's screen. The photo highlighted the fact that the corner of the chisel end was partially broken. Following this, one particular timber chock filled the screen with an indentation circled in red. Then a small plaster casting of the indentation in the timber chocks was shown, also indicating the broken edge. The Crown contended that the timber chocks were a failsafe to support the old Jaguar in the event the jack failed.

"What do you deduce from these photographs, the plaster mold of the indentation in the timber chocks and the broken end of the crowbar?" the witness was asked.

"There is no doubt that the broken chisel end of the crowbar caused the indentations. Given that the chocks were supporting the vehicle, there is every likelihood that the impact caused them to give way and for the car to then fall onto the faulty jack.

We know from the reports related to the coroners inquest that the jack failed, and the car dropped, crushing the head of the deceased."

Arun now added a further notation to his notepad. The notes were numbered, not by importance, but by the order in which they had come to him as the evidence was led. In order they read; 1. Confirm with M, nature of jersey; 2. No evidence it's the same jersey.; 3. No evidence of date jersey arrived at workshop; 4. Workshop not a secure crime scene for 20+ years. 5. IF crowbar caused dents in chocks, no proof it happened on DOD. Finally point 6 was, IF crowbar caused dents in chocks, no proof of involvement of M. This last entry, however, had been heavily underlined.

The evidence of the forensic officers continued to paint a picture that pointed to the fact that the coroner's two options for the cause of the death of Leonard Krause might be incorrect. The next revelation was again related to the crowbar with the prosecutor revealing to the court that this was the evidence that had convinced the police in the first instance that this old case had to be reopened.

Before she left Brisbane for Dalby, Marion Kent had been accused of theft as a servant, and while the case wasn't proved, her fingerprints and palm prints were in the system. The prints on file coincided with the prints later taken from the defendant at the watch house at the time of her arrest.

Following further questioning by the prosecutor, the police scientific officer revealed that testing showed that the crowbar had been in Marion's hands, possibly at the time of Lennie's death. When asked why he had reached that conclusion the officer said, "The accused's prints were found in numerous places and positions along the length of the crowbar. One set was midway along the crowbar, positioned the way they would need to be if she were using the chisel end to strike something.

The prosecutor thanked the witness and he was excused, she then addressed the Court. "Your honour, the Crown contends that it is also instructive to the case, that the crow bar had obviously been removed from the immediate proximity of the deceased and propped against a wall in the corner. Arun immediately put a series of large question marks beside point 5 and 6 on his list and added item 7 that read– "M's sprints could have been added months prior to the death."

Written evidence was then produced by way of Marion's doctor in Dalby and from the Royal Brisbane Hospital in Brisbane. The doctor's records revealed that Marion had been pregnant some seven months prior to Lennie's death, and that she had apparently had the pregnancy terminated in late

September 1979. The records further confirmed that Marion had visited the doctor in Dalby on the day of Lennie's death and that she had been advised during that visit that her second pregnancy was too far advanced for a termination. The hospital records and an entry from Birth Deaths and Marriages Registry also confirmed the date of her daughter's birth in Brisbane. The date coincided with her Dalby doctor's estimate of the date she was due. The forensic officer advised that DNA evidence also confirmed that Leah was Lennie's daughter.

Alan Fitzgerald was then recalled by the Crown. He was referred to the recent evidence about the crowbar and asked if he knew its provenance. Fitzy looked blankly at the prosecutor and asked for clarification about the term.

The prosecutor apologized and rephrased the question. "Mr. Fitzgerald, do you know anything about the crowbar in question, specifically where it came from, who might own it, and how long it was likely to have been in the deceased's possession prior to his death?"

"Yes the crowbar is mine. I had broken the chisel end at a job in Charleville and brought it back to have it patch welded. I recall my father suggested I have Lennie do the job and he dropped it off to his shed when he came into Dalby for an Australia Day function. I know it is mine because our family paints the top half of our tools white, so we can identify what is ours."

Just to ensure the point was well taken, the prosecutor then asked, "So that particular tool was only in the deceased's possession for some fifteen days, from January 26th, 1980 until he died on February 9th, 1980"

Fitzy responded in the affirmative and was once again excused.

The next witness called to the box was the lead CIB detective Conrad Peters, who had been working closely with Fitzy and others over the last few months. It was the prosecution's contention that the homicide detective would testify that the Crown had obtained confessional evidence from Marion proving that she was at the workshop on the day of Lennie's death. He further revealed how Alan Fitzgerald came to be on the Gold Coast working with police, and the method used to obtain the incriminating evidence.

Following the explanation of the procedures and precautions used, a transcript was handed to the court and a copy given to the defense table. The tape recording that resulted from the wire Fitzy had worn during his meetings with Marion was then played. It started with Marion's sales pitch to a client who would never buy.

"Alan, I can see you have a genuine interest in the unit and it is fantastic value, but if you don't want to miss out, I suggest you have me submit an offer in writing as close as possible to the listed price.. I will

fax it to the owners in Sydney and with a little bit of negotiation back and forward, we can have the deal all agreed upon and sorted by tonight."

There was then a short pause during which time, Marion no doubt thought the buyer was considering his options.

Instead, the next voice on the tape was that of Alan Fitzgerald. *"How is your daughter, Leah, doing?"*

A clearly shocked Marion had stammered a response indicating that her daughter was now living with her latest boyfriend in Melbourne. As the tape continued, it was apparent that Marion's anger levels were rising. When the recording reached the section where Fitzy continued to press Marion as to why she had failed to tell Lennie's grieving mother about the birth of her only granddaughter, Marion leaned noticeably forward in her seat and looked accusingly, first at the detective and then at Fitzy.

The tone of Marion's voice in the tape revealed that her anger had overpowered any thought of self-preservation or suspicion. Her voice was loud and terse.

"Alan, my time is valuable, and you are fucken wasting it. I didn't tell her because I just wanted nothing more to do with that family. Dalby was a mistake that was behind me. Len got me pregnant, and I went over to tell him that I was leaving town to have an abortion. That loser mate of yours was laying

329

on the ground covered in grease as usual, working on this old Jag. Some dad he would have made!

"It turned out I had left it too late and I had to go ahead with the pregnancy. In the meantime, Lennie topped himself, the <u>stupid</u> prick. Now if you don't mind, I have some real clients I have to look after. I'll see you out. And Fitzy, go fuck yourself."

For once Marion didn't get the last word in. The final words on the tape were Fitzys', *"Marion, you are a lying bitch, you lied then, and are lying still."*

Again, Arun noted down that the wire transcript did not necessarily place Marion at the scene on the day of the death. The visit she referred to could have been days before the death, and it might have been during this visit that the jersey was returned. Her inquest statement, however, had stated that she hadn't been at the workshop for likely two months. At the very least, she had been there after Australia Day as that was when the crowbar arrived, and her prints were on the crowbar. The number of falsehoods in Marion's statement to the police for Lennie's inquest continued to grow as did her reputation as an unreliable and dishonest witness. Alan Fitzgerald's final words on the tape were ringing very true.

When the prosecutor indicated that he had completed his case, Arun rose and informed the court that the defense would not be calling any witnesses. He checked for his client's reaction at the evidence presented, but she refused to be drawn, and simply turned her head away.

The magistrate thanked both sides for their attendance and revealed that he would give his determination within the week but may yet recall the court if he required clarification on any matter. In the event the matter was recalled, the prosecution requested the right to present further evidence should it come to hand. The magistrate granted the request and advised the defense that he would extend them the same courtesy should they change their mind about calling witnesses.

There had been no quick "get out of jail free" card as Marion had hoped. She took the opportunity to have a quick conference with Arun to assess how he interpreted the strength of the prosecution case and to determine if they had taken the right tack in not calling witnesses.

"Marion there is no right answer to that question because we weren't aware of the Crown's evidence until after it has been led." Arun went back through the notes he had been taking and continued. "The Crown's case is compelling but it is not complete. There was still a chance the magistrate might dismiss the charges, but I have to be honest and tell you that is unlikely." He asked for further time to evaluate everything he had heard so he could reassess tactics. He however promised that he would contact her shortly for a more comprehensive evaluation. "Remember", he finished, "that this is just one stage in a lengthy process."

Marion's initial confidence was seriously dented however, and it fell further when she was led out of the court and taken back to the correctional centre on remand.

While Marion and her solicitor were in conference, Fitzy and the CIB detective were having a little debrief of their own. Peters took the lead and asserted that things had gone as well as expected.

"It isn't unusual for the defense not to introduce evidence", he explained. "The usual process is for them to extract as much information as they can, and offer nothing back in return."

Fitzy wasn't sure if he was supposed to contribute to the conversation. He was well out of his area of expertise and had made the decision to just tell it as he saw it and let the cards fall where they may. The way the detective was looking at him however, seemed to suggest that he expected his star witness to express an opinion of his own. Fitzy thought on it a while, weighing up in his mind everything he had said and heard and just said, "So your name is Conrad eh? Fuck I thought you must be Greek or something with a nickname like Con."

Chapter 35

As had become his habit, Fitzy conveyed the outcome of events to Brian Jarrett. Brian, while grateful for the update, was still concerned about how to get involved; he didn't just want to be looking on from the sidelines, getting secondhand information. He wanted to ensure that the Crown case was being conducted as well as could be expected. If there were holes in the case, he wanted professional advice on how to patch them. If Marion was guilty, he wanted to be sure she was convicted, and if she was convicted, he needed to know that he was intimately involved in that outcome.

Brian had decided that John Cameron was the only person he knew who had any understanding about the law. He had never held his lawyers or his barrister responsible for his conviction, the only person he had ever blamed was his ex-wife. He did, however, feel that they owed him to some extent. John Cameron, after all, was the person who had introduced him to this latest chapter in the ongoing saga of Marion Jarrett. When he suggested to his solicitor the idea of becoming more personally involved, Cameron told him that he needed advice from a barrister with experience in criminal law.

A few phone calls later and Brian's original barrister had agreed to act in a consultancy capacity but not before both men had met with him. Once they were comfortably seated around a coffee table in the barrister's plush office, both John Cameron and the barrister pointedly, and explicitly explained, that they were offering nothing but their opinion on how the matter was progressing, and any advice that they tendered would be based on the accuracy of the information Brian was to provide. They clarified as well that the advice would extend to their view of any weakness in the Crown case, and to also cover how a good defense barrister might counter the Crown's counsel.

Neither men, Brian was told, would brook any suggestion that they should bend the law in any way. To ensure the information he was feeding back through his lawyer to the barrister was as accurate as possible, Brian was asked to keep voluminous notes of the hearings. He was also told that it would be a good idea if Joy could help to compile and type them out.

After their second meeting, it was the considered opinion of Brian's new consultant team, that the magistrate would commit Marion to trial. It was their view that the Crown had a strong case but was also lacking in a few respects. They believed that the delay in the magistrate handing down his decision was because the Crown had insufficient evidence to prove a case of murder. They had many things in their favour. Marion was proved to have lied on numerous occasions in her statement to police at the inquest. This proved her testimony would be unreliable, and strongly indicated that she was hiding something. From the point of view of the original inquest, it also cast serious doubt on her alibi. The crowbar evidence was crucial, as it proved she was in the shed holding the potential murder weapon in her hands within weeks of Lennie's death. They had forensic proof that the same crowbar had been used to cause the indentation in the chocks.

They had a strong motive with Marion finding out that she was once again pregnant to the deceased, and that she was compelled to proceed with this pregnancy. She was also aware that the father of the child was in no position to be of financial assistance. These issues combined with her proven temper could well sway a jury.

On the side of weakness was the fact that the site of Lennie's death had not been a secured crime scene for over twenty years. The main weakness in the case, however, related to a lack of concrete proof that Marion was at the scene at the time of his death.

Cameron conveyed their final piece of advice. "The Crown needs to prove that she had the opportunity to cause his death. If I was on the prosecution side, I would be concentrating my efforts in plugging this gap. If I were at the defense table, I would be pointing this failing out and concentrating on the coroner's findings of death by misadventure, or suicide over twenty years ago. This report favours Marion as it was a contemporaneous finding. That is it had been made right after Mr. Kraus' death and as such it would be argued that this report should be given considerable weight."

Brian pondered the broad advice and went back over the copious notes he had taken following his conversations with Alan Fitzgerald. Late that night, he awoke abruptly from a restless sleep. He had been dreaming that he was the defense barrister and that he had all but convinced the jury that Marion was as pure as the driven snow, and that Lennie Krause had taken his own life. His mind was a whirl, and it took a concerted effort to settle down and get back to sleep.

Next morning, he woke early, still fatigued from the poor night's sleep, and went into the kitchen to make an early morning coffee for Joy before his young son disrupted the day. They spoke of his concerns for a short while, and he then crept back out of bed and went into his study which had notes strewn across the desk. His stupid dream last night about proving it was a suicide was nagging at him. He asked himself the question, "Why had the Coroner decided on an open finding? Why had he not found that suicide was the proven cause of Lennie Krause's death?"

The answer was fundamentally the lack of a suicide note. It had always been suspected that if such a note existed, it would be found written on the section torn from the diary on the day he died. It had been concluded that either it was never written or if it was, it must have been blown away.

Brian was now as conversant as anyone as to the broad details of the case, and the advice he had received was that they needed to concentrate on confirming that Marion was with Lennie at the time of his death. Brian scrounged around the papers to confirm the actual date and remembered the specific piece of evidence that referenced this date: the half page torn out of Lennie's diary. It wasn't just that it was the only page that had been disturbed, it was the page on the day immediately prior to Lennie's body being discovered. It had to be more than a coincidence, and it had to have some major bearing on proceedings. Maybe it was the plug that was needed for the major hole in the case.

He wrote down his thought process in sequence on a pad and picked up the phone to call Fitzy, who had already returned to "Kilmarnock." He outlined his thoughts on the relative strengths and weaknesses of the case with a particular focus on that missing half of the diary page. He suggested to

Fitzy that he wanted to drive out to Dalby and meet both him and Con Peters at the site.

"I want to bring Joy with me too, she has been typing everything up for me and has it all in her head. We will bring our son too. You can introduce me as someone who has an intimate knowledge of how Marion thinks."

Fitzy raised the idea with Peters who was less than enthusiastic about involving Brian. But after Fitzy pressed the matter, the detective agreed that they would meet at midday at Di's old property, but that he didn't want a circus. He couldn't stop Brian and his family from attending but they couldn't come into the workshop itself. Brian was gratified that he was becoming more hands on, even if the directive from the detective was "strictly hands off!"

The following day, they all arrived at the house and the introductions were made. Brian and his family, however, had arrived late afternoon the day before. Together they had toured the town and managed to visit many of Lennie's old haunts that Fitzy had referred to, or had been discussed in the court proceeding. They had driven past the hospital and the footy ground, and had even had a counter meal at The Imperial.

While Brian was becoming more embedded in the process, he didn't make the best of impressions on Detective Peters when he revealed that he had been getting professional advice on the weaknesses in the case.

"I do this for a living, Mr. Jarrett," came the quick response when the issue was raised. "But you are right about that missing diary page, we are going to turn this place upside down. If it is here somewhere we will find it." The detective suggested that while he was precluded from allowing Brian into the workshop, the house itself was not involved. "Why don't you go through the house property again and see if you can turn something up?"

Brian eagerly accepted, glad at least that he had initiated a further search for the missing page, then headed off with Joy in tow, carrying her young son on her hip.

Just as he reached the stairs, he stopped and turned back to his car to retrieve a hot six-pack of XXXX cans. He walked back over to Fitzy and said, "You wanted to see if that old fridge was still operational. Turn it on, drop these in, and hopefully we can toast a successful search later on."

Peters looked knowingly back at Fitzy as if to say, "Well he is out of our hair."

After opening up some louvres at the end of the shed, to let a little air in, Fitzy plugged in the old fridge and put the hot cans in the small freezer section. They then got back to their search for that one specific missing item. Two hours later, Brian arrived back at the rough perimeter that Con Peters had laid out as his "no go zone," to announce that he had found nothing of interest in the house. Fitzy and the detective reluctantly admitted that they had also been unsuccessful.

As they were heading back to their respective cars, Brian turned and patted Fitzy on the chest. "Shit, the beers."

Two days later, the DPP lodged a request with the Court to submit new evidence. Since the magistrate was due to reconvene the case the following Monday, the request was approved. After numerous meetings with his client, Arun was still of the view that they would not be calling witnesses of their own at this juncture. He was concerned, however, that this tactic might require a change, particularly if the new evidence was in the least compelling.

Monday mid-morning arrived, and the court was duly called to order. After the usual procedures, the prosecutor called Alan Fitzgerald back to the stand where he was reminded that he was still under oath. The prosecutor then tendered Lennie's diary. She indicated to the magistrate that she particularly wished to point out a number of critical matters.

She first turned to the page assigned to February 9th, reinforcing the point that this was the date of Lennie's death and asked the witness if he had any knowledge about the missing half of the diary page.

Fitzy nodded and said that he did. Before a follow up question could be asked he volunteered, "The CIB detective, Con Peters, and myself, have always wondered why half a page from Lennie's... the deceased's, diary—from the very day he died, would go missing. It has been suggested that the deceased must have written his suicide note on this missing section of diary, but I figure no one writes a suicide note and doesn't leave it out in the open."

Counsel for the Prosecution then led questions about prior searches for the note and their lack of success, until Fitzy volunteered, "We knew the shed had been searched from top to bottom a couple of times but figured they had been looking in the open because they were looking for a suicide note."

The prosecutor then tried to take back control of the questioning. "So, what was different about the approach of yourself and Detective Peters this time," she asked.

He responded, "Well we acted on the basis that the note wasn't a suicide note and that if the torn page wasn't out in the open to be found, there was every chance it must be hidden somewhere. You understand, if it was hidden somewhere, it wouldn't be a suicide note, no one hides their suicide note." Fitzy went on to explain that in the week prior, he had arranged to meet with the detective back at the shed in Dalby where the death occurred to have a final scout around, but that this time, he was at pains to emphasise they would be looking for something hidden, not something just missing.

Frustrated, the prosecutor cut in, "And did you find anything hidden?"

Fitzy replied, "We spent a good couple of hours turning the place over again with no success. We were about to retire to the pub when the very mention of a beer pricked my memory."

"And can you explain to the Court just what you mean by that?" The prosecutor asked in exasperation.

"Well, I had turned on the shed's fridge earlier and put a hot six-pack of XXXX cans in there to test if it still worked." Fitzy continued, "As I said, we had given up our search and were in the process of leaving when I was reminded that the cans were still in the fridge. When I went to get them, I found the cans had frozen to the bottom of the little freezer section. I had to shake them a bit to loosen them and when I did, an extra panel at the back of the freezer section popped out and there was a secret spot behind it."

The prosecutor paced a little for dramatic effect, and to relieve the frustration she was feeling at her witness's lengthy explanations. She then asked Fitzy to explain what he meant by "secret spot."

"Well, like most small businesspeople, Lennie was apparently keen to keep a little of his turnover back from the tax man. I remember that the last time I visited the deceased at the workshop, just before Christmas, that Lennie had gone to the old workshop fridge and come back with some cash and asked me to go and buy a couple of cartons of beer. The fridge was obviously the secret spot where he hid that cash."

"And what was hidden in that cavity, that secret spot, Mr. Fitzgerald?" the prosecutor continued in a tone that indicated that the answer would be of critical importance to the case.

Fitzy replied, "There was an old Vegemite jar, the lid nearly rusted shut."

"And what was in the jar, Mr. Fitzgerald?" the prosecutor asked in a frustrated tone, certain she was getting in with the question just before the magistrate.

"Well, Detective Peters pulled on some rubber gloves and pulled the jar out. He unscrewed the lid and inside was a tightly rolled up old style original paper $50 note. We took it out into the light for a closer inspection, unrolled the money and inside it, we found the missing half page of Lennie's diary."

The prosecutor excused Alan and called the CIB detective Conrad Peters back to the witness box; she showed him the $50 note and the torn diary page, and after the detective confirmed it was the one he had found, both were entered into evidence.

The prosecutor asked the witness to inform the court of the words written on the note. He cleared his throat and read out loud, Lennie's last written words.

"Farewell visit from the bitch just now, good riddance. Tickled pink - going to be a dad after all. First down payment today on my kid's education."

Arun had his note pad at the ready and was quick to add "note on diary still no confirmation M at the scene on DOD."

The prosecutor then asked the detective if that was all that was written on the note. Peters adjusted himself in the witness box then removed a pen from his inside pocket. He used it to point to a few disjointed words, "..fter 6," that were also written on the torn section, immediately above the news about Lennie's pending fatherhood.

Further evidence revealed that the note discovered in the fridge was the bottom half of the page torn out of the deceased's diary, with forensic testing showing a simple match. The second point was as telling. The prosecutor then drew attention to the full entry on the remaining section of the page in the diary for February 9th. It read: *"Joe Youngman's old Jag - brake job – in at 12. If finished today call him a.."*

The words on the note found in the freezer completed the sentence in the diary. It confirmed the note on the torn section of paper found by Alan Fitzgerald and Detective Peters was written after the Jag was delivered on the morning of Lennie's death. Arun put a wriggly line through a number of points on his notepad.

The magistrate again offered the defense the opportunity to introduce witnesses of their own and again they declined. He broke proceedings for lunch, indicating that he would reconvene in a few hours after further considering the new evidence. It did not take quite that long. Almost immediately after the scheduled lunch adjournment the magistrate reconvened and announced that he believed that the Crown had presented sufficient evidence in the case, such that it required that the defendant be committed to stand trial. He directed Marion to appear at the criminal sittings of the Supreme Court in Brisbane at a date to be advised.

Without the anticipated "get out of jail free" card, Marion initially sat in stunned silence. Arun hovered over her about to offer advice and support, but she angrily waved him away while she composed herself. "Where to from here," she thought, "now that there is to be a trial? How long will I be in jail before it comes around??" Then the reality of her possible situation came crashing down. "What if I lose at trial?"

Eventually the bailiff approached, preparing to lead her back to the cells, so she motioned Arun across and they had a quick debrief. While Marion was undeniably shell shocked, Fitzy and Con Peters were visibly delighted. After a few self-congratulatory back slaps, Fitzy took out his mobile phone and conveyed the news to Brian and Joy.

Chapter 36

Over the next few weeks, a transcript of the committal hearing along with copies of the witness statements and evidence led by the prosecutor was sent onto the DPP for a decision on what the formal charge should be. They considered the matter for some weeks before advising Aram that his client would be charged with murder. He was unsurprised, given what had been revealed at committal, however, he still vigorously objected to the murder charge in a written submission back to the DPP.

His position was that while his client maintained her innocence, the Crown did not have evidence that would prove intent, and that if the matter were to proceed as had been determined at Committal, the charge should be downgraded to manslaughter. While the DPP pondered his submission, he went to work trying to unravel the police case against his client.

By the time her trial approached, the near perfect life Marion had created for herself, had seriously unravelled. Her leased BMW was no longer, and her income as a high-flying commission only salesperson had obviously evaporated, as had her reputation. She had taken out a mortgage on what had previously been her unencumbered Gold Coast home to pay for general living expenses, but more particularly to cover her ever-mounting legal bills.

In pretrial discussions with his client, Arun laid out her options. "Marion, the charge is serious, and the prosecution case is now very comprehensive. I have to confess that my efforts thus far to disprove their case hasn't been that successful. On the positive side I believe that they have a major weakness regarding the timing of when you touched the crowbar."

"How so?" Marion asked.

"Well, they have now proved you were there that day, but they have not proved when you touched the crowbar. We now know the crowbar arrived fifteen days before Lennie's died so your prints could have been added weeks before the death."

Marion breathed a little sigh of relief, before Arun continued, "Of course, this theory is weakened by your earlier lie in your statement to the coroner that you hadn't been at the workshop for months. The other evidence tendered that you were regularly seen wearing that distinctive jersey around town until at least early February weakens things further but it's something." Arun finished by suggesting that the only other weakness he could discover was that the DPP might be trying just a bit too hard with a charge of murder.

"To be successful with a charge of murder," he explained, "there must have been intention to kill. The Crown can now place you at the scene very shortly before Lennie died. The prosecution has shown you handled the crowbar, and that its use was likely the cause of the car falling off the jack. They have proved you lied at the inquest and that you were pregnant for a second time with the deceased's child. But even with all that, they have no proof that there was an intention to kill."

Arun always kept Marion aware of his endeavours to weaken the police case, but he had to admit to her now, that though technically the Crown still needed to prove it, he had not designed a compelling rebuttal. He reiterated that the main weakness he could find was a lack of proof of intention to kill. This was the basis of Arun's original written submission to the DPP for the charge to be reduced to manslaughter.

Reality had set in for Marion since that unsuccessful submission so she asked Arun, "I am nothing if not a realist, I know it wasn't sounding good in there. What is the likelihood of me being found guilty, what would be the likely sentence if I was indeed found guilty, and what options are open to me?" Before he could answer a little of the "classic" Marion Jarrett resurfaced , when she added, "And what sort of compensation would I get from the government in the event that I am not found guilty?"

Arun answered the last question first. "It doesn't work that way, Marion, this is a criminal matter. If the verdict is not guilty there will be no refund, no compensation. That is the cost of justice. As to your other questions, I can tell you a not guilty verdict is highly unlikely. It's my usual practice, to keep a running estimate on the sort of odds you are asking about. I believe the chances of being found not guilty are 20% maybe 30% at best. If found guilty of murder, the sentence would likely be twenty to twenty-five years imprisonment, with the usual prospect of earlier release for good behaviour."

Marion asked for some time alone to consider her options. When the meeting reconvened, she asked Arun, "What would be the likely outcome if I change my plea to guilty, but to the lesser charge of manslaughter?"

Her solicitor did not try to dissuade her from considering this option. "Marion," he said, "I think this is the right course. We have tried for a reduced charge before, but the difference is that with the last submission, you were still maintaining your innocence." Arun already knew the estimated numbers for the alternative charge, as well.

"Marion if they were to accept your plea to the lesser charge, the outcome would likely be a sentence of twelve to fourteen years imprisonment. It does get a little better though, as this would likely be further reduced with good behaviour and allowance for time served. I would expect you would be released in seven years." He emphasized that the decision was hers alone to make, and that if she agreed, he would need to prepare a fresh submission to the DPP.

"I hope that the addition of a guilty plea this time, will make the difference, and that they will accept the reduced plea."

Marion pondered these odds and asked her solicitor for time to consider her options. She knew she had to do what best assured her the earliest release. It wasn't that Marion was particularly stressed with prison life, over her time of life on remand, she was handling the stresses of trial preparation in her stride. Her early fears that someone with her profile might be attacked had also not eventuated.

In her new 'home" she was not considered the highflyer she thought herself to be. The prison had a full complement of nefarious characters, including drug dealers, drug addicts, thieves, arsonists, sex workers, con women, larcenists, psychopaths, even murderers. Marion had now been confined in various institutions for some months, and as always, she was a quick study. She had quickly determined how to recognize potential conflict and how best to avoid it. As it transpired, none of the other inmates had posed a particular threat to Marion, her main enemy was boredom.

Chapter 37

For a few days, Marion pondered the options her lawyer had given her. Based on his estimates, she calculated that she would already have been on remand for over a year by the time her trial date came around. There was every chance she would turn fifty during the trial itself. The prospect of being free again at fifty-seven with the remnants of her personal worth still available to her, sounded a lot more attractive than the idea of being released when she was seventy or older. For God's sake, her mother was already dead by that age, she realised.

Eventually she arranged for Arun to meet with her so she could tell her own account of what had happened in Dalby twenty years ago. If he was comfortable with her revised story, she would ask him to prepare the submission to the DPP. Her revised statement would form the basis of this submission. Once Marion decided that she would change her plea, she had been working meticulously on how to put the best spin on her version of events.

She and Arun sat down, and he removed a small tape recorder from his briefcase and asked her permission to record the interview. He advised Marion that he would then create a statement from the recording which she would have to approve and sign. She agreed to the process, and he asked her to speak slowly into the microphone and explain exactly what happened on that night over twenty years ago. She endeavoured as best as possible, to stick to the "script" she had practiced in her head over the last few days.

When she finally fell silent, Arun looked at her, waiting for her to acknowledge that she had finished. He told her he would create a statement based on her recollection of events and remove the language, and the emotion. She would then be required to sign it as a true recollection of events.

They met again early the next morning, and he bought with him two copies of the statement. He asked her to read it, and if she agreed to the written testimony, to sign at the bottom. If she wished to make amendments, she should note these on the spare copy. After reading through it twice she looked up at him, nodded and then signed both copies. The final statement read:

"Lennie and I had our moments; for a short time, I thought the relationship might go all the way. He was a very positive and caring person with a really strong work ethic. He loved his mum, and was a very devoted son. He was a very good sportsperson and a gifted mechanic who had a growing business. Some people

who have given evidence at the committal hearing have made much of the fact that we argued, but there was never any violence, and really, our rare arguments were no more nor less than any couple our age had; not more than lover's tiffs really.

When Lennie had his football accident I endeavoured to be as much help as possible, while still holding down a demanding job. I was essentially his nurse for many months, afterward. Unfortunately, he changed after the accident. He became very depressed and demanding. I felt like I was no longer appreciated, and that he was just taking advantage of my better nature. In the end, I just decided that we just weren't meant to be a couple. I broke the news as best as I was able to, and explained to him that I was moving out.

We had been broken up as a couple well over a month before he died. I had moved on with my new life, I had a new job, a new flat, and new friend, and had put my old relationship with him behind me. Then I became suspicious that I might be pregnant again and so I went to see my GP.

The doctor confirmed that I was going to have a baby. Shortly afterward, I found out that I was further along with my pregnancy than I thought. This meant that Lennie was the father and meant as well, that terminating the pregnancy would not be an option. I had never wanted to have children of my own. I came from a broken family with an abusive and alcoholic father. He regularly beat both my mother and I, and we went without so much because of his drinking and gambling addiction. Then just after I started at school, he abandoned us, and my mother had to raise me alone.

After I had my own daughter, Leah, I even had my tubes tied so there couldn't be any further mishaps. Not only did I not want to be a mother, I didn't want to ever have to abort a child again. I suppose my view on motherhood was due to my abysmal unhappy childhood. Before I was advised of my pregnancy, I had already decided to leave Dalby. Once it was confirmed that I was to be a single mother, there was no way I wanted to have to exist as a single mother in a small country town with no family support.

When I first suspected I was pregnant, I telephoned Lennie at his workshop and told him I was pregnant again, and that I had already had a second termination. The reason for this was simply because I didn't want him to think he could talk me out of it.

When I realized I would have to proceed with the pregnancy, I decided to go around to Lennie's workshop, admit I had lied to him about the termination, and tell him that it had turned out that I had to keep the baby. I also wanted to tell him that I expected that once he was back on his feet, he needed to live up to his obligations as a father and be responsible for the cost of raising his child. It was critical to me that my child did not have to endure a deadbeat dad such as my own.

When I arrived at his workshop, I noticed that he was drunk again and my fears about my baby having an alcoholic father like my own intensified. As a peace offering, I bought back his old jersey, but instead of being grateful, he just used it to clean his grubby hands and dropped it with a bunch of other rags. He heard what I had to say, but then he used the vilest language to abuse me, and then just turned his back on me. I felt I was being abandoned all over again and in my time of greatest need. I left, but I was incredibly angry with his treatment of me. He had ruined my life, was the father of my unborn child, yet apparently had no intention of helping out, or so I thought at the time.

I walked away from the workshop defeated, but from halfway up the driveway I could hear him inside just listening to the radio as if nothing had changed in his life and I thought I won't take this. When I stormed back in, he was laying on the floor in a ball crying drunk. It made him look like a weak excuse of a father, because I should be the one crying not him. I told him I'll give him something to cry about, but he either couldn't hear me or was ignoring me. I banged on the jack handle, but it was covered in grease, so I picked up this long steel pole and banged on these timber blocks to get his attention. Well, you know the rest.

I don't know the foggiest thing about mechanical stuff, I didn't even know what the wood was there for. The pile of wood tumbled, then the car dropped toward me and stopped. Then straight away whatever it fell onto gave way too, and the whole lot fell on Lennie. He had taken the wheel off, to work on the hub, and when the car fell, his head popped like I had dropped a watermelon on the ground. It was obvious he was dead and there was nothing I could do.

I was sick with shock, it was frightening. I panicked; I was walking around in circles crying; I was an absolute mess. I had a baby on the way, I was in a pile of trouble, I had no money, no job and no prospect of help. I raced around, putting things away. I cleaned myself up as best I could, then I just legged it out of there back to my mother in Brisbane. I never went there to kill him; I went there to get a commitment from him that he would support me financially to help raise his own child. When I got to Brisbane, my mother and I went over everything that had happened. I told her that I should go to the police to explain everything.

Her concern was that I would go to prison and that she would have to bring up the baby, so together we cobbled together the story. We both signed statements to the police and life moved on. As it turned out, mum died in 1991, a few years after I got married. My husband was a deadbeat, and it also turned out he had abused my daughter. He ended up in jail for that so as it turned out, for the most part, I did have to raise Leah all on my own. I could not have done that from prison. I did the right thing by my daughter to stay out of prison, but I never murdered Lennie. It was all a horrible accident."

Their line of argument in the submission to amend the charge would simply be that there was insufficient evidence of intent to kill. Marion had not the foggiest understanding of mechanics, she was unaware that simply hitting the chocks would cause the Jag to fall to the extent it did. She would have been unaware that the car falling onto the jack would cause it to fail, and she could not have known where Lennie's head would be at the time the car fell or even if such a fall would result in death.

The submission was rounded off with the comment that all evidence was impacted by the effluxion of time, and the fact that she was in a highly emotional state at the time, having just discovered that she would need to continue with the pregnancy of her ex-boyfriend's child. Further, that she was of the firm belief from his response at the time, that he had no intention of helping financially with the baby. Her anger at the time was justified because she felt that she had been abandoned by the father of her baby, just as her real father had abandoned her as a child.

A series of conferences followed the arrival of the submission at the offices of the DPP. Following these, the Crown prosecutor had to acknowledge to herself that she still had reservations that it would be possible to prove intent to kill. Other than this soft spot, they looked at the specifics of the case.

Firstly, the death was twenty years old and while this did not reduce its seriousness, the lack of immediacy would play in the accused's favour. The deceased also had no living relatives, and the defendant came from an abusive dysfunctional background. If this was insufficient to arouse a degree of sympathy, it transpired that after the event in question, she had married a man who was later sentenced to jail for sexually abusing his step-daughter. The DPP considered all these issues, the strength of the case and how it would play with the jury.

After due consideration, they responded to Arun that the Crown had agreed to accept to amend the charge to manslaughter and the plea on the lesser charge to guilty. There was one proviso though; Marion must read her statement into the court record.

When Arun conveyed the decision to her, Marion realized that she never thought the day would come when she would be happy to know she was going to prison. She had one more performance now to ensure she received the lightest possible sentence.

Chapter 38

When the day of the trial arrived, Marion arrived in court in a much more conservative manner of dress. There was no power suit this time and certainly no "killer heels." As she was ushered into the courtroom and placed in the dock, she glanced up to see her daughter, Leah, sitting alone in the second row. They stared at each other intently, and Leah's impression was that her mother's demeanor was somehow different; she wasn't presenting as the self-confident, assertive matriarch her daughter knew.

The judge entered the courtroom, and everyone stood. His associate directed Marion to remain standing while he read out the indictment, which now set out the reduced charge of manslaughter. To the judge's question of "How do you plead to the charge?" she simply replied, "Guilty your honour."

Marion was then asked to read her prepared statement to the court. She produced a typed copy of the statement that Arun had created for the submission to the DPP. As she read her statement, however, she was able to include emotional pauses, and even managed a few sobs and the occasional tear.

Sentencing was reserved, allowing the Crown and the solicitors for the defense to prepare submission as to what the term of jail should be, and the reasons. More tears ran down Marion's cheeks, though whether these were tears of relief or guilt, only she would know. She took a long breath as she looked skyward, then at her daughter and then the smallest smile of conspiracy crossed her lips. When the bailiff released her from the dock and led her from the court, Marion noticed two familiar men and a pregnant young woman in animated conversation in the back row of seats.

"How in God's name" she thought, "did Brian Jarrett come to be hugging Alan Fitzgerald?" Then she realised she just didn't care; the fight wasn't quite over, but she had won this round.

As Brian and Fitzy discussed the best venue for a celebratory drink, Brian noticed that his wife was engaged in a deep conversation with a slightly overweight but nonetheless attractive twenty-something woman who was standing just inside the doors to the courtroom.

"I think you know who I am, Leah, and I am sorry to be raising this with you at such a difficult time, but I just have to grab the opportunity."

"You're Brian's new wife, aren't you? Joy isn't it?" Joy nodded her head in acknowledgement.

"It's not such a surprise really," Leah said, "It's about what I expected she would get," she said in a surprisingly matter-of-fact tone.

This gave Joy the courage to ask the question that had bedeviled her married life. She didn't ask if Brian had done what he was convicted of doing; she had known the answer to that before they even married. She simply asked, "Leah, why did you lie about what happened with Brian? It makes no sense. What did you hope to achieve?"

Leah didn't raise the slightest suggestion of denial. She just shrugged her shoulders and said, "Listen, the only real family I have ever known was my mum and grandma. Mum told me my dad, Lennie, was a drunk who committed suicide before I was born. Lennie's dad was already dead before she even met Lennie, and she told me that my other grandma died just after the suicide. I liked mum's mum, but she died when I was a kid." Joy listened intently as the young girl explained her reasons.

"So, to answer your question, in my mind, there was really just the two of us that counted, mum and me. Brian came along, but he wasn't much of a stepdad, just another bloke in the house as far as I was concerned. Then he decided he was going to dump us, so when mum told me what to tell the police, I just did." Leah finished her answer with a simple shrug of her shoulders, an action that was irritatingly apathetic.

"But you ruined his life," Joy said with barely concealed anger.

"How was it ruined?" Leah quickly replied. "He got rid of mum, spent what, 18 months in jail? He got remarried to you and you seem nice. And he has a kid with you now too, doesn't he?" Looking down at Joy's swelling belly she added, "And another on the way by the look of it?"

Joy willed her to go on, still unsatisfied with her answer. "He got to keep all his dad's money too, and anyway, he knows he didn't do it. He knows he just got played."

"That's the thing, Leah, he has always known he wouldn't do it, but because of all the dope he was smoking, he has never been absolutely hundred percent sure that he didn't do it."

"Well you can tell him from me, hundred percent….he didn't. That might cheer him up. Fuck me, he was always fast asleep after a smoke."

Leah slung her handbag over her shoulder and walked out the court doors, a carefree jaunt in her step, as if her last statement was of no import whatever.

After a few beers back at The Treasury, Fitzy headed off to the gents, and Joy grabbed Brian's shirt, pulled him close and kissed him. She told him about her conversation with Leah, how she had finally confirmed the whole thing was a fiction. "Revenge must be sweet honey," Joy said, looking to her husband for a reaction. She was unsure if that reaction would be elation, dancing in the street, anger, satisfaction, vindication, but a statement of resignation was the least expected.

"It just doesn't matter, babe, the damage is done." Joy was disappointed and confused; her husband had taken on this challenge with a passion only exceeded by Alan Fitzgerald. But she didn't have to ask him for an explanation. Brian could see the confusion and concern in her eyes and so he continued. "I am told Marion will likely be in jail for five to seven years. People will think about this case for a few days max. Some will say she meant to do it, others that it was an accident, and still others will say she was a victim of circumstance. Either way, they will all say that it happened long ago and when she is released, they will say she served her time and that will be the end of it."

Joy looked at him with pity knowing he was correct and nodded in agreement. But Brian wasn't done. "Marion manipulates people and the truth. She took one life and tried to ruin mine, ours, and she seems to get away with it every single time. Ten years they reckon, fuck!"

The more Brian considered the result the less satisfied he was with what Joy had seen as justice. "Revenge might be sweet, but it isn't justice. What's the expression? 'Justice Delayed is Justice Denied.' That's my situation and Lennie Krause's too. Not only that, but I was thinking throughout her trial you know, that even a charge of murder doesn't leave as big a stain as I have on my character. Innocent or not, I am marked for life."

While the team for the prosecution was enjoying their celebratory drinks, Marion was being processed to head back to the remand centre, and arrangements were being made for her to be transferred to the newly completed Brisbane Women's Correctional Centre at Wacol. She was ushered to her single cell where she found no more than a single cot, dresser, and a toilet and shower in the corner. She had hardly time to acquaint herself with the new facility and its routines when word came through that she was to head back to court for the sentencing hearing. Once again, she dressed conservatively and clothed herself as the victim, with no knowledge of how her actions of twenty years ago might cause the death of her ex-boyfriend.

It transpired that Arun's assessment on sentencing was marginally on the high side. Marion was sentenced to ten years imprisonment with the standard time off for good behaviour, and allowance for the nearly fourteen months of time already served. She had every intention of being the model prisoner, and so calculated that she should be released in six years and home in time for her fiftieth birthday.

As soon as the sentence was handed down, Marion contacted Leah, who by that time was back in Melbourne. She had been hopeful of convincing her to move back to the Gold Coast so that she would at least have a regular visitor to help pass the time. She also reasoned that having Leah as a trustworthy local contact who could access her funds, would also ensure that she continued to enjoy a few of life's luxuries.

Leah, unfortunately, was now fully immersed in the Melbourne culture, and was enjoying the night life and music scene. She had moved on from her last boyfriend and was now living with the manager of one of the clubs she loved to frequent. "I might not be able to visit mum," she said, "but we can speak regularly by phone, and if you give me some advance warning about what you need, I am sure we can arrange to have it delivered to Wacol."

While Marion was disappointed not to have Leah right at her beck and call, she soon proved that she could be very useful even from Melbourne. To begin with, she had helped arrange for her old estate agency to find a quality tenant for her house meaning that the small mortgage was covered, and she had access to a healthy monthly balance, more than enough to cover the regular requests for special treats. After almost 18 months of these regular calls, Leah noted that of all the complaints her mother made about prison life, the two most common related to overcrowding and the fact that she was just plain bored.

Marion complained, "Even the colours are boring; everything is the same bloody colour, even what we have to wear is the same colour as the walls. I think that just makes it worse."

Leah felt her mother's boredom was partially self-inflicted. She knew from Marion that the opportunity was offered for vocational educationl and training, but none of the courses were of interest.

"Some of the inmates could do with it, but I was successful before I ended up in here. Some of the other inmates though, are so dim they are learning how to read and write." Marion did take advantage of the pastoral care offered by the chaplain, but she explained to Leah that this was just to accrue brownie points for the Parole Board when it was time to assess the reduction for good behaviour. She also explained to Leah, that while everyone had to do some sort of work in the prison kitchen or cleaning the cells, for instance, that these were also mind-numbingly dull. On the rare times she was involved in work the prison had contracted to undertake, such as small manufacturing jobs, she was always lumbered with the most menial of tasks.

"I'm overqualified for this sort of work", was her standard position.

The overcrowding complaint came from the fact that the authorities regularly forced two prisoners to share a cell designed for one.

"If the cell has to house two prisoners, one prisoner gets the single cot and the other has to sleep on a mattress on the floor with their head close to the open toilet and shower. Of course, I always get the cot, a little kicker to the prison officers makes damn sure of that," she told her daughter. "But you would not believe some of the people they stick in with you."

Then Marion's voice dropped down to a conspiratorial whisper. "I am sure the mousey little runt they put in last week is a lezzo. Some of the women in here turn that way out of convenience. This one I am sure, came in that way." She went on to explain that her latest cell mate was in for heroin possession and trafficking.

"I get the impression that she is no stranger to this life because a few of the other girls know her, and I am guessing they didn't go to school together. She is ticked off big time that I get the cot and we have had a few words, so I am working on getting her moved elsewhere" The topic then turned back to how best to break the boredom, and Marion explained to her daughter that she had been cooking up a scheme that she was sure would keep her entertained for months and should be a nice little pay back to her cell mate for giving her grief.

She then asked her daughter the strangest of questions. "I have been thinking about something, honey, and I need your help with this scheme. What do you think about becoming a lesbian?"

Chapter 39

Always the observant one, Marion had noticed that when the mail was delivered to inmates, one or two were particularly eager. These were also the ones who always received more than their fair share of correspondence. She made some discreet enquiries and was told that these two particular women were working the "pen pal" scam. A few bars of chocolate were then produced which encouraged the informants to reveal a little more about how this scam worked.

Apparently, some men just loved the thought of all these women together in prison; their imaginations ran wild. The idea was to find likely candidates, create a story about the difficulties of life in prison, and then start some correspondence. There were myriad ways to find such men, but most frequently, a contact outside prison found a likely lonely prospect and suggested they contact their sister or close friend, who was a wonderful person but who was having it tough inside. Over time, this correspondence would become more intimate, and the man was soon hooked. Once hooked, he could be persuaded to help the poor suffering inmate with the odd cash injection, on the promise of her everlasting love once she was released.

There were a couple of reasons that this particular scam ideally suited inmates. As they were in prison, their mail was always appropriately postmarked, so whatever they wrote to their pen pal was believed. The next benefit was that their "pen pals" usually could not visit them due to distance, and even if they could, visiting was restricted. This was why the best "marks" were those who lived well out of the state. The last benefit was the best of all; there was no limit on the number of "pen pals" they could accumulate. One relatively attractive girl apparently had five guys contributing to her at one time. And even if they did get caught, what was the downside? They would just say it was a relationship that went wrong and worst case, they couldn't be sent to prison.

Marion had no need of the income but marveled at the design of the scheme. Every mail session, she watched those girls playing the game, and noted how it filled a big part of their lives. This was when she realized that she could play the game as well, but this time with a twist.

The next time Marion spoke on the phone, she raised the idea she had in mind. Leah was more than a little confused by her mother's question about her future sexuality, but a huge smile swept across her face when she heard the explanation. The smile wasn't because of the ingenuity of the scheme, it was just the realization that prison hadn't much changed her mother. What Marion had proposed wasn't designed to be a scheme to make money, in fact, they would be the ones paying money instead. The scheme was fundamentally to help Marion pass the time in jail, and to fuck with the mind of her irritating cell mate. Leah thought the whole thing was a huge joke and couldn't sign up quick enough to the scheme.

To put it in place, Marion gave her daughter the run down. "Your new lover's name is Toni Bradley, I am not sure of her prisoner number, but she will supply that when she writes back because the mail gets through quicker if the number is on the letter. You know the postal address here."

Marion then passed on all the preliminary information that she had managed to glean about why her cellmate was sentenced, and where it happened. She asked Leah to use that to do as much research as she possibly could on the woman, such as finding newspaper articles about her case. Armed with all her history, she was then to write to her in prison and establish some ongoing correspondence.

Marion kept an eye on her cellmate every time the mail arrived. Her observations paid off a week later when she received a pink envelope, the signal mum and daughter had arranged to know that things were underway. Marion could immediately see that the letter came as a complete surprise to Toni, who was soon laying on her mattress on the cell floor eagerly reading the message. Marion didn't know the exact wording, but what was being read was close to what she imagined that Leah had created.

"Dear Toni,

You don't know me, but I saw the story about your case in the Byron Advertiser and immediately felt that we had a connection. I have been through a similar experience where my partners have taken advantage of me, and where I have had to pay the price for things they have done. Fortunately for me, this hasn't resulted in the prison sentence you are having to endure.

The article in the paper has a photo of you leaving court, and you look so sad, cute but sad. I hope things are not too difficult for you in there. I would love to write to you on a regular basis and to financially help a little as well, if you need anything. If you would like to write back that would be wonderful."

Your new friend,
Erica Donald,
Flat 1/146 View Street Highett Victoria.

Over the next few days, Marion watched her cellmate open and reread the letter on a number of occasions until eventually she retrieved a pad from amongst her meagre possessions and began to write. Marion knew the game was afoot and this was confirmed during her next call with Leah.

"She got right to the point, Mum; wanted to confirm that she was right to assume that I liked the ladies."

The new scheme occupied most of the calls between mother and daughter, as they devised ways to enmesh Toni into her new love life. One week Toni even received two letters on the same day, which was a means they devised to show Toni just how keen "Erica Donald" was to develop the relationship. This seemed to be the trigger for Toni to feel sufficiently comfortable to turn the correspondence in a much more personal direction. She began to explain how she became enmeshed in the situation that led to her being in jail. She briefly touched on her troubled early life in Sydney, before explaining that the opportunity had presented itself to live a more idyllic life in the hinterland of Northern New South Wales with her lover.

As money had become tight, however, they had reverted to their old ways and ultimately moved into growing and selling their own pot. This became a lucrative exercise but soon led them to a closer association with some bad old contacts back in Sydney, who suggested they might like to offer their clients a few more exciting options. Toni confessed that moving up that food chain was ultimately the biggest mistake in her life, because she started to sample her own wares. Soon she was on the needle, and was doing whatever she was asked just to ensure her next score.

Ultimately, she came unstuck and was currently serving six years for dealing in Class 2 drugs. But the worst part, she confessed, was that it was her lover who had assisted the police in her arrest. The sentence was longer than expected due to her prior arrests in Sydney and because of a Breach of Bail conviction associated with those old charges. The only positive of finding herself back in jail, she told "Erica," was that she had received treatment for her addiction and was committed to never backsliding again.

In her response, "Erica" congratulated her on her commitment and promised to stand by her when she was released. Soon it was "Erica" confessing to all manner of confected stories about her own troubled early life in Melbourne; how she knew from an early age that she was gay, and how her own very religious parents had disowned her when she confessed this to them. Marion had almost burst out laughing when that suggestion had been made during their regular calls. Once their respective backgrounds had been established and confidence established, the correspondence became more sexual and Marion delighted in Toni's response, when one of these letters arrived.

"This is such a riot," she thought to herself. "Tough old Toni Bradley has been bringing herself off to a letter written by a fictitious character created by her own cellmate. She is being royally fucked over and isn't even aware of it!"

Chapter 40

After Marion had been sentenced, Fitzy invited Brian, Joy and their young son, Matt, to "Kilmarnock" on several occasions. On every occasion, the topic eventually came around to how Marion would be enjoying her new life. Brian and Detective Peters had become much friendlier during the trials, with the detective having to acknowledge that Brian's approach to the missing page was what had finally broken the case. Brian had asked him to keep a track on how Marion was progressing, as he and Fitzy were keen to ensure that she served the full term, if possible, with no time off for good behaviour. Unfortunately, the detective could only pass on reports and information provided by prison authorities, and these seemed to indicate that she was a model prisoner.

About eighteen months into Marion's sentence, Fitzy called Brian to announce that there was a new lady in his life, Helen, and he hoped to introduce her to them the following week. Of course, he also wanted to meet the newest member of the Jarrett's household, another boy who they had named Roy, after Brian's father.

As soon as she caught the edge of her husband's conversation, Joy, ever the matchmaker, was keen to know more. She had grown very fond of the big grazier, partly because the circumstances of their meeting had been so intense. She believed Fitzy deserved more happiness in his life. Not only because of the series of tragedies he had suffered, but because without him they wouldn't have lifted the veil on Brian's situation. After heavy questioning from Joy, Fitzy revealed that Helen was in her early fifties and had divorced some years earlier.

"She had been struggling financially since the divorce and decided to go back to teaching. Lucky for me, she took up a posting at Kaimkillenbun State School, and we have been getting along like a house on fire since we met."

Brian's initial response to the news wasn't about Fitzy's love life; he wanted to learn more about the town with the strange sounding name.

"Just call it The Bun, everyone else does. It's on the coast side of Dalby only about 25 km from town, so not much more than an hour's drive from Kilmarnock. It's a small school and they have multi age classes." At this point, Fitzy confessed uncertainty about Helen's actual role. "She teaches years four to seven, or four to six; one or the other."

He went on to explain that the school was having its annual fete the following Sunday and that this was to be followed by a big social at The

Bun pub later that night. He invited them to stay at Kilmarnock for the long weekend and confirmed that Helen would be joining them there.

"I've got a couple of dirt bikes out here. After Helen arrives and the girls get to know each other, we can head out to the mountains east of here on Saturday."

Brian took the Friday off. And they set off first thing that morning and arrived at "Kilmarnock" around midday, just in time for an enormous lunchtime meal that had been prepared on the verandah by Von, his housekeeper. Joy could never come to grips with the expanse of the place. Their own riverside home was considered large by Brisbane standards, but Kilmarnock homestead always seemed to look substantially larger. On reflection she decided that this was because "Kilmarnock" was like an island oasis surrounded by established lush gardens in what was otherwise a treeless expanse of golden cultivated fields.

Fitzy loved playing rough with young Matt, who was now walking and quite the handful. When Joy introduced him to Roy, he picked him out of the cot with his huge, calloused hands and could not have been more gentle. When Joy asked if there might be kids on the horizon for him if things panned out with Helen, he laughed off the suggestion.

"Sure, we are serious, but our baby-making days are well and truly behind us. If everything pans out, I will just have to be happy with the company of her two kids, a girl and a boy in their early twenties." Then in a lower voice he confessed to Joy, "Helen—she worries about my fixation with the case. We had a long and very deep conversation about it a few weeks back which really helped me understand it myself. My grandfather died after service to his country and working himself into the ground establishing this place, dad died of hard work, mum after a long full life, Phoebe and my brother Spud, well they died tragically and too young, but Lennie didn't die, Lennie had his life taken from him and that makes all the difference. Life is precious and someone took his."

Not long after breakfast next morning Brian noticed a long plume of red dust on the horizon. After a few minutes, it was apparent that a little red car, driven at speed toward the homestead, was raising the dust.

Fitzy soon joined Brian on the verandah, and as he walked down to greet her, announced, "This is Helen. She loves her little car; drives like a maniac."

The little Mazda 323 came to a stop, followed by the dust trail which soon caught up with Helen as she hopped out of the car and ran toward the new love of her life. Helen was a tall thin woman with her auburn hair pulled back into a ponytail. She had made no effort to conceal the streaks of grey that started from her forehead and she wore only the most basic of makeup. Fitzy turned his back to the dust to shield her, then bent town to kiss her on the nose and hug her close. "Come on in and meet Brian and Joy and little Matt and the new bub, Roy. Matt is a real handful."

Then, as he grabbed her small overnight bag, he wondered about her early arrival and so asked, "Have you eaten yet?"

She whispered her response in his ear as they ascended the steps onto the wide Kilmarnock verandah where he made the introductions, and asked Von to prepare Helen a small breakfast of toast and Vegemite, and to make everyone another cup of tea. While Von was busy in the kitchen, they all retired to the big outdoor setting and got to know each other.

Helen's experience with small children was soon apparent to all, because within minutes, she had little Matt in howls of giggles. Helen was aware of how her man, "Al", had come to know the young couple from Brisbane, so she made a point of directing the conversation away from that topic that had been consuming him of late. Fitzy knew what she was up to, and despite her efforts, was keen to discuss it privately with Brian. Once the girls were apparently comfortable in each other's company, he reminded them of his intention to show Brian around the property by bike. As they headed to the machinery shed, Helen and Joy were already deep in conversation about Joy's life as a new mum, Helen's life as a new rural schoolteacher, and the upcoming dance at "The Bun."

Brian was no slouch on a dirt bike but was still impressed by the skill that his much larger companion was exhibiting. They eventually got to the far end of the property, an area of less arable country suitable only for cattle, and stopped near an outcrop of boulders shaded by a large gum tree. In no time at all, Fitzy raised the issue of the court case and Marion's sentence. He revealed that not long after the case had finished, he had spoken to the local police sergeant about how things had transpired. He told Brian that he had apparently become something of a local celebrity for a short time, and that the police were impressed by his doggedness in getting an outcome for young Lennie.

"I sometimes think getting congratulated for my efforts only makes it worse. Like you, I think she got off light."

Brian was also conflicted by the outcome. "I always knew that a result wouldn't change my own case," he said, "but at least she is paying something for past deeds. There is no doubt she talked her way out of it. I don't know about the finer legal points, but even if she had no intention of killing Lennie, the fact is she didn't much care what the outcome might have been. Like she didn't much care about how her accusations would impact me."

Even though they agreed that Marion got off lightly, the issue was that the trial was over and nothing could be done.

Fitzy ultimately shrugged his broad shoulders and asked, "What more can we do but accept the judgement and move on? From what you tell me, Con Peters says she is behaving herself, so I suppose we better prepare for her getting an early release." The way Fitzy phrased this last sentence, Brian took it as more of a question that needed an answer he could not give right now.

It was a great weekend of bike riding, good company at Kilmarnock, loads of fun, too much food at the fete, followed by a great steak meal, and dancing and music at The Bun. For all the weekend's distractions, Brian didn't forget the question that Fitzy had posed. Based on his experience with Marion and his knowledge of the way she worked, he now thought he had the germ of an answer. Before his return to Brisbane, he asked Fitzy if he thought Marion would change her ways in prison.

"Brian, she fucked Lennie around big time, and ultimately killed him. She did a major number on you too."

Brian interrupted Fitzy's response. "Exactly, it's who she is. She may be in prison, and the authorities may think she is behaving herself, but I think it's a cert that she is up to no good in there too. I reckon we need to have someone who lives in there with her, to get us some dirt on what she is really up to. The question is who and how."

They discussed what they knew of her situation from the information provided through Con Peters. He had made a few well-placed calls and arranged for prison staff to brief him on Marion's activities. The detective was informed that she seemed to be keeping to herself and was largely the model prisoner. The only issue was that Marion was sharing a cell and, apparently, had taken a dislike to her lesbian cellmate. Peters was told that to ease the friction, the authorities were in the process of transferring the current cellmate and her "gallery," to a separate cell.

When the detective enquired about this "gallery", the prison officer had laughed and then filled him in on the latest scuttlebutt. "Kent's cellmate is a Toni Bradley, mid-level druggie from Byron Bay who was caught dealing in Brisbane. A little while back she started to receive some unsolicited "fan mail" and now is apparently desperately in love or in lust with this chick from Melbourne. Half her cell wall is covered with photos of the girl."

None of this information, however, was considered extraordinary and it certainly would not adversely impact Marion's prospects of early release.

But Fitzy and Brian suspected there was a lot more to it.

"While you have spent time inside, Brian," Fitzy said, "I am guessing none of it was inside a woman's prison. I know someone from Byron though and while she hasn't been inside, I can guarantee that she knows people who have been."

Fitzy went on to talk about his wayward sister-in-law, Gaye, and to suggest that he would contact her to see if she could find out a little more on Marion's activities. It was two weeks before he heard back from Gaye and was provided with a lot more inside information.

Toni Bradley and her ex-partner were well known to anyone who wanted to score any serious drugs in the Byron Bay/Ballina district. While Gaye didn't know them personally, she knew a few people who did, and who could be persuaded to contact her in prison. She called in a few favours and soon was able to tell Fitzy that Marion's cellmate's new lover was an Erica Donald, from an address in suburban Melbourne. Toni had apparently told her little clique about the new love interest she had from down Melbourne way, and how she even intended moving to Melbourne to start a whole new life with her when she was released.

Gaye even arranged for her contacts to have Toni send them a photo of Erica which she immediately sent to Fitzy. She also advised that the new "relationship" had apparently upset a big Samoan "lifer", Tamar Ioane. Tamar had been in the process of establishing a relationship of her own with Toni before the pink envelopes started to arrive.

It was now six months since the first of those envelopes had been delivered and Toni was well and truly hooked. It was the highlight of Marion's day to see her reading and re-reading the letters and carefully storing and filing them according to dates. The pleasure Marion derived from orchestrating the scheme was heightened substantially when she discovered that her lezzo cellmate had started recounting stories about her new love interest to anyone who would listen.

After Fitzy received the collated information on Marion activities, he immediately arranged to meet with Brian at his Brisbane home. They discussed their suspicions, then Fitzy put him in contact with the PI he had used to make his initial investigations about Marion some two years previously. Brian briefed the PA with his suspicions, offered to cover all expenses, and asked him to determine if their suspicions were well founded. If they were, he was to compile a comprehensive fully documented report.

A week later the verbal report came back, and their suspicions were confirmed. Flat 1/146 View Street Highett Victoria, the address used by the imaginary Erica Donald, was in fact occupied by one Leah Jarrett. Brian immediately commissioned the full report and when it arrived, the evidence of Marion's scheme was irrefutable. The report contained a copy of the lease agreement to Leah, photos of Leah coming out of the property, and photos of her dropping a distinctive pink envelope into a local mailbox. The girl in the photos did not resemble, in the least, the photos that Toni Bradley had posted on her cell wall.

The photos on that wall did, however, bear a more than striking resemblance to another photo in the report, this one was of a young single woman who lived in the adjacent Flat 2, at that same address. The name of the woman from Flat 2 was not Erica Donald either. The imaginary Erica Donald was, in fact, Leah Jarrett's unsuspecting next-door neighbor. Brian gleefully reported the findings to Fitzy, and then he had a brilliant thought. He dug through his old photo albums and found the most recent one he had of his ex-wife, a photo that he never thought that he would allow to see the light of day again. He put the photo in an envelope with a cardboard backing sheet and posted it back to the PI with some instruction on how he should amend the final report and who the addressee should be on the large manilla envelope.

Chapter 41

The day that Marion had been looking forward to had finally arrived. The authorities had informed her about a week ago that due to a few recent releases and transfers, her cell mate would be relocated and she would be getting the cell all to herself once more. As Toni packed up her gear for the move and began taking down the photos of her lover, Marion couldn't help but contribute another dig.

"It will be good to have a wall clean of that skank's photos. The place was starting to smell all fishy!"

When the mail was delivered the following day, Toni Bradley didn't receive a pink envelope. This time she received a rather heavy buff manilla envelope containing a substantial bound file.

Brian had informed the PI, that from his own experience as a prisoner, the authorities would carefully vet a package of this size. Hence, it was important that the contents conveyed the intended message to the recipient but did not raise the suspicions of the prison authorities. The PI had therefore done his best to disguise it as a property report and had attached an unsigned covering letter to the front with an oversized paperclip. The letter explained that the file represented the assessment of the rental property at View Street Highett that Toni had enquired about. If it wasn't for the address in Melbourne that the report referred to, Toni would have thought that she was sent the envelope by mistake. She was confused at first, but because she recognized it as Erica's address, she began to read the contents in full.

The report contained a copy of the current lease agreement for unit 1, with a photo of the tenant pinned to the corner. The agreement showed that the existing tenant for unit 1 was not Erica Donald but rather one Leah Jarrett. That last name immediately rang alarm bells for Toni because she had heard that surname yelled out six times a day for the last nine months. The file also contained a number of photos, all with date stamps showing they were taken at various times over the weeks prior.

One photo showed the front of Unit 1, with a twenty-something girl leaving the front door. The person in the photo was not the Erica Donald she had come to believe was her new love interest, rather it was the same person in the photo that was attached to the lease agreement. The next photo was a close up of the same girl depositing a bright pink envelope into a mailbox. The text under another photo revealed that all the units in the complex were in the same condition. This photo clearly displayed the face of the tenant in flat 2. The woman in this photo was clearly the woman that Toni knew as Erica Donald, however, the caption read, *"Adjacent tenant Marilyn Thompson has lived here two years and confirms the complex is well managed."*

There were a few filler pages showing maps and the location of shops and other facilities but the last page, which was designed to look like the signature page of the report's author, was the most telling. It contained two photos, an old photo of Marion, with her name clearly typed underneath. The second photo was of Leah, with the name Leah Jarrett underneath. Again, the photo of Leah was clearly recognizable as the girl leaving Unit 1 in the earlier photo. The report ended with, "Always at your service, Erica Donald Real Estate." Under this were the handwritten words, *"We are happy to have clarified any misunderstanding. Once you have assessed the contents of this report, we trust you will take the appropriate action as opportunities to do so rarely present themselves."*

Toni read and re-read the report to fully absorb its contents. Once she realized that she had been the victim of a cruel hoax, she experienced dueling emotions; sadness, embarrassment, anger, and a deep desire for revenge. She had spent enough time inside to know to hide her feelings and took the report back to her new single cell to read again. She removed all the photos of her faux lover from the cell wall and then sought out the company of the giant Samoan girl and let her emotions flow. With Ioane's arm over her shoulder, she explained the contents of the folder, let her know just how much the scam had hurt her, and suggested how grateful she would be if her old cellmate was made to pay the price.

Apart from work in the kitchen, garden, laundry, and cleaning, prisoners were occasionally offered work in the prison's bulk storage facility. This work was generally spasmodic unless the prison secured a contract on commercial terms from an outside business. Most prisoners loved these opportunities as they represented a variation from the day-to-day monotony of prison life; and they paid better as well. Ioane was in the happy position of having undertaken a forklift course via the prison service and so was generally guaranteed bulk storage work when the opportunities came. It was some months before such work was offered after the prison had secured work in the basic assembly of components for a firefighting system. The big Samoan had already been involved in the storage of the heavier components that comprised boxes of sprinkler heads, hose reels and hoses. These had been delivered on pallets and she had stored them in racks using her forklift skills.

When the prisoners were assembled to undertake the basic assembly training, Tamar was initially the centre of attention. In front of the designated prison officers and other prisoners, she was at pains to follow all the pre- operational procedures she had learned when securing her forklift license. She meticulously walked around the machine, checking the fork arms, particularly checking the locks into the bridge, she checked the hydraulic hoses and chains, the rollers in the mast, tires, gas bottle and hoses on the gas system. She then pulled her bulk up into the cab, struggled to do up the seat belt and began checking that all the electricals were operational. She started the machine and checked that all the brake, indication, and safety light also worked. Next, she began using the various levers to check all the lifting components, back tilt, forward tilt, left and right side shift, then lifting the mast to its fullest extent and lowering it.

Everyone seemed impressed by her professionalism; this wasn't the Tamar they were used to seeing. She put the machine in gear, released the handbrake, and drove just short of the pallet stacks. She raised the mast to the required height and moved forward again slowly so that the forks were about a third of the way into the pallet. She lifted the mast again marginally, then slowly reversed out, carrying the pallet. Some of the girls squealed in delight and one even clapped.

Marion, bored and unimpressed, just chuckled and turned her back on proceedings. She was so busy reflecting on just how easily impressed some of these losers were that she didn't see Tamar tilt the mast forward instead of backward, turn the machine sharply to her left then brake. Marion wasn't in the least prepared when over a ton of component parts came to rest on her self-absorbed skull.

About the Author

Photo by Robyn Hills Photography

Geoff Glanville was born in Brisbane and is a retired property professional. While he has contributed many articles to industry magazines and the general press on this subject, "Justice Denied" is his first work of dramatic fiction.

Geoff started his career in property on the Darling Downs as a cadet rural valuer in 1970, and the characters he met there influenced him to set his work, in part, in this region.

His Covid lockdown experience, coincided with an unexpected cancer diagnosis followed by the recurrence of an earlier cancer; a battle he had hoped he had already won. These events gave Geoff cause to reflect on his life's achievements, and to retrieve and complete his book that he started some 15 years earlier.